The Tavie
Colony
on the Bayou

The Tavie Colony on the Bayou

Darla Daley

Dedicated to my mother and father

As she listened to the brewing storm outside with the flashes of lightning and strong gushes of wind rustling the tree branches, she hoped the storm would only last through the night so her trip with her grandfather would not be cancelled. Finally the rain came, casting a dark and unsettling fear over her. Thunderstorms in Louisiana could cause much damage to a community. This storm moved in and was gone within an hour. Now Jacy could relax and get plenty of rest for her trip.

Jacy Ann Hebert, pronounced "Ay-bear," had been born and raised in Louisiana. Her mother was from Yelgar, Louisiana, and her father was from a swamp town in southern Louisiana called Gator Crossing. He had come to Yelgar as a young man of twenty. His father had captured and sold alligators to zoos all over the country. He had also been an alligator hunter. He would kill the gators and sell their hides to makers of luggage, shoes, and other accessories. His nickname had been "Hack" Hebert.

No one knew exactly why, but everyone in Louisiana had a nickname. Jacy's father's name was Murphy "Man" Hebert. After his father died, Murphy had continued with the only trade he knew, alligator hunting. His wife, Jacy's mother Lucille, had worked in a small bait and grocery store that her mother and father owned. Murphy and Lucille met and were married two years later.

Lucille's father and Jacy's grandfather Pierre Bellard was a carpenter and creator of many beautiful objects—furniture, lamps, figurines, and many other designs. These creations were all made from the cypress trees in the swamp. He sold some of them in his small store on the bayou. Pierre's wife Macy managed the store with Lucille helping.

Murphy became like a son to Macy. He had lost his mother at thirteen years old, so he felt very close to Macy. Murphy said that many of his family members thought she had died and others said that she could not take her husband's lifestyle and had walked away—never being heard from again. Whatever had happened, Murphy was all right with it and had moved on with his life. If she had left, he harbored no hard feelings. Murphy was a very kind and gentle man.

Murphy and Lucille had been married for three years when Jacy was born. Because they had both been only children with no brothers or sisters, they had hoped to give Jacy both a brother and a sister. But it never happened because Lucille had developed some female problem that her mother had and had not been able to have any more children after a miscarriage. They had decided not to adopt and to thank God for the child they did have.

Jacy was twelve when her grandfather Hack Hebert died, leaving only her mother's parents Pierre and Macy to spoil their grandchild.

Jacy was now twenty-one years old. She had graduated from Yelgar High School at eighteen and gone to work in her grandparents' store where she was learning to craft cypress creations. The small items were sold out of the store while the larger items, like furniture and chandeliers, were sold and shipped to businesses around the country.

Pierre was a very good craftsman, and his work was praised. He was grateful that Jacy was learning the trade, though he had not expected a woman to achieve such a high level of expertise. Jacy had refused to go to college and insisted on remaining in the family business.

Shortly after Jacy's graduation, Murphy and Lucille told her they were moving to Baron Rouge. They had saved a great amount of money, and because they had connections with gator hunters and fur trappers, they were going to open their own business processing the skins themselves into sellable items.

Now Jacy had to make a decision. Yelgar was a small town of fifty-five thousand people. This was her chance to move to the big city. She did not have many friends—at least none she could not live without. In high school she'd had a few dates and a boyfriend. Then after high school she had dated several different boys. None of those relationships had been serious, so there was no boyfriend to hold her back. The only problem would be leaving her town that she loved and her grandparents that she adored. At twenty-one she could make her own decision, and after a week, she did. She would stay and pursue her career of working with cypress.

Her parents were sure she would be all right and told her she could stay in their home for a year until she could get her own place. The apartments in Yelgar were limited, especially the ones close to the swamp area where Jacy lived. Yelgar bordered the swamp. You could travel unlimited miles into the swamp from Yelgar. The townspeople said no one had ever gone completely through the swamp. Many had tried but never returned. The swamp was a treacherous thing. It was alive—the swamp as a whole. Unless you marked your trail, you could go around in circles and see the same thing for the rest of your life. Newcomers to the area never went into the swamp without a guide. A few tried, but again, never came out.

The big talk of the town centered on tales of bright lights coming and going in the swamp. Jacy's grandfather said those stories had been going around since his childhood. When he was younger, he had seen the lights many times while night fishing. Many thought they were fireflies or swamp gas, but no one was completely sure about what to think.

Miss Susan, a friend of Lucille's, swore she had been abducted. She would go into great detail about how her abductors had put her on a table and put her through tests. Occasionally serious men in dark suits would arrive in town to tour the swamp because of the stories going around. Helicopters were also a common occurrence in Yelgar. All of a sudden there would be four of them flying around. No one knew where they came from or where they went. Many of the old-timers said there was an oasis in the middle of the swamp, but very few had actually seen it. No one really believed it existed.

Pierre's supply of cypress was running low because most of the trees in the area had been cut down. He and Jacy had been using the knees of the trees. The knees were roots that had grown up vertically near the trees. They had been making the knees into lamps and other decorative household items. But now even the knees of the cypress were gone. Pierre would have to go deeper into the swamp for more cypress.

Pierre's good friend Roy, who was a trapper and fisherman in the area, knew the swamp just as well, if not better, than anyone in Yelgar. He had lived there all his life and had ventured farther out into the swamp than anyone in the town. Roy sometimes brought home weird tales of the swamp. The last one was that he had smelled home cooking twenty miles into the swamp. There are banks in the swamp in different areas, so maybe someone had found one and cooked a feast. But they would have had to fight the alligators and snakes for the resting area. The smell was probably just Roy wishing he had some home cooking because he was hungry.

Roy had made a good find for Pierre though. He had found many small cypress trees in an area about thirty-five miles into the swamp—an area that was very dangerous. The boat's motor could only be used in certain areas of the swamp. In other areas you had to row or use long mud sticks. The closer you got to the swamp banks, the shallower the water. Once in the swamp, the boat was the only dry thing around. You had to completely rely on your boat. It must be rigged out with lanterns, food, all your essentials, and mosquito nets. You must also have medicines for snake bites because tree snakes could fall into the boat. There were many species of swamp snakes, and some were poisonous. The elements of the swamp were definitely against anyone who ventured out into it.

Like anything, the bad qualities of the swamp were balanced by its good ones. The swamp also possessed a beauty incomparable with any other in nature. In the spring, flowers covered the water with all colors and assortments—truly a sight to behold. Beautiful plants and vines not to be found elsewhere hung from the trees. The moss was home to many insects, and birds of many colors and species flew around searching for food. Food was very plentiful.

The most gorgeous residents were the butterflies in flight. Their colors—reds, yellows, blues, blacks, whites, just about every color of the rainbow—made them a joy to watch.

Roy told Pierre that he would draw him a map that showed where he had located the cypress. Pierre was thrilled that he could continue his work with Roy's cypress find. Roy explained that he should not try to cut the larger trees by himself because they were in a dangerous area; he would definitely need help. There was no land in sight, so he must take a long float on the back of his boat to drag the trees back. Pierre must wait for heavy rain so the swamp would be full of water, which would also make travel much easier. In a drought, you could get caught in the mud and have to stay there for weeks until it rained. The deeper water meant that the trip would be safer. Pierre definitely wanted a safe trip.

Roy drew the map for Pierre and then showed him shortcuts so he would have a better chance of not getting lost. Pierre was now ready to find himself a helper to take to the swamp for his journey. He asked Jack "Bubba" Smith, a thirty-year-old man he had known for many years. Bubba had helped Pierre many times in his wood shop and store and was willing to take the trip with him. Pierre knew that Bubba could handle himself in the swamp; he was very strong and could tolerate the elements.

Pierre had a flat-bottomed boat with a tiny room for the commode and a small corner they called a kitchen. The boat could sleep three people and carry enough supplies for a month. But it could only float in the deeper waterways and sections of the swamp. Pierre would have to take special routes through the swamp.

Jacy had been promised by her grandfather that she could take the trip with them and was very excited. She hardly slept the night before they left. It was her first trip so deep into the swamp, where the animals and plants were more plentiful and larger than normal.

By sunrise, Jacy, Pierre, and Bubba were packed and ready for the trip. They wore jeans, long-sleeve shirts, and a hat with a brim to protect them from the sun and the many biting insects. They also brought goggles for those sections of the swamp where swarms of insects threatened to get into your eyes and block your vision. This could be very painful without eye protection of some kind.

As they left the shore, Pierre waved to all their loved ones on land. The trip could take as long as one or two weeks, and there would be very little communication. The short-wave radio on the boat was just for emergencies. Even in the event of an emergency, small airplanes or helicopters were the only way to locate people in trouble. Trying to give your location was not an easy task.

Jacy sat on the side panel of the boat and put her feet up as she enjoyed the cool breeze generated by the boat's slow pace. The weather was perfect. It was mid-September, and the temperature was seventy-eight degrees with low humidity that made for a comfortable day. The boat moved slowly, which made the ride very relaxing.

Bubba picked up his fishing poles, hoping to catch that big one for lunch. They had no refrigerator on the boat, so food they caught or food out of a can were the only meals available. Grilled fish was probably going to be their meal every day, and that was fine with the three explorers. They looked forward to their fishing enjoyment.

They were not able to see Yelgar landing anymore. They were at least two miles into the swamp. The waterways were still deep, and there were swamp shanties all along the banks. Shanties were small houses built on stilts that sat high up out of the water. They had no electricity or running water. The owners lived in the swamp and depended on it. Boats were their only transportation to get back and forth into Yelgar for their supplies. Most of the shanties were built where the banks were high along the deep waterways. The residents trapped and fished for a living and loved their lifestyle. Swamp shanties were usually found no farther than five or six miles into the swamp. Some people had a home in Yelgar and a shanty, spending time in both places. They used the shanty like some people used a campground, except often it was where they made their living.

Most shanties had tin roofs on a small-frame house with a porch built on one side for fishing. The people were very happy to have guests and welcomed them. As the boat passed the shanties, they waved to each other and nodded hello and good-bye.

Around noon it was time to stop the boat for lunch, and Jacy got her fishing pole ready. They had to decide which bait to use because there were different types of bait for different fish. Jacy decided on crickets because all fish like crickets. They had to use poles instead of rod and reels because of all of the stumps and trees in the area. Bubba brought out the bucket of crickets. They were so jumpy that they lost a couple of them. Finally, they managed to get the bait on their hooks and dropped their poles into the water.

Jacy soon had a bite. She jerked her pole up quickly, but to her surprise it was a medium-sized turtle. Turtles were eaten regularly in Louisiana, but today it was too much trouble to clean. Jacy dropped the turtle back into the water and watched it swim away. Then Pierre's line sunk rapidly in the water. He jerked his line up and saw it was a large catfish. Bubba grabbed the net and dropped it into the water while Pierre fought to land the big fish. Pierre finally dragged the fish to the net, and Bubba pulled it up. This fish weighed at least seven pounds and would be perfect for lunch. Bubba skinned the catfish and prepared it to be grilled on the hot plate. Jacy knew that seasoning and cooking the fish was her job and expertise. She grilled the fish and opened a can of beans. It was a marvelous first lunch for their trip.

At four o'clock the sun was not as bright as it had been, and the cool air was taking over. The temperature had already dropped to seventy-two degrees. Pierre and Bubba prepared the mosquito netting for the evening. The net hung from a bar over half the boat and then attached to the sides of the boat. Many areas of the swamp had swarms of mosquitoes so thick you could not breathe. The netting protected you until you were out of that area.

As they went deeper and deeper into the swamp, the air became thicker, and as night came on, fog covered the water and made it difficult to see. It was quiet except when a feeding animal's prey yelled out. The sound echoed across the water. The moon was beautiful with the clouds partially covering it, making it a tranquil moment, and they began to feel sleepy.

Bubba took out the transistor radio tape player, put a Cajun music tape in it, and turned the volume very low. They sat and munched on crackers and cheese before going to bed. Bedtime in the swamp was when the sun went down.

Pierre anchored in a deep area of water so there was no way they could drift into the mud. All they did to prepare for bed was brush their teeth and wash up. They would sleep in their clothes and wear them again the next day. Changing clothes was something they would do about every two or three days. They would wash their clothes by laying them on a rack in the boat to let the rain clean them. Rain in September was usually every day or every other day. They hoped to have plenty of rain to keep the water high.

Their beds were small, a set of bunk beds and another bed secured halfway up the wall. The area was not enclosed, so they depended on their mosquito nets to keep out pesky intruders. The night was a cool fifty-eight degrees—perfect for sleeping.

Jacy, being the smallest at five feet five inches and 125 pounds, got the top bunk. Pierre, at 185 pounds and five feet ten inches, would sleep on the bottom bunk. Bubba was 170 pounds and six feet tall, so he got the longer individual bed. Everyone slept very well that night.

As daylight shined in and the sounds of the swamp got louder, Jacy jumped up to make the coffee for the crew and pulled out some cinnamon rolls she had packed up. Bubba and Pierre were grateful for her thoughtfulness. Breakfast was soon over, and they were ready to start the motors and get underway. They still had quite a way to go.

Their first day had been very slow because they had taken their time to enjoy the scenery. Today they were going to try and cover at least six miles.

There had been no rain the day before, so the water level would not be high in some areas, which would definitely cause some problems. They needed a good rain today or tonight.

The swamp was getting thicker, and the trees were closer together and had more moss on them than in other areas. Sunlight did not get through, so there were lots of mud spots. Because of the boat's size, Pierre had to cut the motor and use the paddle and mud sticks. The water was full of driftwood and lots of reptiles. There was no way of knowing how long it would take to get out of this area. The only nice thing about the delay was the coolness in the shade of the huge trees.

Many snakes hung from the branches of the trees as they waited for a meal of bird or lizard. Jacy watched them carefully in case one fell into the boat. She kept a paddle close to throw it out or whack it.

After about six hours, they saw sunlight up ahead. They kept paddling and finally reached the open space. Now they could rest and have lunch. They kicked back and had a nice lunch of canned meat sandwiches because no one was in the mood to fish.

After lunch, Pierre started the motor up and tried to keep with the map Roy had given him. He had gone into the swamp many times for different reasons, but never this part of the swamp. He had no idea what was ahead. And things often changed in the swamp areas. One month of dry weather could make an area completely impossible to get through. Roy had made the map under the assumption it would rain every other day and this would be a passable route to the cypress.

As evening fell, still no rain came and concern filled Pierre's mind. "I know it will rain tonight," said Pierre. "This is our raining month."

Bubba agreed, and they prepared for bed. It had been a hard day for Pierre and Bubba because they'd had to use the mud sticks and paddles. They were very tired and ready to go to sleep early.

Morning came, and they looked to see if it had rained. There was no evidence of rain during the night. This was not good as they were getting deeper and deeper into the swamp. It was now their third day, and they wondered whether they should continue on or turn back now. They would have to decide quickly. They all talked about what could happen but still decided to go forward and hope for rain soon.

Pierre pulled his map out and turned the motor on. There were two motors on the back of the boat. If something happened to one, he could use the other until the broken one was fixed. Debris in the water could damage the motor, or gators. They often followed boats and sometimes got caught up in them.

As Pierre drank his morning coffee, he took out his binoculars and tried to see what was coming ahead. Everything looked clear and passable. It was taking three times longer than they had figured to reach their destination. Roughly guessing, the men thought that between the hours spent using the motors and mud sticks and paddles, they were about twelve or fifteen miles into the swamp.

The water they had brought along was only for drinking. They would use rainwater caught in pails that Jacy had placed on the floor of the boat to clean up, but the pails were still dry.

Jacy was a pretty girl with big brown eyes and shoulder-length auburn hair. She was an outdoors type who only used makeup on special occasions, and jeans were her main wardrobe. But even though she was not a fussy girl, the only thing she dreamed about right now was washing her hair and cleaning up in the rain.

Pierre and Bubba had different worries, and they were getting more intense. As they traveled slowly watching for any signs of cypress, Bubba pointed at a sign nailed to a tree. It read "Roy was here." They knew they were following the map correctly and should reach their destination soon now. If not today, then tomorrow for sure they would run into the cypress.

Jacy made more sandwiches for lunch. There could be no fishing in this area because there were too many gators and snakes. They would catch them on their hooks, and the only way to get them off would be to cut the fishing lines.

Bubba took out his compass just to see if they were still going in the right direction. The compass moved left and right and would not come to a stop. He called Pierre over to see this in amazement. Pierre had heard that a compass could not be used deep in the swamp and that sometimes short-wave radios would not operate either. Bubba wanted to know why not. Pierre guessed that maybe it was because of a magnetic field of some kind. Bubba said he had dropped the compass in water before they left on this trip; perhaps that had broken the compass. Pierre just smiled and kept guiding the boat. Gazing over the swamp waters, he sighed. Roy had told him he would be doing some trapping in this area. Knowing that Roy was somewhere nearby was comforting.

The boat was moving slowly, so Jacy decided to drop a fishing line into the water to try to catch supper. She put a wiggly worm on the hook and dropped it into the water. It only took five minutes before she had caught another catfish. This one was not as large as the last, but it was enough for a nice supper. Bubba skinned the fish and prepared it for Jacy to grill. This kept Jacy's mind busy. She put a country and western tape in the tape player and turned the volume down low as she swayed with the music. After supper they all discussed what tomorrow would bring. If there was no rain tonight, going home would be the best idea.

With the water level dropping, gators and snakes were more easily seen, and mud spots were popping up. This was very bad. Pierre had to forget the map and use his own instincts to stay in deep water, and night was on its way. They dropped the mosquito net and hoped for rain so they could continue on their venture. Finding a deep place to drop the anchor was not easy anymore. The worry of snakes crawling into the boat was a real concern.

As they lay on their beds, they agreed that if it did not rain that night they would head home. Night fell and no rain came. Nothing else mattered now. Getting home alive was the only important thing.

As Pierre got up from his bed, he spotted a snake coiled up on the side panel of the boat. He took the paddle and knocked it off into the water and carefully looked to see if any other snakes had crawled into the boat during the night. There were none that he could see. He had to get the anchor up and start moving the boat. Gators were all around the boat, so Bubba took a mud stick and hit them until they moved away. This would be a bad time to run over one and lose a motor.

Pierre only wanted to stay in high water areas and head back to Yelgar, but he was not sure of his location because he had never been in that area before. The best he could do was follow what looked like a marked trail in the tree line Everything seemed to look alike. Still hoping to run into Roy, he kept his binoculars close at hand. They had to be at least twenty-five miles into the swamp by now.

Without any rain, the temperature got up into the middle eighties. This was a very good indication there would probably be storms soon. Bad storms could be dangerous while in the swamp. They would have to tie the boat to a tree.

The sun was glaring down, and the water was alive with life. It was only morning; what would the afternoon be like? The humidity was so bad that they could hardly breathe, and flying insects had become bothersome. Swarms of gnats were everywhere. They had to put on painters' masks on so they would not inhale them.

Pierre got on his radio and tried to reach someone—anyone. The static was so bad that he could not hear a response. The radio would be no help. They were on their own, and the swamp was against them.

The float on the back of the boat was starting to drag and hit stumps in some areas. It caused the boat to sway and made it hard to control. If they could not find a more passable area, they would have to release the float, tie it to a nearby tree, and come back for it later.

With a quizzical look around, Bubba asked, "Where are we? I think we are out of our parish."

Pierre had to agree. "I have no idea where we are," said Pierre. "I know we are no longer following the map. The landmarks don't appear the same. We are lost for now, but not for long. I will get us home."

This being the fourth day, Jacy had only changed her clothes once. She asked Pierre if they could spare some water for washing her hair and cleaning up.

Pierre shook his head. "Jacy, I love you, but you can only use one cup of water. We are having a crisis here, and I don't know how long it will last."

Jacy nodded and did her best with the one cup of water.

"Girls," Bubba said. "Worried about their hair in the middle of the swamp."

Suddenly, birds were everywhere in a feeding frenzy. There were pelicans and cranes, hundreds of them as far as you could see. Some had snakes in their mouths, while others had fish. As the boat passed, the birds continued feeding without interruption. As the boat got farther away, they thinned out.

"Wow!" Jacy said. "That was a sight to see."

"Because of the low water, the fish are trapped in shallow areas. That is what caused the birds to come in for feeding," explained Pierre.

When Jacy looked down into the water, she could see fish of every size, snakes, and frogs. And the gators were now more aggressive and bit at the boat as they passed by.

Bubba cautioned Jacy, "Don't throw any food out of the boat. The gators will never stop following us."

The three had skipped breakfast that morning. It was now one o'clock and time for a sandwich and some relaxation as the boat moved along slowly. There were no rain clouds in the sky. Ahead was a dark, shaded area, so they dropped the mosquito net, knowing there was likely to be a swarm of mosquitoes or gnats waiting for them. Just as they thought, mosquitoes were everywhere. They took out repellent and used it on themselves as well as the net. The ordeal lasted about an hour, and then they were back in the sun.

A short while later, the float got caught on a stump. Bubba jumped from the boat onto the float and used a hatchet on the stump to break it loose. Jacy wondered how much longer before the boat got stuck on a stump or mud bog and they had to get out of the boat to free it.

Pierre tried to figure out where they were by watching the sun, but it was only guessing. Seeing Roy would be their only hope of a fast return home; otherwise, it could be weeks.

There would be no stopping that night. Pierre and Bubba took turns steering the boat very slowly. Stopping this deep into the swamp would be an invitation to every animal and reptile to come onboard. Land was all around, but only in small patches. With no rain, the land patches were becoming larger.

They saw huge raccoons, nutrias, minks, and swamp rabbits. Turtles were everywhere, including alligator snapping turtles that had to weigh over a hundred pounds.

Pierre said to Bubba and Jacy, "There have to be trappers around here. Keep an eye out." They listened for the sound of motors, but nothing was heard.

Evening was falling once again. Jacy opened two cans of stew and warmed them up for supper. The men needed something hearty to eat; they would be up all night. She also made a large pot of coffee and toast. The bread was no longer very fresh, so she put several slices in a skillet on the hot plate and grilled both sides. By the time they were done eating, night had fallen. The stars were beautiful in the sky. The wind was picking up, maybe a sign of stormy weather. The humidity was so heavy that it dampened their hair and clothes.

Jacy and Pierre were the first to rest; Bubba would wake them in four hours. Jacy and Pierre would then stay up and guide the boat for four hours. Sleep would not come easily with the heat and humidity. Jacy lay awake on her bunk for a while and thought how happy she would be to get back to Yelgar to see her family and friends. Finally, she fell asleep.

Bubba was being very careful not to run into any stumps as he sipped his coffee and hoped to see raindrops. A lantern hung from the top rail of the boat to provide some light. Suddenly Bubba saw lights in the sky, flickering lights of red, blue, green, and yellow. He yelled at Pierre and Jacy to come quickly. They jumped out of bed in response to Bubba's call.

"Do you see that?" asked Bubba. Jacy and Pierre looked up into the sky.

"Wow!" said Jacy. "What is it?"

"I don't know what they are, but those lights are spotted quite often," answered Pierre.

"They are beautiful and a bit scary," said Jacy. "Could it be an airplane?"

"It could be," said Pierre, "but I don't think so. I've seen them many times before. One second they are there, and then they are gone the next."

Sure enough, in no time they had disappeared completely. With all of the excitement, Jacy decided not to try to go back to sleep. She wanted to stay up and watch the sky. Pierre went back to bed so he could take his turn at guiding the boat.

Within five minutes of the lights' disappearance, they heard helicopters in the area all around. The helicopters were flying as low as they could get. They saw three of them, but none came close to them.

Bubba asked, "Should we signal them to let them know we are lost?"

Jacy said, "Yes, let's send up a flare."

The loud noise roused Pierre from his bed again. "What is going on?" he asked.

"There are helicopters all around us," replied Jacy

"They are responding to the lights," he explained.

Pierre must have been right because within minutes the noise had faded away. There were no more helicopters in the area—and no one to see a flare.

Things had calmed down, but Jacy knew something was very strange about the whole incident. Even Bubba was a little shaken up. He had never witnessed anything quite like it before. He had grown up with weird tales of the swamp, but it was still shocking to actually see it.

Pierre once more tried to go back to bed, but Jacy would not. It was three thirty in the morning.

"How could anyone sleep after this?" Jacy asked.

Pierre answered, "Don't worry. It is nothing to be scared of."

But Bubba trembled and could not keep his eyes off the stars above.

There were no more strange lights or helicopters that night. When it was time for Pierre to take his turn at guiding the boat, Jacy woke him. He got up but was still half asleep. She gave him a large cup of coffee. It was almost daybreak. Bubba took his turn at sleeping.

The sun was coming up on their fifth day in the swamp, and they were still lost. Still, the only thing they were running low on was drinking water. They had plenty of packaged food, and the swamp was full of fish. Eating would not be a problem. If no rain came, they could boil the swamp water and drink it, even though that was not what they wanted to do, especially now that the water was so low and full of small living things that they had no names for.

The sun was completely out, and clouds were gathering in the sky. The wind was picking up, and they welcomed the breeze as it blew the small swarms of bugs away.

Then a few drops of rain fell, and they could see lightning in the distance. A storm was brewing. The thunder roared, and the sky darkened. Pierre was not sure whether to wake Bubba or let him sleep. He had only been sleeping for two hours. But the thunder and lightning were getting closer, so Pierre told Jacy to go wake him up. Bubba jumped up and could not believe it was actually going to rain. The only problem was that this rain was coming in a vicious storm. Pierre told Bubba to take the binoculars and find a tree large enough to tie the boat to so they would not blow away in the storm.

The men decided to tie the float to the nearest tree—any tree. It was causing the boat to sway again.

They pulled the float to a medium-sized tree and used a chain to hold it until they could escape the storm and come back for it. Now the boat moved faster, so they hurriedly looked for a large tree that they hoped would keep them safe.

Bubba spotted one through the binoculars. It was a football field away. The men put on their hip boots, knowing both of them would have to get out of the boat to tie it to the tree because it was in a shallow area. As the boat approached the area, the rain came down very hard. The wind was also strong and pushed the boat. The men jumped out of the boat and put a rope around its handle and tied it tightly to the tree. They were sinking in the mud and finding it hard to move their feet. The gators were getting close to Pierre, so Bubba aimed for their heads with a hatchet while Pierre did the tying. Finally, it was finished. The men slowly walked back to the side of the boat to get back in.

As they grabbed the side of the boat, Bubba screamed, "Water moccasins!"

They had stepped into a nest. The snakes bit their boots and just hung there.

Jacy screamed, "Unsnap your boots and leave them!"

As they unsnapped their boots, they continually sank into the mud. Jacy put a paddle close to them so they could grab it. As they grabbed onto the paddle and tried to get into the boat, at least three water moccasins bit them. Two snakes bit Bubba, and one bit Pierre. They fell into the boat and just lay on the deck. Jacy hurried and got the snake-bite vaccine. She gave them both an injection. Bubba was first because he had been bitten twice. The rain poured down on the men. Jacy helped Bubba to his bunk and then returned to help Pierre. They were out of the rain now, but the storm had worsened. The boat rocked and made cracking noises.

This was the most scared Jacy had been in her life. She had two men's lives in her hands. What was she to do? She got the alcohol out of the medicine chest and applied it to the snake bites, which were on their arms. She then took out the snake bite manual and saw that she was supposed to use a suction cup on the bites. She used the cup on Bubba first and, sure enough, the venom came out of the small holes in the skin. She then helped Pierre, and it worked on him, too. At least some of the venom had been removed. The men were limp and did not move, their speech was slurred. Was it because of the actual snake bites or was it the medicine that had been injected? Jacy did not know, but one thing Jacy knew for sure was that they could not stay out in the swamp. She had to get them home—and fast.

The storm was horrible. The buckets she had put out were almost full. She hoped soon there would be a break in the bad weather so she could send a flare up for help. If anyone was around, they would come to their rescue. The storm had already lasted longer than most storms. It was approaching late afternoon, and the lightning still flashed. If the boat had not been tied up, it would have capsized. The men had saved her life, and she would not forget it. She hoped everything would be all right, but, for the moment, she had two very ill men on her hands.

The water level had risen very high now. The storm had calmed down and evening had arrived. Jacy took the flare box and set one off. She made sure the lantern stayed on and turned her tape player very loud, hoping help would come. She tried the emergency radio but got nothing but static. She was very frustrated. Nothing seemed to work. It had been forty-five minutes since she sent a flare up. In an hour, it would be dark enough that it would be easily seen.

Jacy returned to check on the men. They were quivering and shaking violently. She took off their shirts and wrapped them tightly in army blankets. She wiped their faces with cool water and told them she was trying to get help.

Pierre looked at his granddaughter and said, "Thank God for you, Jacy."

Jacy was so glad her grandfather had let her come on the trip. What would have happened to him and Bubba if they had been alone?

Once it was dark, she decided it was time for another flare. In the darkness it could be seen for miles in the swamp. As Jacy set off the flare, she thought she could hear a motor in the distance. She lowered the volume of the tape player and was sure that it was a large boat motor. She turned the volume up on the tape player so the sound could be heard for quite a distance.

The men were very sick. The bitten places on their skin had turned red and blue. Jacy got out the rest of the drinking water and gave them as much to drink as they wanted. They both felt hot. She could only guess how high their fevers were because she had no thermometer. She did have aspirin, but she was not sure that would help. Instead, she just wiped their foreheads with cool water and prayed to God that they would live and that help would come soon. As she glanced at her watch, the hands moved to eleven o'clock.

She was not in the mood for any music tonight, so she turned the tape player down. She also wanted to listen for the motor she had heard before. It was getting closer. She grabbed another flare and sent it up. She just knew someone was coming to help her. She turned the tape player's volume up again and prayed.

As Jacy walked back into the covered area of the boat, she dropped the mosquito net. She had not slept in two nights and was getting very sleepy. But if she went to sleep, she could not help the men. She poured herself a large cup of cold coffee left out from the day before. Something had to help keep her awake.

Pierre was awake and asked Jacy to take off his shoes because they were full of water. She took off his shoes and socks and wrapped a blanket around his feet. She then turned to Bubba and did the same thing. Trying to make them comfortable was very important. Bubba was not moving much, and his head was burning up. Jacy continued to put cool rags on their foreheads. There was not much more she could do.

The coffee was not working. Jacy was getting sleepier and sleepier. She went to one of the buckets of water on the deck and stuck her head in it. She had to stay awake somehow. All she needed now was another episode of the lights that had appeared the night before. The incident scared her and would keep her awake all night. It was early morning now, and the sun was coming out. She picked up Pierre's binoculars and slowly scanned the swamp in all directions. Coming right at them at a fast pace was a large trapper's boat.

"Maybe it's Roy," Jacy thought.

She watched the boat as it approached. It was Roy. She turned the tape player off and screamed, "Please hurry! They've been bitten by snakes!"

Roy pulled up next to Pierre's boat. By some miracle he had his wife Doris a petite, pretty lady, with him. She was a nurse at the Yelgar Hospital. Roy jumped into the boat, and Jacy explained that water moccasins had bitten both of the men and that Bubba had been bitten twice. She explained how she had administered the vaccine immediately after the bites had occurred. Doris jumped into the boat and immediately went to the men to take their vitals. She asked Roy to put the men into their boat so she could watch them closely. Bubba was in bad shape. He needed another injection.

Together, all three of them helped the two men into the larger boat. Doris gave Bubba another injection. Pierre's vitals were good, but he still needed to be under a watchful eye.

Jacy looked up to the heavens and said, "Thank you, God. Thank you."

Now the men had a good chance to live. Roy could get them home in one day. His boat was larger and much faster.

Jacy told Doris the men had only drunk water and had not eaten the day before. Doris told Jacy she would heat up broth. Heavy food was not what they needed right now. Bubba could not talk, and he was still shaking very badly. Pierre was very sick but was no longer shaking.

Doris said, "Jacy, you saved these men's lives by giving them the vaccine immediately. The poisonous venom should not affect their hearts."

Roy told Jacy to get dry clothes for them. There was more rain coming, and the temperature would probably drop into the fifties by evening. After dressing them, Roy put the men in the bunks while Doris warmed the broth.

The rain had never really stopped completely. It would slack off and then start again, but the thunder and lightning were over for now.

Roy knew he had to get the men to a hospital as soon as possible. But he did not want to leave Pierre's boat in the swamp unattended, so he asked Jacy if she could guide the motor on the boat.

She replied, "Yes, Roy. I've done it many times before."

"Okay," he said, "you follow me as close as possible."

Jacy nodded and climbed back into her grandfather's boat. Roy took out his hatchet and cut the rope that was tightly tied around the tree. The boat was loose. Jacy started the motor. Roy explained to Jacy that he was not stopping for any reason, so she must keep up. The water was high, and they could make good time. If for any reason she could not keep up, she was to anchor the boat in deep water and wait for him to come back for her after he had found medical care for the men.

Jacy asked Roy if she could stop for an hour or so later.

He said, "Sure. Use your binoculars and you will still be able to see me. Just follow at your own pace."

Jacy told Roy she had not slept in two consecutive nights and could hardly hold her eyes open. She followed Roy for at least four hours before she was too sleepy to go on. She put the boat in an area where the water was deep and dropped the anchor. She was very hungry and thirsty and decided that a can of beans and wieners would be a fast, good meal. Her drink of choice was a can of root beer. After eating quickly, she dropped the mosquito net and lay on her bunk.

It was twelve thirty and her sixth day away from home. The rain peppered the roof of the boat. It was a soothing sound. The wind blew a cool breeze, and there was a chill in the air. Jacy grabbed a blanked and fell into a deep sleep.

Hours went by, and evening came. Jacy had slept for six hours. It was now raining harder, and the wind picked up speed, rocking the boat. The noise and motion woke Jacy. As she got up from her bunk, she could see that evening had fallen. It was too late for looking through the binoculars for Roy's boat.

Unsure what to do, she decided to pull up the anchor and start the motor. She aimed the boat in the same direction she had last seen Roy going. She knew that night travel in the swamp was very tricky. Remembering what Roy had told her, she slowed the motor down. He had told her to anchor and not move. But right now that sounded like a waste of time to Jacy. She kept the boat moving for about two hours and then stopped.

By now, Roy should have reached Yelgar. If he had, her grandfather and Bubba were now in the hospital and their lives would be saved—she was sure of it. Roy would likely rest a bit before he came back for Jacy. That meant it would be at least the next day before he returned for her.

Jacy turned on her tape player and made a snack. She just let the wind push on the boat. Jacy knew this section of the swamp as well as her father and grandfather; she was not afraid. Listening to the rain and music was making her drowsy, and before long, she was asleep again.

When Jacy woke up, morning had come once more, and the sun had risen. She got up to make herself a cup of coffee and had a cinnamon roll. She was well rested now, finally having caught up on her sleep. The rain still sprinkled, but the wind had calmed down. The temperature was now in the low fifties. It was a very refreshing cool. She put a windbreaker on and walked to the uncovered part of the boat.

There was a strange calm to this part of the swamp. There were no alligators in sight. She took the binoculars and looked for snakes, but there were none. The only wildlife she saw were a few different kinds of birds. The trees were huge and towered up high into the sky. Moss hung off the tree branches, creating massive shaded areas. She had never seen this type of tree before. It resembled the mighty oak. She was worried but knew she would be found.

She looked once more into the binoculars and could see the huge trees for miles. She also saw what looked to be a sandy beach. Maybe she had found Yelgar or a surrounding town. She started the motor and headed for the beach. As she drew closer, she could see a bright yellow light surrounding it. Maybe the town was having some kind of celebration and the lights were part of it. She got the boat as close to shore as she could go and dropped the anchor.

Jacy jumped out of the boat and just stood in the sand for a while. It felt so good to be on dry land. This was her seventh day in the swamp, and she had finally arrived somewhere. Believing she was in Yelgar, she was anxious to get to the hospital to check on Pierre and Bubba. She ran up a hill and through the light, but as she looked around, she slowed down. An older woman was standing on top of the small hill with her arms stretched outward toward Jacy. The woman looked like she was in her sixties, with a medium build and graying hair. Jacy did not know her.

She met Jacy as she arrived at the top of the hill. "Welcome to the colony. My name is Lavern," the woman said.

Jacy was puzzled. "Colony? Funny, I've never heard of this town. Where is it located? In what parish?"

Lavern said, "Dear, you must not be frightened of what you are about to see. No harm will come to you."

"Where am I?" Jacy screamed and then she turned to run back to the boat.

Lavern shouted, "Please, Jacy. Please don't go!"

Jacy stopped. "How do you know my name?"

Lavern said, "Please, Jacy. I have things I want to show and explain to you."

Jacy reluctantly turned around and walked back to Lavern. They walked a short distance toward what looked like a small town. There were small houses with pyramid-shaped roofs scattered all over. Then they came to the entrance of the small town. The streets were wide and made of brick. The town's businesses looked like something out of a fifties movie Jacy had watched with her grandmother. The huge trees were all throughout the town, and the pyramid-shaped roofs of the buildings were covered in sand. Everything looked camouflaged. As they came into the first section of town, there was a large, round concrete table with a wraparound bench, also made of concrete. Lavern asked Jacy to sit down, and she did. There was no one else around.

Jacy heard a door open, and a chill went down her spine. The man who appeared was not completely human; his features looked otherworldly. He had a bald head, large eyes, and a small nose and ears. His mouth was perfect. He was of medium height and weight.

Jacy closed her eyes and asked, "What are you going to do with me?"

The man answered, "Jacy, open your eyes. You are our guest, and we are happy to have you here. My name is Samuel. I will answer all of your questions—and there will be many. The people here are part human and part alien from another world. They are of every nationality. There are many children that will crave your love, Jacy. Please don't be scared. They will want to touch you. This is how they show affection. We would love for you to stay with us a while. Will you, Jacy? We will not make you if you refuse."

Jacy thought for a while. She did like Samuel. He seemed to have a warm, friendly personality. Mesmerized by her surroundings, she said, "Yes, I guess I can stay for a while. I can't stay long, though. My grandfather and a friend are in the hospital, and I must return to check on them."

Samuel put his hand on top of Jacy's and said, "Pierre and Bubba are just fine. Don't worry about them."

Jacy was shocked. "How do you know that?"

Samuel said, "I will explain it to you later."

Jacy looked up to see the other inhabitants coming out. There were colonists of every age, and all of them had a different look. She tried to hide her fear. Nothing in her life could have prepared her for what was happening. Samuel told her not to be scared. She thought he did not want her to frighten the children. Her heart was beating at a very fast rate.

Children gathered around her. Some were more human than others. They were timid as they came up to her and stared into her eyes. Their smiles were so genuine, and they put out their hands for her to touch them. When she touched their hands, they just giggled and ran away. They seemed to be very playful and happy. And then everyone disappeared as they walked away.

Jacy asked Samuel, "Where did everyone go?"

He told her the adults went back to their jobs, and the children went back to playing games or to their studies. Samuel asked Jacy to go with Lavern to see where she would be staying. She would be able to clean up, and then he was going to give her a tour of the whole colony and let her meet all of its people.

Lavern took Jacy to a small house. They entered into a small living room with a TV and a VCR, a rack of tapes, and a sofa. Through the living room was a bedroom with a bed and a dresser and small bathroom with a commode and shower.

Lavern asked Jacy what size she wore so she could go and purchase her something to wear.

"Where are your shops?" asked Jacy.

"They are on the main street in town, like in any US city," replied Lavern.

"Is everything here like our cities and towns?" asked Jacy. But Lavern did not reply.

Jacy told Lavern she was a size six, and Lavern set out to purchase Jacy an outfit similar to what she had on.

While Lavern was gone, Jacy peeped out the windows and could see many of the residents coming and going. Some of them were on bicycles. Their basic dress was the same as what she wore, mostly jeans and T-shirts. Some of the children were wearing overalls.

Jacy focused on their faces and bodies. Some had more otherworldly features, while some had more human features, but most had the same features— small ears and noses, large eyes, and normal human mouths. Samuel and Lavern spoke English with a Cajun accent. It was like they had lived in Louisiana and adopted all of their ways but without ever having been seen. The residents' skin colors varied from light to dark. Their hair was not as thick as humans, and most of the men were bald.

"Could it be that they shaved their heads?" thought Jacy.

Jacy dropped the green cotton curtain on the window and focused on the TV and VCR. The tapes were all Disney G-rated movies. When she turned on the TV, words came across the screen: "No Access." Not being in the mood for a movie, she sat on the flowered sofa in the small living room and awaited Lavern's return.

It had only been about thirty minutes when Lavern returned. She knocked on the door, and Jacy opened it, anxious to see what kind of clothes she had in the bag. There was a pair of jeans that looked like a familiar brand, except that it had no logo on it, and a red plaid shirt with long sleeves. She had also bought underwear and a pair of slide sandals.

Jacy liked everything and thanked Lavern. Then Lavern showed Jacy where the toiletries were stored and gave her some towels. She told Jacy she would return in one hour, and they, along with Samuel, would go to lunch.

Jacy was now more relaxed and not as frightened as she had been. There was nothing she would enjoy more than a good shower. The bathroom was exactly what anyone would expect to find in a hotel room, along with the mirrored medicine cabinet. The soap and shampoo had no brand name on them. The shampoo she washed her hair with had a citrus smell to it. The soap seemed to be the same. It was a very mild and pleasant smell. As she got out of the shower, she wrapped a towel around herself and opened the medicine cabinet. It contained a toothbrush, toothpaste, comb, and brush—everything she needed. While brushing her teeth, she noticed that the toothpaste was the same as she always used, although it had no label. Nothing had labels. Where did all this merchandise come from? Samuel had said she would have many questions, and he was very right.

Jacy towel dried and combed her wet hair and then debated whether to leave it down or wear it in a ponytail. She decided to wear it down. Then she walked into the bedroom to put her new clothes on. Everything fit her perfectly. She felt refreshed and clean. Now all she had to do was wait for Lavern to return for her.

She lay on the bed and thought, "What is happening in my life? It's like I'm dreaming, but I know I'm not. I should be afraid of what might happen to me, but for some reason I'm not." She got up from the bed when Lavern once again knocked on the door.

Together the two women walked to the town entrance. Samuel was waiting for them at the large, round table. The people in the town had resumed their normal activities. No one even acknowledged their presence.

Samuel stood up and asked Jacy if there was anything else she needed. She said that everything was fine and that she was no longer frightened. Samuel smiled and asked Jacy to follow him. They walked into the town, passing many stores, restaurants, and a variety of businesses. Lavern was right. It looked like any other small town in the United States.

Finally, they entered a restaurant. It had about thirty tables and was decorated in a Cajun style. On the tables with salt and pepper was also some Cajun Spice and filet for gumbo. On the walls were fishing nets with crabs and crawfish in the nets as decoration. Also, on the wall was an old, retired pirogue boat. They seated themselves at a table near a window. The restaurant was half full of people from the colony. None of them stared or even glanced their way. Jacy, of course, looked at everything and everyone in awe. Soon, a waitress came to the table with menus and glasses of water. She wore a white skirt and blouse. Her hair was a light dirty blonde, and her eyes were a bit larger than a human's, slanted and dark green in color. Her mouth was normal, and her nose was very small but cute. She was about five feet two and petite. She looked to be about Jacy's age.

Samuel stood and introduced her to Jacy. Her name was Carol. The two girls smiled at each other and shook hands. Carol then asked the group what she could get for them. Jacy looked at the menu and noticed it was all Cajun seafood. She then looked at the customers around her to see how their meals looked. All of the meals looked great. She asked

Lavern and Samuel what they were going to order. Samuel ordered seafood gumbo, and Lavern ordered the crawfish and shrimp bisque.

"What a decision," Jacy thought. She finally decided on crawfish etouffee.

Carol then asked what they wanted to drink with the meals. Samuel ordered iced tea, and Lavern and Jacy ordered cola.

Jacy focused on the tablecloth. It was a red and white check. On top of the table were sugar, salt, pepper, and gumbo filé. The familiarity of the things around her made Jacy feel more comfortable.

Carol brought out the drinks and set them down on the table. She then returned to the kitchen for their food. Jacy had not had a decent meal in a week. This was going to be a real treat. Carol brought Jacy's food out first, then Lavern's, and then Samuel's. She gave them each a bowl of rice. Jacy was so hungry and it all smelled so good that she immediately began to eat. Samuel stopped her and asked that she first bow her head and thank God for the food. The three bowed their heads and said a silent prayer of thanks to God.

Jacy thought, "Wow, they're religious."

Then they all began to eat their food, and to Jacy's delight, it was very good.

After the meal was over, Samuel asked for the check. A large man in solid white pants and shirt came out of the kitchen. He approached the table and asked Jacy if she had enjoyed the meal. Assuming he was the chef, Jacy raved over how delicious it had been.

Samuel explained to Jacy that the man was the chef and that his name was Big Ben, jokingly adding that he was no relation to the one in England. Jacy smiled at him.

Ben smiled back and said, "This meal is on the house. I welcome you to the colony."

"Thank you very much," said Jacy. "I hope to see you again, Big Ben."

The three then got up and left the restaurant. As they walked down the street, Jacy could not help but notice how clean everything around was. There was no litter anywhere.

They walked a while until they came to what looked like an entrance to a park. Lavern and Jacy followed Samuel as he walked into the park. Once through the entrance, there were pigeons flying all around them, and Jacy saw park benches and water fountains that shot up toward the sky. It was a beautiful sight. The cool sprinkles of water from the fountains splashed them as they walked by. People of the colony were all around. Many of them were reading, and some of the children were feeding bread crumbs to the pigeons. This was a place for complete relaxation.

Samuel sat at a small bench with an attached table. Lavern excused herself, saying she had things to do and would return in an hour or so. Jacy sat beside Samuel hesitantly.

He tried to start a conversation with her. "Do you have any questions, Jacy?"

She answered, "Yes. Why doesn't Lavern have any alien features? She looks like a human."

Samuel said, "I'll tell you why. She is a human as you know her."

"Then why is she here?"

"Because years ago Lavern had a son born to her that was part alien. He has a rare blood disorder

and only her blood can save his life when he gets
sick, and that is very often. Lavern had to make a
hard decision between her two children. She has a
human son who is perfect in every way and well
taken care of in your world, and then she has her son
here in the colony that was dying and could not live
without her. They brought Lavern here often to help
her son by giving blood. The last time they brought
her, she chose not to return. She stayed and took care
of her son, and that's the only reason he lives today."

"Who are 'they'?" asked Jacy.

"*They* are the protectors of the colony. You
will soon meet them."

"How did Lavern have an alien child?"

"She was artificially inseminated by the
scientists and doctors that travel with the protectors.
This is a very deep discussion, Jacy. There will be
time to explain it all to you," said Samuel.

"Does this insemination happen often?" asked
Jacy.

"Yes," said Samuel. "It's been happening for
more years than you can even imagine."

"Why?" she asked.

"Because the protectors want their powers and
existence to survive," answered Samuel. "Their planet
has been failing for many years, and they are
surviving here on earth."

"Do they choose special people?" Jacy asked.

"Yes," said Samuel. "The people are
interviewed and brought to their nearby colony so that
they will come to understand the importance of the
aliens' existence. Without the donors, the aliens'
powers would be lost forever. Their powers are
wonderful. Many can see into the future or know
everything about the past. Many can do both. Some

can do things by concentrating their minds. There are many alien children that look human that have been placed in your world with human families. This has been going on for a very long time."

Jacy looked at Samuel and said, "You are part human. Who is your mother?"

He returned Jacy's gaze and said proudly, "Lavern is my mother. I am the child she left your world for. She chose to save my life, and I am very grateful.

"That's enough questions for now, Jacy. We will continue our conversation later."

They got up from the bench and continued to walk through the park. Jacy took this time to observe Samuel more closely. He was dressed in a long, black shirt that buttoned up the front and came down to the top of his knee. His pants were black, and he also wore black shoes. He was of medium build, and Jacy guessed that he was in his late thirties. His outfit looked like a uniform, but she had not seen anyone else with the same outfit on.

She looked at Samuel as they walked and asked, "Can I ask you one more question?"

He smiled at her and said, "Okay, one more."

"Are you the mayor of the colony, and is that a uniform you have on?"

"Oh," he said, "that's two questions, but I'll answer. This is a uniform, and I have many like it. You will only see me dressed this way. The answer to the other question is yes. I guess you could call me the mayor of the colony. And I have very special powers, Jacy. I'm going to tell you that Lavern is coming this way right now."

As they turned the corner of the brick pavement, Jacy could see the exit gate. Lavern was walking toward them. "How did you know, Samuel?"

"It's just one of my powers."

Lavern walked up to Jacy and asked if she had enjoyed the park.

"Of course," answered Jacy. "It was very beautiful."

"Did Samuel answer a few questions for you?" asked Lavern.

"Yes," said Jacy, "but I have many more for him."

"Well, we will have plenty of time for them later. Would you like to go back to your room and rest a while before we go to supper? We'll also have some entertainment."

"That sounds good," said Jacy.

It was about four thirty in the afternoon, and even though she was not tired, Jacy thought it would be nice to be alone for a while.

As they walked to her room, Lavern reached into her pocket and pulled out a small makeup bag that contained lipstick, foundation, and mascara.

"Jacy, maybe you would like to use this makeup for this evening."

"Thank you," said Jacy. "I surely would. You never know who you're going to meet," she added jokingly.

They reached the small house that Lavern and Samuel called her "room." Jacy opened the door and entered the house. As she walked into the bedroom, she glanced at the dresser and saw that the clothing she had arrived in had been cleaned and left nicely folded on top. She would have to thank whoever had cleaned her clothes. She walked back into the living room and lay on the sofa. She thought about all the questions she had asked Samuel. The answers he had given her seemed very confusing, and she had so many more questions to ask.

Jacy took a short nap and then bounced up from the sofa when she awoke. She went into the bathroom and applied makeup to her pretty face, brushed her teeth, and fixed her hair. She was now ready for the evening. Instead of waiting in the house, she walked out the front door onto a small wooden entrance porch and sat on the top step to wait for Lavern. It was dusk, and the sun was going down. She could see Lavern coming for her in the distance. Jacy stood up and walked toward her.

Lavern greeted her with a big smile. "We are so glad to have you here, Jacy," Lavern said.

Jacy thanked her and thought how nice Lavern was and how being around her made her completely relaxed and confident that no harm would come to her. As they walked into town, Jacy could see a band setting up on the brick street.

"What type of band is going to play?"

"Country and western and some Cajun," Lavern replied. "Tonight is a street dance. Would you like to go?"

"Yes, of course, Lavern. I love music."

"They also have booths around for eating and drinking."

"Do they have beer?" Jacy asked.

"Of course. Remember, we are all Cajuns here. There is no hard liquor, but plenty of beer."

Lavern reached into her pocket and gave Jacy some paper money. It was pastel blue with black stars around the sides of the bill. In the center of the bill, in heavy black print, was a circled number one. Lavern gave her five of these bills.

"This is for food and drinks, Jacy, in case you start dancing and I lose you in the crowd."

Jacy replied, "I will be hard to lose, Lavern. You and Samuel are the only people I know here."

"You will meet many people tonight, Jacy. Relax and have fun."

The music began, and the sound was no different than any other country band Jacy had heard, maybe even better than some of them. It was a large band with ten members. They performed country and Cajun favorites as they played their guitars, drums, fiddles, saxophones, and other instruments that Jacy had never seen before. People came from everywhere and danced to the music. Jacy and Lavern sat down in chairs that had been put out for the event.

Carol, the girl from the restaurant, came by and sat next to Jacy. She talked to Jacy, and the two girls quickly formed a friendly relationship. When Carol got up to dance with one of her male friends, a handsome young man, about twenty-five years old, came up to Jacy. He had short, dark hair and brown eyes. He was very muscular and stood about five feet ten inches. He looked 100 percent human.

He said, "My name is Billy. Would you like to dance, Jacy?"

Jacy answered, "Yes, I would."

Billy held his hand out to Jacy, and she noticed that it was not human. His fingers were very long. It was a slow song, and Carol winked at her as they danced. When the dance was over, Jacy and Carol went back to their seats.

Carol said, "He has your look, Jacy, and he is very nice."

Jacy agreed. He did have human looks, and he seemed to be very nice.

Carol and Jacy got up from their seats to get something to eat and drink. They walked for a while until they spotted a sandwich booth. Carol ordered a fish sandwich. Jacy then asked the young man in the booth for a hamburger.

Carol whispered to Jacy, "We have no meat in the colony. Ask for a veggie burger."

Jacy then looked at the man, who was staring back at her from the food booth, and corrected herself, "I mean a veggie burger, please."

The young man turned to prepare their orders. When the orders were ready, he handed them to the girls.

Carol asked, "How much do we owe you?"

He answered, "One unit each, please."

They each handed him one bill and went on to the next booth to get a drink. The girls each ordered a beer, and the cost of the beer was the same as the sandwich—one unit. The beer was served in a paper cup and was very good. The girls then walked back to their seats.

Lavern was there, and she was dancing to the music. The band was playing an old Cajun song, "Jolie Blonde." No Cajun could ever sit that song out; a Louisiana heritage would not allow it. Just as they were about to sit down, Billy appeared and again wanted Jacy to Cajun dance with him. She put her sandwich and beer down on the chair and took off to the street to dance. As she danced with Billy, she noticed that Carol was also dancing again.

Billy was a very good dancer, and he was so handsome. She tried not to look at his hands but found it hard, so she stared at his eyes. "What beautiful eyes they are," she thought.

The song ended and another started without a pause. Billy grabbed Jacy and hugged her close to him. She put her arms around him and lay her head on his shoulder. "This," she thought, "is very good."

They slow danced and swayed to the music. The song stopped, but Billy and Jacy continued swaying to the music that was no longer playing. After a while, they realized the band had taken a break, and Billy walked Jacy back to her chair. Jacy felt weak in the knees for the first time in her life. Her mom had always told her she would find a special man that would make her weak in the knees. She had always thought that was an exaggeration, but this was definitely no joke.

As Jacy approached her chair, she saw that Carol and Lavern sat with smirks on their faces. She picked up her food and drink and sat down. Billy thanked her for the dance and asked if he could also have the next one. Of course, she said yes.

Carol commented to Jacy that she and Billy had the same rhythm and looked as though they had danced together a hundred times. Jacy thanked Carol for the compliment. She took a bite of her veggie sandwich but realized she was no longer hungry, so she sipped on her beer instead. Her eyes skimmed the crowd to see if she could spot Billy.

Lavern asked Jacy if she was getting tired. Jacy quickly replied, "No, I feel fine."

She wanted to ask Lavern and Carol questions about Billy, but she did not know how to begin. The obvious questions about people did not apply here. He had probably never seen his family, and she had not seen any schools around. She knew time would give her answers, but time was something she did not have. Then a question came to her: would they ever let her go or would they keep her there? After meeting Billy, she was not sure which she wanted to wish for.

The band started again, and there he was, standing over Jacy. She was thrilled but tried not to show it. He once more held his hand out to her. She put her hand in his and again they went out to the street to dance. He held her close once more, and that is how they stayed through three songs. It did not matter whether the songs were fast or slow, close was how they stayed.

The band stopped for a short time, but Billy did not want to let Jacy go. He looked down at her and asked if she would take a walk with him.

She replied, "Yes, but first I must tell Lavern or she will be worried about me."

Billy walked Jacy back to where Lavern was seated. She asked if Billy could walk her home, and Lavern agreed. As they walked toward Jacy's, Billy suggested they walk down to the water first. As they approached an area close to the water's edge, they found benches set far apart and took a seat. Jacy could see the yellow light that bordered the island. She wanted to ask Billy why the light was there but thought questions were not in order right now.

Billy looked Jacy in the eyes and asked, "Do you want to know about the light that borders the island?"

"How did you know?"

"Your mind transferred the question to mine. Sometimes people really don't need to say a word to know what the other is thinking."

He went on to explain the bordering yellow light. "It is a conditioning light. When you leave through this light, everything that happened to you in the colony will be erased from your conscious mind, but your subconscious will always remember. When, or if, you return to the colony, walking through the light will bring all of your memories back to you. Leaving through the light will once more erase them from your conscious mind, but your subconscious will never be affected. The light extends up to the universe as far as the stars. Many planes and helicopters fly around us. The same applies to them. They enter the light, and when they exit they forget everything that they saw. This is how the colonies all over the world have existed for a very, very long time."

Jacy looked at Billy and thanked him for answering her question. He put his arm around her and put his head on her shoulder. In return, she leaned her head on his. They just sat quietly and stared into the night.

Then Billy asked Jacy if he could kiss her. Instead of answering him, Jacy kissed him. It felt like a never-ending kiss. A tingling feeling covered Jacy's whole body. She already had weak knees, but now she had a tingling body. This had to be love. Finally, they stopped kissing and embraced each other. Never wanting to let Billy go, Jacy knew this would be a very complicated relationship.

Billy pulled away from Jacy and looked into her eyes. Then he said, "I love you very much, and I have been waiting for you a long time."

"How could you have been waiting for me?"

"I've always known that you would come to me one day, Jacy. That day is here and never have I ever been this happy."

Jacy looked at Billy and said, "I think I love you too. I have never been this emotional with any man in my life. How could we be so sure of something like this in only five hours?"

He said, "I was sure the first minute I laid my eyes on you."

Jacy smiled and hugged and kissed Billy once more. This time it lasted at least fifteen minutes. In her world, a man would have definitely wanted to take this emotional moment to the next step, which would be having sex. Billy was not of her world, so she had no idea what to expect from him.

Jacy stood up and asked Billy if she could go back to her room. She was. overwhelmed by the whirlwind of their relationship.

He replied with a smile, "Jacy, can you give me five minutes before I get up? Remember, I am mostly human."

Jacy knew then that he was like the other men of her world, and it was a relief to her mind. She smiled back at him with a giggle and gave him a few minutes. As they walked back to her room, the two held hands and walked very close. When they reached the door, Jacy and Billy kissed good night, and he walked away into the darkness.

Floating on a cloud, Jacy went straight to bed and relived the whole night over and over again in her thoughts. She wished her mother and grandmother could be there to share her joy. Then reality hit her. She had to go home soon. Or did she? Samuel would surely have all the answers. She would find him and discuss her life with him the next morning. But what did she want to do with her life at this point? She had no idea. She only knew that Billy must be in her life for always. Complications had once more come into Jacy's life. She closed her eyes and finally went to sleep.

The sun came shining through the bedroom window, and Jacy awakened from a deep sleep. She got up and quickly took a shower and got dressed, not forgetting to use the makeup that Lavern had given her the day before. Looking good for Billy was a priority now. Today was going to be a good day and the beginning of a new life, though the details were somewhat unknown at the moment.

Then there was a knock on the door. Thinking it was Lavern, she rushed to open it. To her amazement, she found a little girl standing there. She looked Native American. She had brown eyes and shoulder-length, straight dark hair. She was very beautiful, with a round face and big dimples. She looked about five years old and was dressed in jean overalls. She looked at Jacy with a big smile on her face, accenting her deep dimples.

"Jacy, are you ready to go have breakfast? Lavern sent me to get you."

Jacy said, "Yes, I am. What is your name?"

The little girl replied, "My name is Cindy, and I am your friend."

Jacy took the little girl's hand and walked with her to a nearby restaurant. Samuel and Lavern were waiting for them at one of the tables. Jacy and Cindy each pulled up a chair and sat down. Samuel had already ordered Jacy some coffee and a piece of toast and oatmeal and orange juice for Cindy.

As Cindy ate her oatmeal, Jacy put sugar in her coffee and asked Samuel for some cream. He told her there was only coconut milk in the colony, so she put some in her coffee and realized it was very good.

"Why don't you have cream or meat in the colony?"

He answered, "We eat no meat or meat by-products here. We only eat fish, crab, crawfish, and other types of seafood. Some of the colonists cannot digest meat or meat by-products. They might get very sick or maybe even die if they do."

Jacy decided to get off that subject. Lavern left the table and came back with a large basket filled with all kinds of rolls and breads. She also had a pot of coffee and variety of jellies. Everything tasted wonderful. The four sat and enjoyed the food and friendly conversation.

Then Cindy got on her knees in the chair and looked intently at Jacy's face. She looked at Samuel and said, "Jacy has a human appearance, just like me and Lavern."

Samuel answered, "Yes, she does have the same look as you and Lavern, but y'all are not alike in any other way."

Cindy then got up and headed for the door.

Lavern called out to her, "Cindy, you will have school in an hour, okay?"

She said she would be back.

That was the first Jacy had heard of any school program. "I thought you said children that have human looks are turned out into the world. Why is Cindy here?" she asked Samuel.

He replied, "She is a special case. She has more ability for learning and a more powerful mind than anyone in the colony. We are teaching her to control her powers and special abilities. Without control, she could be very dangerous to herself and to those around her."

"You would never know. She's such a pleasant and precious child," said Jacy.

"Enough about Cindy," Samuel said. "Let's talk about you and Billy. He's been waiting to meet you for a long time."

"How did he know I was coming?" Jacy asked.

"One of his abilities is looking into the future."

"*One* of his abilities?" Jacy asked. "How many does he have?"

"Billy is a great scientist. He works in our laboratories."

"A scientist," Jacy said. "Who would know? When did he have time to learn to dance as well as he does?"

"He only works eight hours a day, Jacy. No one is a slave driver here. He has a life, and I bet a happier one now that you have finally arrived."

"Does he travel with the doctors and protectors, Samuel?" Jacy asked.

"No, not yet. But soon he will, Jacy."

"How often do they go out into the local areas for the artificial insemination?" she asked.

"Every day," said Samuel. "The babies are taken from the wombs of the selected women at four months. The doctors take them before many women even know they are pregnant. The doctors then put them in an incubation facility until the child is ready for the world. The scientists run tests to see which world they will have to be reared in. They remain in the hospital for a month and then they are given to their prospective parents. Some are put into your world, and some are put into the colony. The protectors try to give all of the children a family. But Cindy was an exceptional case. She could not be put with parents. Lavern and I raise Cindy."

"How come you can't make test tube babies, Samuel?" asked Jacy.

"Because, Jacy, you must come from the womb to have a God-given soul."

"I understand," she said. "Do the married couples of the colony ever have children naturally?"

"Not very often. The object here, Jacy, is to put these special children into the world. Couples are given children to raise as their own, and these children are always from that family's bloodline," Samuel answered.

"If one day Billy and I make a commitment, do you think we would be allowed to have children?" she asked.

"Yes, I think you could probably have two children that would look human, but the third would probably show alien features. The studies through the years prove this is true. Billy is three-fourths human, maybe even more. He was the third child of a couple that thinks they are human. He had to be taken from his mother at four months and brought to the colony. Do you know why, Jacy?" he asked.

"Yes," she answered. "His hands are different. But it doesn't matter to me. I love him. Does he ever get to see his family here in the colony that he was taken from in my world, here in the colony?"

"Billy has family here in the colony that loves him very much. He is happy here. He knows his history and where he came from. The rest is left up to Billy to pursue. He's very intelligent and has total control of his life."

Jacy accepted that and dropped the subject.

Samuel told Jacy he had plans for her.

"What are they, Samuel?" she asked.

"I want you to mingle with the colonists and get to know all the people here as you know your friends from Yelgar."

"If Cindy will accompany me, it will be a pleasure."

Lavern stood up and asked Jacy if she wanted to go shopping. Jacy agreed and then the door opened and precious little Cindy walked in ready for school. She wore jean overalls and an eager smile on her dimpled face. Samuel took Cindy's hand and asked her if he could walk her to school.

She said, "I want Jacy to come too, please. Please?"

Samuel told Cindy that Jacy would visit her later. She agreed and hugged Jacy very tightly. "I will see you later," she said. Then she walked off with Samuel down the brick street.

Lavern and Jacy walked behind them. Jacy took her eyes off Samuel and Cindy to glance at a jeans shop. She had only looked away for maybe thirty seconds, but when she looked back they had disappeared.

"Lavern, what happened to Samuel and Cindy? I wanted to tell Cindy good-bye. They've disappeared. There's nowhere they could have gone."

"Samuel will answer that question later on today, Jacy. Now let's just shop and enjoy an hour or so before Samuel comes back for you."

Jacy thought things were getting a little strange. They walked into a clothing store, and Lavern told her to pick out another outfit.

"Another one? You have already given me a nice outfit, Lavern."

"No," she said, "that one was compliments of the colony. This one will be from me."

"Why are you being so thoughtful and nice to me?" asked Jacy.

"Why? Because being around you makes me very happy, and I wish it could last forever. I went to spend all the time with you that I can"

"I have enjoyed your company too, Lavern. You make me feel safe, and I thank you for that. I'm sure you could be doing other things, but instead, you are entertaining me. I am enjoying my stay here at the colony."

"Enough talking. Let me see you try on some of these clothes, Jacy."

Lavern took some nice slacks and a lightweight sweater off the racks and asked Jacy to try them on. There were no salespeople around, just one lady at the register. Lavern led Jacy to a small changing room where Jacy tried on the new clothes. Jacy thought the black and gray striped slacks and the light gray, long-sleeve sweater looked good on her, but she wanted Lavern's opinion.

As she walked out of the changing room, Lavern shouted, "You are beautiful! Those colors work wonderfully with your eyes and hair color. Please get this outfit, Jacy. I love it on you."

"Okay," Jacy said. "I like it too. Do you think Billy will like it?"

"I think Billy will love anything you put on, but he will especially love this outfit on you."

Lavern walked to the counter and reached into the pocket of her dress. She pulled out a change purse with money folded inside. Jacy noticed that this time the bills were a pastel purple with black stars around the edges and a circled number ten in the center. She gave the lady behind the counter three of the bills.

"Thirty dollars is a real bargain," Jacy thought. "In Yelgar, the same outfit would have cost at least eighty dollars."

Lavern told Jacy that she wanted her to wear the outfit she had just purchased when she went out with Billy that night. Jacy wanted to ask her what the occasion was but already knew what Lavern would say. She always answered with, "Samuel will tell you later."

Jacy took the bag, and she and Lavern headed for the door, thanking the lady behind the register. She still wondered what had happened to Samuel and Cindy. She could make no sense of it. "People just do not disappear into thin air," she thought. "Or do they?"

Lavern and Jacy walked back to her room to leave the package. She did not want to carry it around all day. Jacy opened her door with the key and set the clothes on the sofa. She then went back outside to meet Lavern, who was waiting for her on the porch.

"Well, what's next?" Jacy asked.

Lavern answered, "Let's take a walk to the orchards."

"Orchards? I haven't seen any orchards."

"Just follow me, Jacy."

Lavern walked toward the park area Jacy had already visited with Samuel. But instead of entering the park, she walked past the entrance about seventy-five feet to a small dirt path that went toward the water. They followed the path, and sure enough, fruit trees soon came into view. First, there were lemon trees bunched together, and then there were satsuma trees. After walking a little farther, they saw pear trees and persimmon. There were many trees that were native to Louisiana. Best of all, Jacy saw mayhaw trees located on the water's shore.

The morning breeze blew through the trees, producing a fragrance that Jacy knew would be unforgettable. It was heavenly, clean, and very citrus. The two women sat on the grass under the trees and enjoyed the wonderful smells.

Jacy turned to Lavern, looked at her very closely, and said, "I can see why you chose not to return to our world."

At that remark, Lavern jumped up and said to Jacy, "Let's go now. Samuel will be looking for you."

Jacy was puzzled. "I'm sorry, Lavern. Did I say something wrong?"

"No, Jacy. Let's forget it."

As they walked back toward town and the round table at its entrance, Jacy wondered what she had done that upset Lavern so much. Maybe Lavern missed their world and tried not to think about it. Samuel had said that she'd left one son there to save another.

"That's it," Jacy thought. "Being reminded of leaving her son and family was too painful for Lavern to talk about." Jacy was very sorry that she had upset Lavern and decided not to bring up the subject again.

As they got closer to the town's entrance, Jacy saw Samuel walking toward them. They continued to walk until they met up.

He said to Jacy, "Are you ready to go to school?"

She replied, "Yes, as ready as I'll ever be."

He took her hand, and they walked toward a large stone in an open area that was shaped like a pyramid. It looked to stand about five feet high. He waved his hand across the top, and a red light appeared in an indention about halfway down. He told Jacy to place her hand in the indention. She did as he asked, and the light went from red to green.

"Now, remove your hand," he said.

She did as he said, and the light turned green again. But this time a door going down into the ground rolled back. It was large, about a hundred feet long and forty feet wide. As she looked down into the massive area, she noticed a wide section of stairs. On the side of them was a sliding board made of stone.

"Probably for the children," she thought.

Next to the slide was a narrow pole that led down into the underground world. She looked at Samuel, and he told her to take the steps down into the learning facility. As they walked down the first section of stairs, the door closed behind them. They continued down the stairs, which consisted of about thirty steps, and she was amazed at what she saw around her. The walls were constructed of marble and stone. As she entered the huge open area, she could see there was a large hall with doors leading to the rooms straight ahead. Chairs made of marble were placed all around the open area and had adults and children seated in them.

'This is amazing," she thought.

The temperature was perfect, and the lighting was not from electricity, as it had been above ground. It was a brilliant white light that flowed from a large bubble floating in the corner of the ceiling. The light was beautiful and soothing to the eyes.

As they continued walking toward the hall, Jacy looked up at Samuel and asked, "Where are we going?"

He said 'It's a surprise. Just come with me."

They passed up at least twenty doors leading into rooms on both sides of the hall before he finally stopped at one door. She was very glad he had stopped; they had walked at least fifteen minutes to reach this door. He pushed the handle, which looked strange. It was shaped like a small horseshoe.

The door opened into what looked to be a laboratory for scientists. Samuel had brought Jacy to visit Billy. There were different types of laboratory equipment everywhere, but there were no animals to run tests on. From a distance, she saw the love of her life appear. Billy was dressed in white scrubs. He walked hurriedly toward her. Samuel told Jacy he would return for her later and that Billy was going to give her a tour of the laboratory. Jacy was so excited that she could not hide her emotions.

Samuel smiled and said, "I thought you might want to come here first."

"Oh, thank you, Samuel. Thank you," she said.

As Billy approached, his dark hair shined in the brilliant light. His eyes were piercing, as though he could see into her soul.

"Yes, there is definitely something going on here," thought Jacy. Her emotions were going haywire and out of control. She got the shakes, and a rush went through her body when he touched her hand. She knew this was the man. She could not deny anything. He was her soul mate.

Billy could not hide his joy at seeing Jacy. His smile burned, and his spirit was so strong it covered Jacy like a cloud of protection. He kissed her very passionately and told her once more that he loved her and had been waiting for her visit. Then he asked her if she would like to visit the baby section.

As she looked into his very handsome face, she said, "Yes, very much so."

They walked to a side doorway not far from where they were. Billy put his thumb on a button, and the door opened automatically. As they walked into the room, she saw hundreds of babies attached to an imitation navel. They were floating in square boxes made of transparent material. The boxes reminded Jacy of aquariums. The first few babies she saw were so small they could fit in a cup. As they walked on, the babies she saw were larger and larger. Billy stopped at the full-term babies.

"Jacy, do you know Miss Susan, the lady that talks about us to everyone?" asked Billy.

"Yes, she's a friend of the family, and she's always saying she's been abducted many times. No one actually believes her, including me," said Jacy.

"Well, she's a product of the colony, and she has control of her subconscious. There is no way of erasing her memories. I'm about to show you her little girl that is about to be born. She was taken from Miss Susan at four months and is part alien. She will remain in the colony and be placed with a loving family after her birth. We will name her Wendy."

As they talked and looked at Wendy, the water began to bubble very fast. Two doctors quickly appeared with a small hose. They screwed the hose into a circular valve located in Wendy's tank. They drained the water and then opened the front section of the box. They disconnected the navel cord and removed the baby. One of the doctors held the baby by her feet and rubbed her back until she cried. She was beautiful, but she had alien features. Jacy watched as one of the doctors carried the baby to another room. Billy grabbed Jacy's hand, and they followed.

A man and woman were in the room and staring at the baby. Billy told Jacy that they would be Wendy's parents.

"They are family and will take care of each other. This man and woman of the colony will not be allowed to produce children and will be given another child later."

Jacy asked, "Do they get to take Wendy home?"

"No," he said. "We will keep Wendy for observation for about a month to see if she has any special abilities. Each child goes through the same testing. If she does have special abilities, the teachers will help her develop them."

"Who will test her?" asked Jacy.

"I will," Billy replied. "That's one of my duties."

"Is that all you do in the laboratory?"

"No, I do many other things, some involving experiments for curing diseases. I will soon travel with the doctors, scientists, and protectors."

"Is that good? Are you looking forward to this?" she asked.

"Yes, Jacy. I'm thrilled to be a traveler part-time. We help your world's people, mostly through disease control. Your scientists meet with ours, and they are given formulas for the cures of many diseases. Your people are our people. One day we will all live together."

"Billy, please don't say my people are your people. We are the same people. I love you, and you love me. That makes us one, doesn't it?" asked Jacy.

"Yes, but we are from different worlds, even though they are only thirty-five miles apart. So close, but yet so far away. That saying was meant for us. True love always finds a way. And, Jacy, this is really true love. It will never ever end." Then Billy hugged Jacy so closely that she could feel his heart pounding very fast.

Jacy felt as if he was not telling her something. Billy released Jacy and asked if she was ready to visit another part of the laboratory. She reached into the tiny bed where Wendy lay with her eyes wide open and touched her.

"Can I kiss her on the head?" she asked.

"Yes, you can," said Billy.

Jacy bent over the bed and kissed Wendy on the forehead. Wendy reached up with her tiny hand and touched Jacy's face.

"Did you see that, Billy? She likes me."

"She does like you, and you may visit Wendy later, as many times as you would like."

Jacy was satisfied with that answer and followed Billy into another part of the laboratory. He led her down a small hallway and through a tunnel into a room that was completely dark. He sat her in a chair next to the entrance. She could hear him turning on switches. The universe suddenly appeared in front of her eyes, just like at a planetarium.

"It's beautiful, Billy, just beautiful."

He was standing next to a control system, moving dials and pushing buttons. "First of all, Jacy, I'm going to zoom in on the planet that our people's ancestors are from. The planet's name is Tavus, and it is located between Venus and Earth."

Jacy asked, "How has no one from Earth discovered this planet?"

"The planet is cloaked at all times," replied Billy.

A huge round world moving slowly on its axis appeared on the enormous screen. Billy focused in on the mountains that consisted of only rocks and dirt.

"At one time, this land was green with plants and wildlife, just like Earth. Look at the mountains now; there are no streams anywhere. There is no vegetation anywhere. No animals live there anymore. Nothing can survive in this mountain environment." Then he removed the mountains from the screen and focused on a desert area unlike any Jacy had ever seen. There was black sand everywhere. It looked like it had been burned in a fire. There were no cacti and no snakes or scorpions anywhere. There was nothing, not even bugs.

Billy said, "This is why the Tavies came to our earth, Jacy. They did not come to harm anyone; it was just so they could survive." He pulled Jacy close to him and looked into her eyes. Then he lifted Jacy's chin with his long alien fingers.

She looked down at his hands, clutched them between hers, and kissed them tenderly. "I love all of you, Billy. All of you."

He smiled and kissed her gently. "I want you to visit one more section of the laboratory," said Billy. "This section is where you can get many questions answered directly from those who know."

He reached for Jacy's hand, and they walked toward another entrance. They walked back through the laboratory and into the hallway, passing doors again, except this time Jacy noticed a beam of light that looked like a tunnel. Billy, still holding her hand, pulled her toward the light.

Jacy stepped back. "What is this, Billy?"

He answered, "Don't worry. No harm will come to you."

Having confidence in Billy, she walked into the light of the tunnel with him. The light was golden and seemed to move with them as they walked. After a short distance, they entered a large room with bubbles of golden flowing light in the ceiling corners.

Jacy and Billy walked a while and then two men approached them with their hands held out to welcome Jacy. The men were aliens from Tavus. They had no human in them at all. Billy introduced the men as Zen and Qua. They were both dressed in tight-fitting, royal blue uniforms with long sleeves. The collars came up high on their long, slender necks, and their pull-on boots were black.

The Tavies' bodies were slender, and they stood about five feet eight inches tall. They had large dark eyes with hardly any white showing. Their ears were not as large as a human's, and their lips were very thin. They looked as though they had slits for mouths. The noses on the alien men were somewhat different but both small. One of the men had a nose that pointed upward, and the other had a nose that pointed down. They had no hair on their heads or faces. Their hands had five long fingers on them. When they smiled, Jacy could see that they had teeth in their mouths.

As she looked at them, she thought about how man was created after God's image. "Their bodies are slightly different from ours, although also the same, with everything in the same places. We are all God's children, just from different worlds. But how many different worlds are there? Zen and Qua are handsome and seem to be very nice," thought Jacy.

Something told Jacy that they knew what she was thinking as Zen and Qua looked at each other and chuckled.

The group walked to an area with chairs and tables. Jacy looked around the large room. One wall was covered with small screens and an enormous control system on the side, just like the room where Billy had shown her the planet Tavus. The rooms were very similar except that this room had more screens and a larger control system. The wall extended as far as she could see. The opposite wall displayed what looked like otherworldly items, and Zen confirmed these items were from the planet Tavus.

Zen got up and walked to a machine. He tapped it once, and cookies and orange juice appeared. It was just enough for the four of them. He picked up the tray and set it in the middle of the table.

"We will have refreshments," said Zen.

"Thank you," replied Billy and Jacy together.

Lunch was still an hour away. Billy and Jacy sat across from each other, and Zen and Qua sat on both sides of Jacy. As she looked at them closer, she could see their skin was a khaki color and flawless. She was not scared at all. The alien men did not have round faces, like most humans. Their faces were larger at the forehead and tapered down into a chin that formed a V. Their bald heads were perfectly round, and their eyelids had no lashes.

As Billy reached for his orange juice, so did Qua. Jacy observed the long slender fingers of the men. Billy was definitely with friends, possibly even family. Zen and Qua did not look at Jacy while she took everything in. It was obvious they were giving her time to focus before they started a conversation.

They sat there quietly for a good five minutes while Billy watched Jacy observe.

Zen turned to Jacy, and speaking in perfect English with a Cajun accent, he said, "Billy says you would like information on the destruction of our planet Tavus."

"Yes," Jacy answered. "Very much so."

Zen stood up and went to a lighted square board about eight by eight feet. On the board was a drawing of the planet Tavus. With a pointed stick in his hand, he began to point at different areas on the planet.

"Thousands of years ago, our planet was hit by a barrage of meteors that pushed it closer to the sun. The temperature slowly became so hot that no life could survive. The Tavies knew that they must find new worlds to live on. As Noah built his ark to survive, we had to build spaceships to survive. Some of them are as large as your cities. Your world was the closest, so we chose Earth for our home.

"When we first started landing on Earth, it was untamed. Through the years the Tavies taught your people many things. Some of your greatest scientists and inventors are products of both worlds.

"The planet Tavus has only one section where there is life." He pointed to the lower bottom part of the world. "Soon, or within the next five hundred years, this part of the planet will also become unlivable. By then, there will be no pure-blooded Tavies. But our bloodlines and intelligence will always exist here on Earth. There are colonies all over Earth where our people exist. Most are mixed and have both human and Tavie features."

Zen then turned to Jacy and asked, "Are there any questions?"

"Yes," Jacy said. "Do you ever return to Tavus?"

Qua then stood up and said, "Yes, we go home once a month. As the planet deteriorates, we are constantly moving our people. Some live on spaceships. Our world did not have great bodies of water on it like the oceans on Earth. We only had large rivers and streams. The Tavies cannot live in highly humid places—only climate-controlled places."

He then pointed to the bubbles floating near the ceiling. "These bubbles provide us with the climate we can live in. We could not survive long above ground because of humidity. Our children can now survive in both climates, above ground and below, because of our mixed Tavie and human blood." Qua sat down again.

Billy asked Jacy if she had enjoyed her visit with the Tavies. She looked at Zen and Qua and thanked them for their time. She told them it was an honor to meet them and shook hands with each of them. They smiled at Jacy and she smiled back.

As Billy and Jacy stood and headed for the door, Jacy looked back at the aliens and said, "I hope to see you again soon." They just nodded at Jacy and said nothing.

Jacy and Billy went back through the tunnel of light and into the laboratory. They then exited and went back into the great hallway. This time, Billy led Jacy back to the entrance of the underground facility and sat with her as they waited for Samuel.

Jacy asked, "Billy, can you have lunch with Samuel and me?"

"I can't," he said, "but I can meet you for supper."

"Will you come to my room to get me?" she asked.

"Yes," said Billy.

Jacy was pleased that she would be spending another evening with him. It would be wonderful.

Jacy heard the sound of the large doors opening and saw Samuel walking down the steps toward her. Billy stood and kissed Jacy on the cheek and told her that he would see her at six. He turned and walked away. Jacy began to walk toward Samuel when Cindy ran up to her and hugged her around the waist.

She shouted, "Can you visit my class, please?"

Samuel said to Cindy, "She can visit your class later, but now we are going to lunch. You can come with us, Cindy."

Cindy walked up the steps holding Jacy's hand and hopped from step to step. When they reached the door, Samuel once more asked Jacy to place her hand into an indention against the wall. Once more, the light turned red and then green. She removed her hand. She knew she was now in the system. She placed her hand back into the indention, and the door rolled open. The entrance was also the exit.

It was a beautiful day. As they walked toward the town entrance, Cindy skipped as she stayed close to Jacy's side. Samuel led Jacy and Cindy to a local sandwich shop. They sat down at a table for five, expecting Lavern to join them.

Cindy asked Jacy what she wanted. Jacy said, "The same as you, Cindy."

"Okay," Cindy said. "We are going to have a fish sandwich and French fries."

"That sounds good," said Jacy.

"What do you want, Samuel?" asked Cindy.

"The same, Cindy. The same as you and Jacy."

"Okay'" she said. "I'm going to order. Can I, Samuel?"

"Yes, you may, and add one more for Lavern."

Cindy walked to the counter and ordered four fish sandwiches, four orders of French fries, and her favorite drink, orange soda. Cindy pointed at the door as Lavern entered. Lavern went to the counter with Cindy to pay for the food and to help her carry it to the table. She put the tray on the table, and Cindy gave Jacy her sandwich, fries, and drink first. She then gave Samuel and Lavern theirs and took hers off the tray last.

"What a nice and thoughtful little girl you are, Cindy," said Jacy.

Cindy looked directly into Jacy's eyes and said, "I don't want you to leave, Jacy. Not ever."

Lavern glanced at Cindy and said, "Cindy, eat your food. You have to return to class in forty-five minutes."

Jacy did not know how to respond. Lavern obviously did not want Cindy to talk about the leaving subject, a subject Jacy herself was not sure of. Samuel said nothing. He continued eating his sandwich and did not look up.

As they finished their meal, Cindy asked Samuel if she could take Jacy to look at the water lights. She said, "I don't want to go back to school. I want to be with Jacy."

Samuel and Lavern looked at each other and got very quiet. Samuel then took Cindy outside and talked to her for about five minutes. They returned and came back to the table.

Precious Cindy had a big smile on her face. "Jacy," she said, "can I show you the water lights?"

"That sounds good," said Jacy.

Cindy took her hand, and they walked down the brick street toward the surrounding swamp area. Jacy asked Cindy where the water lights were. Cindy pointed down to the sandy water's edge where red, blue, green, and yellow lights were shining up through the water as far as she could see. The whole swamp area was lit up. It was more than beautiful.

"What causes these lights, Cindy?" asked Jacy.

"It's Philip and the protectors. They sometimes stay down in the water."

"You mean it's a spaceship?" asked Jacy.

"Yes," Cindy said. "They travel out into the universe. There are many small aircrafts that stay in Philip's spaceship. Sometimes they fly around the colony and swamp areas. My friends and I watch them at night. Sometimes they wink their red lights at us. They are making sure we are safe."

Jacy asked if they only came out at night.

"No," said Cindy. "They are around all the time. There are probably some of the smaller crafts out there right now."

"How long does the ship stay down in the water?"

"It will be coming up soon. It's never underwater more than a few hours at a time."

"The lights are very beautiful, Cindy. I'm glad you brought me here."

Just as Jacy finished her sentence, she could not believe her eyes. The gigantic spaceship lifted from the water. It was round and a shiny silver, with lights at the bottom of the craft. She could not hear a sound as it lifted straight up into the sky and shot off like a bullet.

Cindy waved to the spacecraft as it lifted. Saying in a soft voice, "Bye, Philip."

The two girls held each other's hands as they walked back into town. They took a seat on a bench beside the street to have a conversation with each other and met some of the colonists as they passed by. Cindy did not have a shy personality. She was very outgoing. Carol walked by, and they asked her to sit down with them a while. She agreed and took a seat on the bench with them.

Carol asked Cindy why she was not in school. She replied that Samuel said she could be with Jacy for a while and just spend time.

Carol said, "I will enjoy spending time with Jacy, too."

Cindy just smiled and squirmed in her seat as she sat between the two women.

Suddenly a shrill sound rang out. It sounded like a warning of some sort.

Carol screamed at Jacy, "Go down below," as she ran as fast as she could to the facility below ground.

Jacy grabbed Cindy and held her close. The colonists were all heading to the underground facility. Seeing this, Jacy walked very fast as she followed them, holding Cindy in her arms. Cindy held on so tightly that she was squeezing Jacy's neck. She kept saying, "I'm scared, Jacy."

Jacy stopped to loosen Cindy's arm grip, and within seconds, an alien appeared in front of her. He had stepped out of a beam from a spaceship that was hovering in the sky. The alien looked just like Qua and Zen, but he was wearing a silver jumpsuit and did not look nice. He grabbed for Jacy while she was still holding Cindy.

Cindy looked directly into the alien's eyes and clenched her fists together as tightly as she could. She made a humming sound, and the alien began to bleed red blood from his eyes, ears, nose, and mouth. He screamed in pain and stepped back into the beam. It took him up into the spaceship.

By this time, Samuel was running toward Jacy. At the same moment, the foreign spaceship was surrounded by three Tavie spaceships. They were shooting colorful beams at each other. Samuel put his arms around Jacy and Cindy and held them close. Their hearts were beating very fast. The whole event lasted maybe four minutes and then the hostile spaceship disappeared.

"Who are they, Samuel?" asked Jacy.

He looked at Jacy and replied, "They are from Tavus. They are not allowed to land here because they are very evil. Sometimes they take some of our people to evaluate them. They very seldom try to land here."

Jacy looked at Cindy and kissed her on the cheek. "You saved my life, little girl. Thank you."

Cindy smiled at Jacy and hugged her as Jacy held her in her arms. Samuel sat down on a bench, and Jacy and Cindy joined him. The people of the colony were now coming out of the underground facility. They looked up into the sky and saw the three smaller spacecrafts still lingering in open view. The bad guys had taken off and escaped, although one had left with a very bad headache.

Samuel told Jacy that Cindy was very powerful and needed to learn control of her abilities. He did not need to tell her anything else. It was self-explanatory after what Jacy had just witnessed.

"Teaching Cindy control is very important. What she did was bad."

Cindy looked at Samuel and said, "I had to. They were going to take Jacy from us."

He answered, "Sometimes, Cindy, we must do what is necessary at the time. What you did saved you and Jacy. We will forget it this time. Please don't do it again."

"Okay," she said. "I'll only use it on the evil ones."

Samuel put his head down and smiled, thanking God that she had disobeyed her teachings this one time.

Lavern came running up the street looking for Jacy and Cindy. They waved at her, and she ran up to them, expressing her concern and happiness that they were safe. It had been quite an ordeal. Everyone was now relaxed, and they just watched the skies.

Suddenly Jacy felt a touch on her shoulder. She turned around and looked up to see Billy with a very worried look on his face.

He touched Cindy on the head and said, "You're the best, Cindy. I'm glad you were with Jacy through this."

Cindy smiled at Billy and said, "Jacy is my friend."

It was late afternoon now, and what a day it had been. Jacy hoped the evening would be less stressful. She was looking forward to being with Billy.

Lavern sat next to Jacy and put her arm around her shaking body. "This could have turned out really bad if the alien had gotten you into that beam, Jacy."

"I had no idea there was danger here, Lavern."

"Yes, Jacy, there is good and bad in every species. They don't come here often because of the protectors, but every once in a while they slip through the shields. They will not return for a while. The skies are being watched very carefully."

As Jacy turned her head to look for Billy, he looked down at her and told her good-bye. "I will see you this evening. I am so sorry this happened to you. Thank God you are safe." He turned away and walked back to the laboratories below.

Lavern touched Jacy's hand and said, "I want you to wear the outfit I bought for you tonight."

"Okay," Jacy answered. "I'm excited. It will be just me and Billy alone, like a real date." Then she stood up and told Cindy that she had to go back to her room.

Cindy said, "Okay, Jacy. I will walk with you so you will be safe."

Everyone standing around giggled at Cindy's remark. It was not very often that a child had to protect an adult, but in Cindy's case, she could be capable of saving the whole colony.

Jacy walked slowly to her room with Cindy skipping along at her side. Everyone stared at them as they walked by. This was the only time the people of the colony had focused on her. Jacy felt like she was under a watchful eye of protection, and it felt very good. She felt as though all of them accepted her now. As they reached her door, Cindy told her good-bye and skipped back into town to meet up with Lavern and Samuel.

Jacy walked into her room and fell onto the sofa. She put her hand on top of her forehead and just lay there in confusion. "What is happening in my life? Where is it going? Do I have a future here? Why do I love Billy so? What are my parents and family doing right now?" So many questions went through her mind at one time. She closed her eyes and realized she had no answers to any of the questions. Trying to clear her mind of so many worries, she concentrated on her prospective future with Billy. Those thoughts made her very happy.

In all of her twenty-one years of life, Jacy had made many friends. Some of them she had liked better than others. But in the colony Samuel, Lavern, Cindy, and Billy were not just her friends. They had formed a special bond, something that could only happen once in a lifetime. Before she had come to the colony, she had thought that a person could only bond with immediate family. Being in the colony had proved her wrong. She loved all of these people, and all in a different way. They made her very happy. Just the sight of them made her feel warm inside.

Jacy's thoughts always went to the same things when she was alone. She had so many questions about her stay. How long would she be there? Would they send her home and never let her return? Could she live without Billy by her side? Could she do without seeing and being with precious Cindy? Would she ever see Lavern and Samuel again if she left, the mother and son team that made her feel so welcome and gave her security during her stay? She wanted all of these answers, but deep down she was scared that the answers would not be what she hoped for. For now, she would just have to enjoy life and pretend her life in the colony was never going to end. Her short stay in the colony was, so far, the best part of her life. Although she loved her parents and grandparents very much, they did not seem to need her in the way her new friends did.

Jacy got up from the sofa to get ready for her evening with Billy. She tried not to think of the negative possibilities in her life. For now, she was going to live for the moment. When she was with Billy, she was very happy.

After her shower, she put on her new clothes and then fixed her hair and makeup. As she looked into the mirror, she felt pleased that she left her hair down. It fell beautifully around her pretty face. The red in her hair was shining especially pretty in the evening light. Lavern was right. The light gray sweater looked perfect on her, and the slacks fit her very well. She felt like a princess waiting for her prince charming in a fairy tale.

Jacy heard a knock on the door and felt her heart skip a beat. She walked toward the door slowly and opened it. Billy stood there with a bouquet of daisies. He was gorgeous. He was dressed in a tight black sweater that showed his broad shoulders and the curves of his muscular upper body and black pants that accented his small waist. This man was perfect.

He looked at Jacy and said, "You are the most beautiful woman in the world."

She smiled and gave him a big hug. Then she took the flowers, and they walked toward town.

Billy said, "I have a surprise evening planned for you, Jacy. It will be just for us, and hopefully very romantic."

That pleased her, and she hoped it would be a long evening.

As they walked into town, Billy led Jacy to a small building with a yellow door. He opened the door, and she noticed that the lights were very dim. There was a small round table with two chairs in the middle of the room. There were candles burning, and food was set up buffet style. Slow country music was playing. The room was not very large, but romantic indeed. The smell of citrus filled the room. Billy took Jacy's flowers, put them in a vase with water, and placed them in the middle of the table.

He pulled her chair out, and she sat down. He sat across from her. They stared into each other's eyes without saying a word. She remembered what he had told her before about reading each other's minds, so she tried not to imagine what it would be like to make love to Billy. The thought kept recurring, and she turned her head in embarrassment.

Billy said, "It's okay, Jacy. We love each other, and I live to make love to you. Would you like to dance?"

"Yes," she said, as she shyly tried to think of something else.

They got up and danced, saying very little. She wrapped her arms around him, and he held her close. Nothing needed to be said at this point. Holding each other tightly was enough.

As they danced, a song from a female country artist played. It was a very seductive love song. Listening to the music, their sexual desires became too much. Billy pushed Jacy against the wall and passionately kissed her. They slowly slid down the wall to the floor, and he pressed his body against hers.

There was a knock at the door. Billy took a deep breath, stood up, and walked to the door slowly. Jacy got up and sat in the chair. It was Samuel. He walked into the room, and the two men just stood and looked at each other. After a few minutes, Billy shrugged his shoulders. About five minutes later, he nodded his head yes. They did not say a word. Jacy thought that they must not have wanted her to hear what they were saying. They were communicating through telepathy.

Finally, Samuel looked at Jacy and said, "I hope you enjoy the rest of your evening." He then started toward the door.

Jacy called to him, "Samuel, please stay and eat with us."

He turned and answered, "Yes, I would like that."

Billy got a stool from the corner and pulled it to the table. They spoke very little as they filled their plates from the buffet. Jacy knew Samuel had stayed because he hoped things would cool off between her and Billy. He knew what was about to happen. It would have been a mistake, and he stopped them from making it.

After they finished their supper, Samuel excused himself and left. Billy then told Jacy that they needed to take a walk. They both definitely needed some fresh air, and the two headed down the street toward the water.

Billy said, "I'm very sorry for losing control. I lost my self-discipline for a minute there, Jacy. It is not the right time for us to make love."

Jacy said, "I'm not the innocent one here. You didn't hypnotize me, Billy."

"Believe me," he said, "it was my fault. I took advantage of you by reading your mind and seizing the moment. That was wrong, Jacy. I never realized how human I really am until you arrived."

He was walking so fast that she could hardly keep up with him. "Billy, slow down," she said. "You are almost running."

Jacy knew he was trying to work out his frustration. Finally, he slowed down as they reached the water's edge. They sat down on a bench and looked up at the stars. It began to sprinkle, but the two did not run for shelter. They remained sitting and staring at the stars and moon as clouds rolled in to hide them. Jacy got closer to Billy and put her head on his shoulder. The rain came down harder, but they still remained sitting. They were drenched with water. After becoming completely soaked, Billy told Jacy he would walk her back to her room. There was a chill in the air, and they were getting cold.

When they got to her porch, he kissed her and told her that he would be back the following evening. "I love you very much," he said.

Jacy could not imagine what Samuel had told Billy, but whatever it was had caused Billy to become somewhat distant. Their evening had been cut short, but the feeling of closeness between her and Billy for that moment when they kissed still lingered in her mind. Jacy was tired and fell asleep quickly.

Two days and nights passed. Jacy had spent them getting better acquainted with the people of the colony and hanging out as much as possible with Lavern and Cindy during the day. Her evenings were spent with Billy, taking long walks and enjoying relaxing dinners in nice restaurants. Samuel, of course, checked on her to make sure she was content.

She had not gone underground the last two days but was anxious to revisit that wonderful section of the colony.

On her fifth day at the colony, Jacy awoke from a deep sleep. Today she was to go underground to the learning facility for a visit. She hurriedly dressed and had breakfast and then headed for the underground. She put her hand in the pyramid indention, and the large door opened. She rushed down the stairs and saw Cindy and Lavern standing at the entrance.

Cindy spotted Jacy and called to her, "Please come with me to class. I'll teach you mind control."

Lavern said, "Cindy, you can't teach mind control."

Jacy asked Lavern if she would be allowed to visit Cindy's class.

"I'll ask the teacher."

She then went into the classroom and returned a short while later. The teacher had agreed to let Jacy visit Cindy in class. She followed Cindy into class, and Jacy took a seat. The children were lined up one behind the other. There were only fifteen children in the class. Ten marble balls sat against the wall. The weights marked on them ranged from five to fifty pounds. Each ball sat in a circular hole to keep it from rolling. Cindy explained that each child was to levitate one of the balls straight up in the air and then set it back down.

The teacher called on the first child in line to focus on the ball he chose to raise. The little boy was about seven years old. He had chosen a ten-pound ball. He stared at the ball with wide eyes for at least a minute. The ball barely rose up and then plopped back down. He went to his seat, and the teacher told him he had done well but needed to work on his concentration.

The next child was a little girl around six years old. She also concentrated on the ten-pound ball. She raised the ball slightly and then it fell back down. The teacher patted the girl on the head and gave her the same instructions as the little boy before her. She wanted her to practice on her concentration.

Next in line was Cindy. She looked at Jacy shyly and told her to watch. The teacher walked up behind Cindy and put her hands on Cindy's shoulders, something she did not do with the first two children. Cindy started with the twenty-pound ball. She raised it up to the ceiling and dropped it back into its holder, perfectly. Jacy smiled at her proudly. Cindy was supposed to go back to her desk but did not. Instead, she concentrated on the fifty-pound ball and floated it all around the room. Jacy clapped in amazement.

The teacher then said loudly, "No, Cindy. Stop. Put the ball up."

Cindy lowered the ball back into place.

The teacher said to Jacy, "Please do not clap. Just remain silent."

As Jacy watched the other children, she realized that they were not supposed to raise any balls that weighed more than twenty pounds. For their age that was the limit. No other child but Cindy could move the twenty- and fifty-pound balls.

After all the children had practiced their concentration and mind control, they went back to their seats. The teacher looked at them and then told the class to write down on a sheet of paper what subject she was trying to transfer to them mentally. The small children took out their pencils and paper.

They looked at their teacher and once more went into a state of deep concentration.

Cindy was so busy looking at Jacy that she hardly glanced at the teacher. Jacy pointed to Cindy's paper and moved her hand in a writing motion. Cindy got the message. She drew a picture of the sun and under the picture wrote "sun." She then raised her hand. The teacher called on her, and she showed her paper to the teacher.

"Correct," said the teacher.

The other children then began to raise their hands, one by one, and all had answered the question right. The teacher then told the children to turn around in their desks to face the person behind them. They were to pair up and practice telepathy, holding conversations with each other mentally. Because there were fifteen children, one child would be left alone. The teacher called Cindy's name loudly and said she would be her partner. Cindy went and sat next to the teacher on a stool. The class then silently conversed with their minds. Jacy thought it was amazing. The oldest child in the class could not have been over eight years old.

The children often looked toward Jacy and then back to their partners. Jacy knew she was everyone's subject. The children sometimes waved at her, maybe thinking she knew what they were saying to each other. She waved back and grinned happily.

The children were mixed Tavie and human. Cindy was the only one that looked human, yet the children accepted her completely. But their looks were deceiving. Cindy looked human but had to be more than 50 percent Tavie. Her abilities did not come from her human blood.

Jacy decided to leave the classroom to visit with some of her friends. As she walked down the hall, she could see Carol in the distance. She called to her.

Carol turned around. "Hi," she said to Jacy. "Would you like to go to the library with me?"

"Yes," answered Jacy. "I would like that very much."

The two women walked down the hall and through a door that led into a huge room. There were books and computers everywhere.

Jacy looked at Carol and said, "Never have I seen a library so huge."

Carol replied, "There's a lot of history here. Anything we want to know about Earth or Tavus we can find right here in the library."

Carol walked to a long wall that had "Tavus" printed on it in large letters. Carol took a book from the shelf and then sat at one of the tables. Jacy sat beside her. Carol opened the book. It contained illustrations of buildings and homes on Tavus. She pointed to structures shaped like pyramids and told Jacy that some were office buildings and others were dwellings made from the same stone and marble that had been used for the underground facility. Some of the buildings towered high in the sky. They were all gorgeous.

Jacy then got up and went to the opposite wall of the library that was labeled "Earth." She found an E encyclopedia and took it back to where Carol was sitting. She opened the book to the Egyptian pyramids.

"Look," Jacy said. "We have those same shaped buildings on Earth. We call them pyramids."

Carol looked at Jacy and said that Egypt was the first place the Tavies settled when coming to Earth. "If you study some of the drawings from many years back, you will see the Tavus spaceships in them. Egypt was the best suited for the Tavies. The environment was more like Tavus than any other place on Earth. Like most places on Earth, they have always practiced Tavie teachings. Those underground tombs were designed by the Tavies to last forever, if not disturbed.

"The Egyptians were very intelligent, and the mixed blood of the Egyptians and Tavies produced handsome, brilliant people.

"Think about it, Jacy. Did they really look like everyone else on Earth many years ago?"

Jacy thought about it for a while and then answered, "From their drawings, they wore dark makeup designs around their eyes and faces. Their bodies were slender. I guess not. They did have their own look, unlike anyone else on earth. No one on Earth has ever figured out how they moved some of the large stones needed to build their pyramids. Now, I know," said Jacy.

"Without a doubt it was levitation," Carol said. "You are correct. It is how the saying goes, mind over matter. Enough about Egypt, let's find another subject."

The girls talked a while and then Jacy asked Carol what information was in the computers.

"Different computers hold different information," said Carol. "You can visit every colony in every country on Earth or find out about your family bloodline. Everyone in the colony is registered on these computers."

Carol then sat at a computer and brought up her own name. She typed "Carol" and pushed enter. A picture of her came up. Under it was her family tree, listing her Earth family as well as her Tavus family members.

As they studied the information, Jacy noted Carol's parents' names and locations. Her mother was from a small town just fifteen miles from Yelgar; her name was Marie Guidry. Her father was from Tavus; his name was Ebe. There was a picture of both of them on the computer screen. Her mother was very pretty. She had the same color eyes and hair as Carol. Jacy looked at Carol and told her she was gorgeous like her mother.

Carol smiled. "She is very pretty. One day I would like to meet her."

"I hope that day comes for you soon," said Jacy.

Then they looked at her father, Ebe. He looked like Zen and Qua.

"Have you ever met your father, Carol?"

"Yes," she said. "I see him often. He is a doctor and spends most of his time on a spaceship with the protectors. He's a very handsome man, and a good one. I love him very much. I would like you to meet him, Jacy."

"That would be great, Carol. Anytime is fine. Just let me know."

As they continued looking at Carol's long line of ancestors, Lavern and Samuel walked into the library. They walked up to the girls and observed. Jacy looked up and saw them standing there.

"Hi, Lavern and Samuel. Need any information from the computer on your heritage?"

Samuel looked at Jacy and said, "Type my name in the computer."

Lavern stood very upright with a solemn look on her face as she stared at the computer screen.

"S-A-M-U-E-L," said Jacy as she typed his name into the computer. When she pressed enter, a picture of Samuel came up with the names of his parents. "Samuel, the son of Lavern Hebert, human, and Philip, living in the colony, is of human and Tavie descent."

As Jacy examined Philip's picture, she looked for a resemblance to Samuel. Surely there had to be one as Philip was only half Tavie. That would make Samuel about three-fourths human.

She looked at Samuel and asked, "Do you know Philip?"

"Yes, I do. He is based on a spaceship. He is the captain and a man of great authority."

She then looked at Lavern's picture and name. "You have the same last name as I do, Lavern."

Lavern nodded, and Jacy moved on to the next of kin. Under Lavern's name and picture it stated that she had one other son by the name of Murphy. Jacy read the name and age of Lavern's son and then looked up at Lavern.

"My father's name is Murphy Hebert. Are you my grandmother?"

Lavern smiled at her and said, "Yes, Jacy, I am your grandmother."

"Oh my God!" Jacy jumped up to hug her and kissed her on the cheek. She then looked at Samuel, who also had a wide smile on his face, and said, "You are my uncle." She hugged Samuel. "Uncle Samuel."

The excitement was evident to everyone in the library. Jacy wiped tears from her eyes and asked why they had not told her sooner.

"We did not know how you would react."

"I'm happy," she said, "and I love both of you."

Carol sat back with a look of astonishment on her face. She could not believe her ears. "Congratulations, you three family members."

Jacy, brimming with pure joy, turned to Carol and gave her a big hug too. Then she turned back to Lavern.

"My father could never answer my questions about where his mother, my grandmother, was."

"You know the circumstances now," said Lavern. "Not one day of my life did I ever stop thinking of my son Murphy and his family. I have always loved y'all with all of my heart. Samuel and I have always kept in touch, but of course, you could not know this. We have watched you grow up to be a beautiful woman."

"Thank you, Grandmother, for saving Uncle Samuel's life. You definitely made the right decision. My father is very happy. If he knew of Samuel, he would be proud to call him his brother, as proud as I am to call him my uncle. I need to tell someone about this wonderful find."

Her thoughts immediately went to Billy. "I must tell Billy."

"He knows," said Samuel. "He has always known, but he doesn't know that you've learned the truth."

"Is he still working in the laboratory?" asked Jacy.

"Yes, he is," said Samuel.

Jacy hurriedly left the library and walked down the hall toward the laboratory where the love of her life was working. She reached the door of the lab and pushed on the small horseshoe-shaped doorknob. As the door opened, she saw Billy walking toward her.

She shouted, "Lavern is my grandmother, and Samuel is my uncle!"

Billy hugged her and said, "I am glad you have finally found out the truth."

"I felt it, Billy. I felt we had a connection."

"You were right, Jacy, a very close connection. Lavern and Samuel love you very much."

"We should celebrate," said Jacy. "Can we celebrate tonight?"

"Of course we can," said Billy. "It will be fun. I'm looking forward to it."

Jacy hugged and kissed Billy before she said good-bye.

Still very excited, she headed back to the library to meet up with her friend Carol and her family members. She peeked in the door. Samuel and Lavern were no longer there, but Carol was sitting at the same computer. Jacy quietly walked in and tapped Carol on the shoulder.

Carol looked up from the computer and asked, "Want to go for a walk and talk for a while?"

"Yes, that would be nice," said Jacy.

It was almost time for lunch. The two women went back above ground to take their walk. The temperature had dropped, and the feel and smell of fall was in the air.

Carol told Jacy she wanted to grab a sandwich and drink and go to the park to talk. They ordered their food and walked toward the park. On their way,

Jacy could hear and see helicopters coming and going.

"Carol, they are looking for me, aren't they?"

"I suppose so, Jacy. You have been missing for a while now. Your parents and grandparents must be really scared that something bad has happened to you."

Jacy dropped her head in sadness, knowing that what Carol had said was true. If only she could give her family a message to let them know she was all right. But that was not possible. Jacy was torn between two worlds, even though they were located in the same place. She wondered if this had ever happened to anyone else, with the exception of her grandmother, Lavern. No one had yet approached her to ask when or if she wanted to return to Yelgar. Maybe she had no choice. Maybe someone would make the decision for her.

When they reached the park, they sat at a table. They were both in deep thought as they ate and watched the birds flying around and the water fountains shooting up to the sky. Jacy hoped her family was not going through too much agony and suddenly became filled with guilt for causing them pain.

She stopped eating and put her face in her hands. Tears ran down her face, and she asked Carol what she should do.

Carol put her sandwich down and walked behind Jacy, placing her hands on Jacy's temples. "I'm going to clear your mind for now. I'm going to take your sadness away."

Within seconds, Jacy's sadness was gone, and she finished eating her sandwich and drinking her soda.

"Thank you, Carol. I don't know what you did, but it worked."

Carol answered, "It is only short-term, Jacy. Your sadness will return."

Jacy changed the subject and asked Carol what her special abilities were. Carol answered, "My abilities are limited." She was not as mentally gifted as others from the colony because her human blood was dominant. She seemed to be a serious person. Jacy had not seen her smile much. But she was a nice girl, and Jacy liked her a lot. She was a good friend.

"So, Carol, how is your love life?" asked Jacy.

Carol looked at her and replied, "What love life?"

"Come on, I know there's someone that you are interested in."

"Well," she answered, "there is one person I like."

"Who is he?"

"His name is Louis. He is a fisherman that comes here three times a week to deliver seafood to the colony. He lives in your world but comes and goes from the colony. He has human looks but is part Tavie. I see him often when he delivers to the restaurant where I work. He's very nice. I've been tempted to invite him to one of our street dances."

"Do it, Carol," said Jacy. "You should invite him to the next dance or celebration. How else will you ever get to know him?"

"Well, he will make a delivery today at two o'clock," said Carol. "I might put my fears aside and invite him."

"What will Uncle Samuel say if he accepts?"

"Samuel will not say anything. Louis has family living in the colony. He's one of us."

"Good luck, Carol. I hope you get your man," said Jacy.

Carol then looked at her watch and noticed it was almost one. Jacy told her to go to the restaurant because Louis would be there in an hour to make his delivery.

"Talk to him. Let him know you like him."

"I am scared of rejection. I look different than he does," said Carol.

"You are pretty," said Jacy. "You do look somewhat different. But he has been coming to the colony a while, so he will appreciate your pretty face and nice personality."

"I'm on my way to the restaurant," said Carol. She left with a smile on her face. Just the thought of Louis made her happy.

Jacy lay back on the bench and looked at the sky, the same sky she and Billy had shared and now would always share. The wind made the huge trees sway. The coolness in the air lessened the humidity, so breathing came easier. She took deep breaths and enjoyed the park. The birds were flying all around, and the fountains were mesmerizing.

"Paradise has to be close to this," thought Jacy. Except for the danger from the evil Tavies, it was a great place to live. But would she want to stay in the colony without Billy? She did have family in the colony and people that cared about her besides Billy. She had little Cindy, her precious little friend, that she loved a lot. Leaving Cindy would be as hard to do as leaving Billy. Cindy also seemed to need Jacy's attention and love. They had formed a special bond that could not be broken. Finally, she concluded that she wanted to live in the colony. It's a home away from home.

Looking at the sun, she thought that it must be two o'clock by now. Carol was probably talking with Louis and maybe showing her true feelings. Maybe Louis liked Carol a lot but was shy. Jacy could hardly wait to talk to Carol later about her meeting with Louis. She decided that lying around for an hour would have been very relaxing, but it was time to return to reality.

Jacy sat up and noticed Samuel at the next table. "Oh, Uncle Samuel!" She walked to the table and sat next to him. "How long have you been here?"

"Just about ten minutes," he said. "I didn't want to disturb your rest."

"You can disturb me any time you want," she said.

Samuel said, "Tonight we will celebrate. There will be a seafood boil for anyone in the colony that wants to celebrate with us. I want everyone to know you are my niece, my blood, Jacy. I am so proud to have you as part of my family."

Jacy jumped up and gave him a big hug.

He hugged her back. "In the colony, Jacy, we are taught as children to suppress our feelings."

"So I have heard," said Jacy.

"Sometimes our human side won't allow it," he said.

"Come to think of it, I haven't seen you reveal any emotion whatsoever."

"You probably won't see it again," he said and smiled at her.

"I'm excited," said Jacy. "What time is the celebration, Uncle Samuel?"

"The town is preparing everything right now. I would guess about six thirty."

"Will there be a band?"

He said, "Of course, but only a small one tonight."

"Great. Does Billy know?"

"Yes, he knows. He will be there."

"Will Cindy and Grandmother be there?"

"Yes, Cindy will be there until about eight thirty, then she will go home to get her rest for school tomorrow. Lavern is helping to prepare for the celebration. She is very excited as well."

"Uncle Samuel, I wish my father and mother could share this joy with us."

"They are in our thoughts," said Samuel. "I must go, but I will see you later, Jacy." Then he walked out of the park and back into town.

Jacy walked back to town and sat down, hoping to see Cindy when she returned from school. As she looked down the street, she saw Cindy, skipping merrily. When she spotted Jacy, Cindy ran toward her with excitement on her face.

"We are having a party tonight honoring you, Samuel, and Lavern. And I can go. I will show you how good I can dance."

"That I am looking forward to, Cindy," said Jacy.

After they had walked for a while, Cindy pulled Jacy into an ice milk and soda shop.

"Let's get ice milk," said Cindy. "I have money."

"Okay. But I thought you did not use milk in the colony."

"We don't use cow's milk, Jacy. We use coconut milk, and it is so good."

"You order, Cindy. Get me a small cone," said Jacy.

Cindy went to the ice milk counter and ordered Jacy a strawberry cone and a chocolate cone for herself.

"This looks delicious," Jacy said.

They found a seat outside the ice milk shop and licked their cones in delight.

"I can't wait for tonight," said Cindy. Her face was brown from the ice milk.

Jacy smiled at her and thought she had never seen such a cute little girl before.

When the girls finished, they walked to Jacy's room. With full tummies, they fell on the sofa and lay there motionless. Then Cindy jumped up and put a tape into the TV's VCR. She made Jacy guess what tape she had chosen.

"*Peter Pan*?"

"No," said Cindy.

"I give," said Jacy as the movie started.

"It's Cinderella," whispered Cindy.

"I love Cinderella," Jacy whispered back.

Jacy glanced at Cindy while they watched the tape. When the wicked stepmother looked meanly at Cinderella, Cindy gripped her fists together. She quickly released them when she saw Jacy watching her.

"It's just a movie, Cindy, and it ends well. Cinderella gets the handsome prince."

"I'm going to get me a handsome prince one day."

"I know you will, Cindy, but right now you should go home and get some rest for the party tonight."

Cindy turned the TV-VCR off. Then she ejected the tape and put it back into the stack of tapes arranged on the side of the TV. She hugged Jacy and told her that she would see her at the party that night. Jacy walked to the door and watched as she ran home. Cindy turned and waved and then threw her a kiss. In the colony, the children were supposed to refrain from showing emotions. Cindy was quite the exception. She was emotional in some situations, showing her human tendencies.

Jacy went into the bathroom to get ready for the night. She again wore the special, pretty outfit her grandmother had bought for her as a gift. The outfit was more special now. She knew it had been chosen for her out of love. She combed her hair and applied her makeup. Now she must wait for Billy. He would not be there for another thirty minutes, so she went outside and sat on the steps to wait for him. The people of the colony were heading for the party area in the street. They looked toward Jacy as they passed and smiled. That was something new. Before, they would not have turned their heads and acknowledged her. She smiled back at them and waved. Since she had almost been abducted, the colonists now treated her differently—like she was special. Each new day in the colony made Jacy happier than the day before.

Billy was walking toward Jacy. He looked really good, as usual. He helped her up from the step and asked if she was ready.

"Yes, I am. I'm ready to party," she said.

He started a strange conversation with her as they walked toward the street where the party was to be held. He talked about dreams and how someone could connect with a loved one through them.

"Connect through dreams?" asked Jacy.

"Yes," said Billy. "Your subconscious stores events from your past, and you can relive them over and over in your dreams."

"Neat," said Jacy. "There are quite a few events with you I'd like to relive in my dreams."

"Remember that, Jacy. Remember me in your dreams."

"'I would rather touch you, Billy. Dreams aren't as much fun as reality."

"You are right, of course. But never forget I love you," he said, and they continued on.

When they arrived, Jacy saw that it really was a feast. There was a huge table filled with boiled seafood. Crabs, shrimp, crawfish, corn on the cob, and small potatoes were all piled up and mixed together on the table. The seafood was extra large, a sight that would make any Cajun smile with delight. There were oysters on the half shell and fish baked in clay on tables all around the party area. And there was plenty of beer served in cans with no labels. Soda pop was also available for the children.

Samuel, Lavern, and Cindy were seated at a table in the middle of the street next to the band area. The band was already set up. There were harmonica players, fiddlers, guitarists, an accordion player, and a washboard player. It was a complete Cajun band.

"What fun this evening will be," Jacy thought.

The band began to play just as Jacy and Billy arrived at the table. Everyone at the event stood up until Jacy and Billy sat down. It proved to Jacy that she was indeed the honored guest.

Samuel stood and looked into the crowd. Everyone's eyes were on him. He did not say a word, yet everyone responded by tapping on the table lightly. Jacy did not get to hear the speech because they were using telepathy.

Cindy got out of her chair and crawled into Jacy's lap. She looked beautiful. She was dressed in a red jumpsuit with long sleeves and a high collar. Her hair was pulled up at the crown and tied with a red ribbon. She lay her head against Jacy's chest and hugged her as though she had lost her best friend.

Jacy looked down at her and said, "Be happy, Cindy. We have been blessed. Your being my friend is truly a blessing, my little angel."

Cindy looked up at Jacy and said, "I'm going to dance."

"Good," said Jacy. "I'm going to watch you."

The little girl got down from Jacy's lap and moved her body to the music.

Jacy reached for Lavern's hand and said, "I love you, Grandmother."

Lavern responded by squeezing her hand back. "I love you too, my special granddaughter. You are so much like your father, my handsome son Murphy, whom I love very much." With those words, the two got quiet and listened to the music. Billy sat next to Jacy and occasionally glanced at Samuel.

Jacy looked into the crowd and saw people of the colony that she had never met before. Everyone was dancing and having fun, just like the people of Yelgar at a celebration. The people here were different, but pleasant. Their looks had shocked her the first time she saw them, but now she thought they were quite a handsome race of people. She focused on Samuel's face and looked for a family resemblance. She thought there must be one as they shared the same blood and loved ones. Her father's brother made her very proud. He must have strong leadership qualities. After all, he was the mayor.

"My Uncle Samuel is the mayor of the Tavie colony in Louisiana," Jacy thought. "Wow!"

A man appeared with a bucket of seafood and emptied it in the middle of their table. He gave each of them a bowl to discard the shells in. They ate and enjoyed their food while they watched the Cajun celebration.

Jacy's loved ones were acting somewhat differently this evening. Instead of happiness, she sensed sadness, especially from Cindy. The little girl was acting depressed for no reason. The sky was beautiful, and the night twinkled with stars and a bright moon. The temperature was in the low fifties, and there was a slight breeze. It was autumn now; Jacy's favorite season. She thought it was a great time for falling in love and turned to look at her handsome beau sitting next to her.

Cindy signaled to Jacy by pointing to the sky. There were three small spaceships hovering over the colony. Their red lights winked at the children. The children were in awe as they stared and pointed at the ships. The children of the colony were deeply loved. It was obvious as the adults stopped what they were doing to observe them. Jacy felt safe with the ships close by. They moved very slowly all around the sky above the colony. The winking of the red lights on the bottoms of the spaceships stopped, and the children returned to their eating and dancing. Cindy was right. The spaceships had been winking just for them.

It must have been a special night because the children were all dressed up. The boys wore dress pants and shirts, and the girls wore brightly colored jumpsuits with ribbons in their hair. All of them were dancing and having fun.

As she watched the crowd, Jacy noticed a bald black man talking to some of the colonists. He was very handsome. He stood about six feet tall, and his body looked as if he worked out in a gym. He was definitely in perfect shape. As she observed him, he glanced her way, and their eyes met. He was human, without a doubt. He smiled and walked toward her. As he came closer, Jacy wondered why he was in the colony.

When he reached Jacy, he introduced himself. "Hi, Jacy. I'm Mark. I am human and have been in this colony for four years."

Billy and Samuel got up from their chairs and asked Mark to sit with Jacy to talk with her. Mark took a seat and asked Jacy if she had enjoyed her stay.

"Very much," she answered, "and it is not over yet."

"I guess you're wondering what I'm doing in the colony," he said.

"Well," she said, "it did cross my mind."

"I'm going to tell you the very sad story of my life before coming to the colony," said Mark. "I was a school teacher in a small town in Louisiana for twelve years. I was married to a beautiful, wonderful woman, and we had two children, a boy who was ten and a little girl who was seven. They were my life, the reason I got up in the morning—my only reason for living. I have no living relatives. My parents died when I was eighteen years old, and I had no sisters or brothers. My family was all I had.

"One afternoon, my wife was taking my son to baseball practice. She and my daughter were going to stay and watch him. I had to go to a meeting and couldn't go with them. On the way to the practice park, there was a railroad crossing. The red lights usually blinked when a train was on the tracks. But this day, the lights had been disconnected for repairs.

My wife was crossing the tracks when a train hit her car at full speed, killing my family instantly.

"Life for me was over. I was no longer loved and had no one to love. I only had the memories of my family. I quit my job, took my money out of the bank, and sold everything in the house that I had shared with my family. I packed a suitcase, threw it in my truck, and headed out to kill myself. Living was too hard. I could not do it anymore. I could not eat or sleep. Memories were the only thing that kept me going.

"Finally, I arrived at a river's edge. I was going to drown myself. I had to find relief from the pain in my heart. It hurt too badly. I couldn't stand it anymore. It was night time, and there were no stars in the sky. The night was still, and it was kind of creepy by the river. I walked into the water. Even though I saw alligators slip into the river and disappear, I still had no fear. There was no pain that could compare with the pain I was going through.

"Tears came from my eyes. I knew I might be doing the wrong thing. I am a Christian and did not want to defy the Lord.

"Then there were colored lights in the sky. They flashed as though they were trying to get my attention. I looked up, and a bright beam of light shot down and brought me up into a small spaceship. Suddenly, the pain in my heart found some relief.

"The Tavies in the spaceship said to me, 'Mark, you have family on this earth that needs you. There are children that carry your bloodline.'

"I was in such shock. I thought I had died, and this was what the hereafter was like. I pinched my arm, and I still had feelings. In minutes we were over the colony, and a beam of light carried me to the ground. Samuel was standing in front of me. He told me to please not be frightened. I followed him, and he led me to a small house, just like the one where you are staying now. He told me I would stay in this colony for the rest of my life. He said my living was important, and I could make a difference in the colony.

"Of course, you know how wonderful it is here, and I thank God that I'm alive. I am a teacher to the children. I teach them their human heritage and history. They love me, and I love them. I can't imagine living anywhere but here."

He then stood up and kissed Jacy's hand. "I'm so glad to have met you." Then he walked away.

"Wow! What a sad story," Jacy thought. "How glad I am he shared it with me. He is such a nice man, and now he has once more found a loving family."

Billy walked back and took his seat next to Jacy. "Did you have a nice conversation with Mark?"

"Yes," she said. "He is a wonderful person. He told me the circumstances of his being here and how happy he is."

"Well," Billy said, "we are all happy Mark chose to stay here to help with the children. The children love him very much."

Billy then asked Jacy to dance, hoping it would get her mind off the sadness she felt about Mark's life before coming to the colony. They danced to the fast-moving music, not missing a step. Lavern and Samuel sat at the table and ate crabs and crawfish as they watched the couple enjoy their evening.

As they walked back to the table, one of the small aircraft zoomed down directly above Jacy and

Billy. A quick flash of light brought them from the ground into the small aircraft.

"What happened?" asked Jacy as the aircraft sunk into a large hole in the swamp.

"We are now in the mother ship."

Just then, the doors in the small ship opened, and they walked through a second set of doors into the mother ship. They entered a large room whose walls were covered with hundreds of TV screens. The screens were flat, and each screen had a different scene on it. It looked to Jacy that they were monitoring many people and places outside of the colony.

Billy walked Jacy to the center of the room. There she noticed a man sitting in a large chair that was elevated off the floor by a block of marble. He looked to be in his sixties and had a nice smile on his face. He was from the colony, probably half human and half Tavie. His eyes were not as dark as most of the colonists' and not as large. His head was bald, and his mouth, nose, and ears were small.

There were many people around the man. Some were 100 percent Tavie, and others looked like the people of the colony. Some of them were sitting, and some stood in front of instruments that navigated the ship. They were all dressed like Zen and Qua.

The man stepped down from the chair's pedestal and put his hand out to Jacy. "I'm Philip, and I'm very glad to meet you."

Jacy stared as she looked at the magnificent man. His body was slender but human looking. He was at least six feet tall, and he stood tall and upright with amazing pride. He wore the same uniform as Samuel.

"I have heard a lot about you, Philip. It is an honor to meet you." Then she shook his hand.

He asked if she was enjoying her stay in the colony, and she replied, "More than you'll ever know."

He smiled again and said, "I bet Billy has something to do with that."

"Yes," she said, "as a matter of fact, he does." Billy just stood beside Jacy as he listened to their conversation.

Philip said to Jacy, "I'm glad you do not fear us. I'm going to tell you the reason for our great ships all over the world. We are the protectors of this world and all that live on it. We do not interfere with the activities on earth, such as wars between countries. We protect the planet Earth from other worlds in the universe that may have bad intentions. And believe me, Jacy, there are many."

Jacy said, "Thank you, Philip, and thank you from my world's people."

Philip then walked up to a screen on the wall and pushed one of the buttons on the bottom of it. Jacy and Billy followed closely. He then told Jacy to look at the screen. She focused on the screen and saw many people moving about. They looked familiar to her, so she looked closer.

"That is my grandparents' store!" she exclaimed.

Philip then picked up an instrument that looked like a TV remote, except it was larger with more buttons.

"I want you to see what's happening in Yelgar because of your disappearance." He stepped on a peg in the floor and a bench rose up. "Please have a seat, Jacy and Billy. You will be more comfortable."

They sat down next to Philip, not taking their eyes off the screen. It was nighttime in Yelgar, and the only lights that were on were the night lights located around the city and bayou boat launches. On the screen now was a picture of Macy and Lucille sitting in lawn chairs. They were watching the waterways with binoculars. Jacy took a deep breath when she saw the sadness on Lucille's and Macy's faces.

Philip spoke up and told Jacy that this had been going on every night since she disappeared. As she watched the screen, Macy and Lucille held tissues in their hands and wiped tears from their eyes.

"I thought my mother and father were in Baton Rouge."

Philip answered, "They came home after your disappearance and have remained.

Jacy dropped her head as she felt her mother's and grandmother's sadness.

"They just sit there watching the water and praying for your safe return."

"What about the store? Who is working it?" asked Jacy.

Philip pushed more buttons on his large remote, and the store appeared on the screen. A large sign was placed on the front door, "Closed."

"The store has been closed since you went missing."

"Where are my grandfather and father?" she asked.

Philip once again pushed buttons, and Pierre, Murphy, Bubba, Doris, and Roy appeared on the screen. They were in Roy's boat, searching the swamp for any sign of Jacy or Pierre's boat. They had binoculars to scan the swamp in the dark, with only lanterns for light. The men did not speak to each other. They just watched the swamp.

"They have been out searching for you since they recovered from their snake bites. During the day, small planes search the swamp. No one has given up on you, Jacy. You are loved in Yelgar. Your disappearance has touched many people. Other boats have gone out during the past week to help in the search. Helicopters with large searchlights look for you at night. This search has been going on since Roy returned and said you were nowhere to be found. The water level is getting dangerously low in some parts of the swamp, and your father, grandfather, and friends are becoming very tired."

As Jacy watched the screen and listened to Philip, Billy moved around on the bench. It was evident he was very nervous. Jacy looked at his face, and he glanced off so she could not read his expression.

Jacy asked, "Are these monitors of Yelgar?"

Philip answered, "Yes, these screens are monitors. The cameras placed in your area are as small as dust particles. They are necessary and have been there as long as your town has existed and will remain."

Jacy looked at Billy and understood now why he had told her he had been waiting for her. He, along with Lavern and Samuel, had to have been watching those monitors for many years. Everything was starting to make sense.

Philip stood up, followed by Billy and Jacy. He stepped on the peg again, and the bench disappeared into the floor of the ship. He then told Jacy and Billy that it was time for them to return to the party. He shook hands with them as they went through the doors from one ship into the other.

Once they were in the smaller ship, she looked at the pilots. They were Zen and Qua, the Tavies she had met earlier in her stay.

"Hello," she said to them. "It is good to see you again." They said nothing.

Billy sat close to Jacy as the ship went straight up, leaving the mother ship. The small ship hovered over the colony, and Billy and Jacy were once more in the party area, except there was no party. Everyone had gone home. Their visit with Philip had been no longer than an hour, but it was late—not late enough for sleeping though. Billy suggested they go night fishing. Jacy agreed, and he walked her back to her room to change into her fishing clothes, those she had arrived in. He told her he would come back shortly, after he had changed into his fishing clothes and found some poles.

Jacy dressed quickly, and thirty minutes later Billy was knocking on her door. She opened the door, and he stood there in jeans and a sweatshirt, holding two fishing poles.

"Let's go," he said to Jacy.

They walked to the water's edge and sat on a bench. He handed her a pole and then reached down into the water to grab a couple of minnows. He put them on the sandy grass. They flopped around as he cupped his hand on top of them and put them on the hooks of their poles. Then they dropped their baited poles into the water. They sat quietly, trying to keep their voices down so they would not scare the fish away. After fifteen minutes without a nibble, they pulled their hooks up. There was no bait. Somehow, the minnows had squirmed off the hooks. They both laughed loudly.

Billy said, "I never said I was a fisherman."

Jacy agreed with him. "You sure aren't."

They took their poles out of the water, rolled the twine and hooks around the poles, and laid them down.

Jacy looked at Billy, and he looked at her. They stared at each other, both knowing what the other was thinking. The subject of Philip's visit would not be mentioned. They would think about any subject but that one. Jacy knew that soon she would have to make a decision, but she still thought maybe the decision would be made for her. Nevertheless, Billy was with her, and she only had eyes for him that night.

They decided to take a moonlit walk. They walked very slowly, holding hands and having little conversation. They walked and walked, staying close to the water's edge. Finally, they stopped, held each other close, and kissed passionately. For them, time stood still.

Jacy stepped back and said, "Maybe we should keep walking. You know the trouble we almost got into before Uncle Samuel stopped us."

"You're right, Jacy," said Billy. "We don't need trouble."

It was now early morning, about three o'clock, and the young couple still had no plans of going to sleep. All they wanted to do was be together. Billy and Jacy walked to the park and took a seat. He reached in his pocket and pulled out a heart-shaped object the size of a fifty-cent piece. It looked like a beautiful diamond with shaded areas of pink running through it. At the top, of the heart was a small hole for a chain.

Jacy's eyes lit up. "How beautiful."

Billy placed it in her hand and closed it. "This is yours, Jacy, from me. It is made of a precious stone from Tavus. The quality is equal to a diamond on Earth. This is proof of my love for you. Every time you look at it, think of this moment. Wear it close to your heart."

Jacy's eyes filled with tears. "Is this like a promise ring?"

"No," he said, "it's way more than that. It is a connection of our souls."

She looked once more at the beautiful piece of jewelry and held it close to her chest with both hands. "Thank you, Billy. I will cherish this always." Then she placed it inside her shoe, as that was the safest place she could think of. She did not want to lose her gift from the man she loved.

It was almost daybreak now. The two sweethearts were cuddled together to keep each other warm. The temperature had dropped into the upper forties. It was still very dark outside, except for a few stars in the sky. The fountains in the park were shooting water high into the air. It made a soothing and relaxing sound. They still would not give in to sleep. They held each other so tight that they could feel the other's heartbeat.

Billy pulled back quickly and said, "I love you, Jacy."

At that moment, the huge mother ship appeared. Its size covered the whole colony. Bright golden lights shone from the bottom of the ship. Everything was completely lit up. It was a sight of magnificent beauty. As Jacy and Billy looked up, a beam of light with golden flares appeared. The beam of light moved slowly toward Jacy and Billy at an angle, instead of straight down. When it reached them, Jacy fell limp. She was now asleep, and Billy picked her up in his arms. The beam carried them very slowly toward the boat she had arrived in. As they continued moving through town, Cindy appeared in the street, screaming and clutching her fists.

"No, Jacy, no! Stay with me. Please don't leave me."

The mighty trees swayed back and forth from the wind Cindy had stirred up with her power. The air was filled with sand, and leaves and debris flew everywhere. Lavern ran out behind Cindy. She grabbed her and held her close, and they fell to their knees. Lavern tried to calm Cindy down, although she was in deep pain herself, fighting back the tears.

"I love her, Lavern," said Cindy. "She is my best friend. Please don't let her leave."

Lavern had a lump in her throat as tears flowed from her eyes and down her cheeks. She could not speak. She just held Cindy as they watched the beam of light carry Jacy and Billy by. Samuel sat at the table of the entrance of town. It was the same table where he and Jacy had sat on her arrival to the colony. His arms were crossed, and he had no expression on his face. He got up and followed the beam to the boat.

As the beam placed Billy and Jacy in the boat, it picked up the boat from the water and slowly pushed it toward Yelgar. Billy continued to hold Jacy in his arms without taking his eyes off her. He kissed her on the lips and then put her down gently. The beam then lifted him out of the boat, placed the boat in the water, and the huge ship disappeared. Pierre's boat was now almost to the boat landing, in plain sight of all the people in Yelgar. It was almost daybreak. Fishermen were preparing for the day ahead but never noticed Pierre's boat.

As the sun peeked over the horizon, Lucille and Macy walked to the water with their binoculars and lawn chairs. They sat down in their chairs and looked over the distant waters. The two women spotted Pierre's boat and began to scream.

"It's her! It's Jacy! She's back. Please, someone go bring her in."

The fishermen that were about to leave for the day jumped in their boats and rushed out to Pierre's boat. The first one there hooked it to his boat and dragged it to shore. Lucille and Macy jumped into the water, and the men helped them into the boat. As they screamed her name, she woke from her trance with tears coming from her eyes.

"Where am I?" she asked.

"You're home, Jacy. Thank God you are safe. Are you okay?" asked Macy. "Have you been sick or hurt in any way?"

"I don't think so," said Jacy as her mother and grandmother helped her off the boat and onto the wharf. Someone had called an ambulance. They could hear the sirens coming down the highway. Lucille and Macy walked Jacy toward the road. As the ambulance approached, Jacy stepped back as if she did not want to get into it.

"Please, Jacy," said Macy. "Just go to the hospital for a checkup. It will reassure us that there is nothing wrong with you."

Jacy finally agreed and picked up her foot to step into the ambulance. She looked at her shoe as she stepped up and said to her mother, "Please don't let them take my shoes off."

"Take your shoes off? Why, Jacy?"

"I want to. … I will take my shoes off, okay?"

"Okay," said Lucille. "You will take your shoes off."

The women all took a seat in the back of the ambulance, and it headed toward the hospital. Jacy never took her eyes off her feet.

Lucille and Macy looked at each other with puzzled looks on their faces.

"What has happened to Jacy? Why is she acting so strange? What is it about her shoes? They are just walking shoes, nothing special about them."

Jacy's eyes looked like she was in a trance. They could not wait to get her to the hospital, thinking that something had affected her mentally.

The ambulance did not have far to go. The hospital was only three blocks from the wharf. The ER nurses were waiting with a wheelchair as the ambulance approached. They opened the ambulance door and pushed Jacy quickly into the emergency room where their family doctor was waiting for her with a smile on his face. They put her on a table, and her doctor immediately began his examination. He told her how worried he had been about her and how happy he was that she was home safely.

Jacy was still not clear-minded. She just looked straight ahead and did not respond to the doctor. As he checked her eyes, he commented that her pupils were somewhat dilated. But he could not find anything else wrong with her. He told Macy and Lucille that she was very healthy and looked as though she had taken a bath regularly, although that would be strange for someone had been stranded on a boat for so long. Of course, it had rained a couple of days while she was gone, which was enough for her to clean her clothes and body.

The doctor gave Jacy permission to go home as long as she was kept under a watchful eye for two days. Lucille led her daughter outside the hospital while Macy motioned to a friend to pick them up in her car. They all climbed into the vehicle and headed to Lucille and Murphy's home, the home they had left for Jacy to live in until she found an apartment. Macy thought that being around family would help Jacy to feel comfortable. Maybe she would relax and regain her senses. Lucille rested her head on her mother's shoulder and closed her eyes. She felt more relaxed now that her daughter was back.

After the short trip home, they got Jacy out of the car and helped her into the house. Macy made sure she went straight to her room and to bed.

Jacy slipped her shoes off first and slid them under the bed. Then she took her clothes off and put on a robe. She lay on her bed, covered up, and went to sleep.

Lucille and Macy walked into the kitchen quietly, not saying a word to each other. They were both deep in thought about what could have happened to Jacy. They sat down at the table for a moment and then Lucille got up to make a pot of coffee. It was still early morning, and a cup of coffee would taste good.

As Lucille poured Macy a cup of coffee, the door bell rang. She went to the door and opened it. To her surprise, there were over two hundred townspeople in her yard and on the street clapping, smiling, and yelling.

"We are here to welcome Jacy home," one of them said.

Macy came to the door in disbelief. Lucille and Macy stepped outside to mingle with the people and tried to answer as many questions as they could. They spent a good hour with their friends from the community as they thanked them for all of their support while Jacy was missing. The local preacher was there and asked everyone to bow their heads to give thanks for Jacy's safe return. After the prayer, the townspeople said good-bye to each other and left.

Lucille and Macy were headed back to the house when someone yelled very loudly, "Mrs. Hebert!" They both stopped and turned around.

What they saw was unbelievable. Media from everywhere were driving, walking, and running toward them. The women stood in shock, unsure whether they should run or just stand there. Microphones were pushed into their faces. Questions were asked by not one but ten people at the same time. Media from as far away as New Orleans had come. Every large town in Louisiana had sent a news crew. It had only been three hours since Jacy had been found.

"How did they find out so quickly?" asked Lucille.

"The power of computers," replied Macy.

The women just stood on the front porch of the house and gazed in amazement at the crowd of media. They did not speak or answer one question.

Finally, Macy raised her hands up in the air and shouted, "Stop! I'm going to tell you all I know." The crowd quickly went silent. "We found Jacy Hebert this morning, at daybreak, near the Yelgar boat landing in the boat she had disappeared in. We got her off the boat and had her checked by a physician. He gave her a clean bill of health. She is still a little dazed and is sleeping right now. There is nothing else we know right now. We will give you more information tomorrow when we have had a chance to talk to Jacy."

The two women then turned and walked into the house. Lucille walked to the blinds in the living room and peeked out to see if they were leaving. Only a few of the vehicles had moved out. The rest of the media looked as though they were planning on camping there for the night.

Lucille went to the bedroom to check on Jacy. She opened the door and saw that she was sound asleep. The noise outside the house had not awakened her.

Macy asked Lucille if she had heard anyone say they had contacted Murphy and Pierre, who were still searching the swamp for Jacy.

"No," she answered. "I have not heard."

At that, Macy picked up the phone and called the game warden station. Nate, a friend of the family, answered the phone. When he heard Macy's voice, he commented before she even asked a question, "We have contacted Pierre and Murphy on Roy's short-wave radio. They are on their way home, and I'm sure they are full of joy all the way."

The men had to be very tired. The search had been long and stressful. Many other residents in Yelgar had also searched the swamp for Jacy. Hopefully, all would be notified. Many of them called in to report every three hours, including Roy.

Lucille and Macy sat down as they were very tired themselves. Macy told her daughter how thankful to God she was for Jacy's return. Lucille agreed with her mother, knowing that Jacy's disappearance had made her mother very sad and miserable.

She turned to Macy and said, "Mother, go back to the store and open it. Jacy is all right. Get back to work and keep your mind busy. Plus, look at all the new customers in the front yard. I promise to call you when Jacy wakes up. I know we both have plenty of questions for her, but the worry is over now, Mom. Go back to work."

Macy grinned at Lucille and said, "You think I should?"

"Yes," said Lucille. "Yes, yes. Everything is all right. Go. Go back to work." With that, she pushed her toward the door.

Macy opened the back door to get into the car and did not say a word to the people outside. She backed her car out of the driveway, trying not to hit anyone, and headed toward her store. When she arrived, she got out of the car and unlocked the door. Then she removed the "Closed" sign.

Some of the media had followed her. They came into the store and bought small items like canned cola, chips, cakes, and candy and made small talk with her. To her surprise, they were very nice and asked no questions. Many of them told her they had prayed for Jacy's safe return.

"Thanks," said Macy. "It worked."

Lunch was approaching, and they asked where to go for the best food in town. Macy named about five restaurants as she tried not to forget any of her friends' and fellow businessmen's establishments.

The crowd cleared out, and there was quiet. She wondered how long it would take Pierre to get home. She did not know what part of the swamp they were in. It could take anywhere from two to twenty-four hours.

Lucille contacted her distributors to start deliveries again. She had no milk or bread, and many of her baked goods needed to be replaced. But the bait section was ready to go. Her friends had taken care of that while she was gone. When her husband returned, life for Macy would return to normal.

"But will it return to normal for Jacy?" she asked the empty store. "She was not herself."

The phone rang, and Macy answered it. It was the game warden Nate. She asked if he had heard from Pierre.

"Yes, they are one hour from Yelgar, and he wants you to meet him at the landing."

"I'll be there," said Macy. "Thank you, Nate."

She hung up the phone and called Lucille to tell her the good news. Murphy, her son-in-law and Jacy's father, was with Pierre. Lucille asked her mother to give Murphy a ride home. She did not want to leave Jacy alone.

"Please also warn Murphy about the media outside the house before he gets here," said Lucille.

Macy agreed and hung up the phone. Next, she called Lucille's friend Miss Susan and asked if she would tend to the store until closing and then open the next morning so she could pick up the men from the landing. Miss Susan agreed and told Macy she would be there shortly.

Miss Susan was not the ideal person to mind the store right now, not with all her tall tales about aliens, especially with the media in town, but Macy had no other choice. She had worked for her before, and she was smart and very trustworthy. Miss Susan was divorced but had no children. She was a substitute teacher at the elementary school in Yelgar and also a practical nurse. She went to the homes of the elderly and helped them by delivering medicines, giving shots, and taking blood pressure readings. She was a well-liked woman in the community.

She and Lucille had grown up together, and she had always talked of her alien abductions since childhood. Everyone listened to her, but no one believed her. At least, no one admitted to believing her.

Some of the people teased her, asking, "Been abducted lately, Miss Susan?"

She always answered in a way that sounded truthful. "Yes, I was abducted last week," or "No, it has been a couple of months."

The person who had asked would then nod at her and walk away smiling, probably thinking, "What an imagination!"

As she waited for Miss Susan, Macy stocked the cola section of the coolers. The media had bought most of the cold colas, and they needed to be replaced. When she looked up, she saw Miss Susan walk in the door.

"I'm here, Mrs. Bellard," she said as she hugged Macy lovingly. "I'm glad Jacy is all right. I'll close up. You go home and take care of your family."

"Thanks," replied Macy.

Macy got into her car and headed toward the landing to pick up the men. On her way, she drove by Lucille's house to see if any media were still there. As she had guessed, vehicles were still lined up on the street. Neighbors were sitting in lawn chairs all over the place as they waited for any new developments about Jacy. They, too, wanted the details of her long disappearance. It was late afternoon now and soon would be night. Maybe they would all be gone by the time Murphy got home.

When Macy drove by, they all turned their heads and watched her pass. She hoped they would not follow her, and to her amazement, no one did. She arrived at the boat landing and parked her car where she could watch the boats come in for the evening. She had not seen her husband or son-in-law for days. They would be a welcome sight. Pierre's and Bubba's recoveries from the snake bites had been very fast because Jacy had administered the vaccine so quickly. The doctor had advised them to stay home and get some bed rest, but the men had insisted on returning to the swamp with Roy and Doris to look for Jacy.

Roy's boat was larger, faster, and better rigged for traveling fast through the swamp. It could hold ten people, and there was no part of the area he had not traveled. If anyone could find Pierre's boat and Jacy, it was Roy. He knew the best paths to travel, where the water levels stayed high. How he had not found her puzzled Macy, and probably everyone else in Yelgar. It was even more shocking how Jacy had showed up at the boat landing. No one had spotted her, even though they had all been looking and she had been so close to land.

Macy looked out over the water with her binoculars and saw Roy's boat headed toward the landing. She was so happy. She jumped out of the car and ran toward them, waving her hands in the air. Roy blew his loud boat horn, and everyone looked their way. All of the people around then waved at the boat, knowing Pierre and Murphy were aboard. As the boat pulled into its slip, the men anxiously climbed out and hugged Macy.

"Where is my daughter?" asked Murphy.

Macy replied, "I will take you to her. She is okay…physically."

They got into the car and headed back to Murphy and Lucille's house. Macy explained about the media on the way.

"She is big news in this area—with a happy ending," said Pierre.

"Brace yourselves; we are almost there," said Macy.

As they approached the house, they could see that the media was still there. The questions started as soon as they got out of the car.

"Are you Murphy Hebert? Are you Pierre Bellard?"

"Yes," the men answered.

Then Murphy said, "We are returning from a long and tiresome search in the swamp for Jacy, and the only thing we want to do now is look at her pretty face and know she is safely home. Tomorrow we may know more and will surely pass any news to you. Thank you for your concern." Then the men walked into the house.

Lucille ran to meet Murphy, and both of their eyes became tearful as they held each other.

"My baby is okay," said Murphy.

"Yes, she is sleeping."

The four of them walked to the bedroom where she slept and stared at her.

Murphy whispered, "Where in the world were you, my little girl? Why could we not spot the boat by air or water?"

It was now evening, and it was evident that the media was not going to leave. Lucille and Macy prepared food for the tired men while they showered and then relaxed as they watched their favorite TV shows. Macy and Pierre decided to spend the night because they did not want to confront the media again by leaving the house. They all had a nice supper and then went off to bed so they would be ready to face the next day.

A new day had dawned, and Lucille jumped out of bed to make a breakfast for the family. She put on her robe and stopped to check on Jacy before going to the kitchen. She was still sound asleep. Lucille picked up her clothes to wash them and pulled her shoes out from under the bed. As she picked up the shoes, she saw something shiny in one of them. She reached into the shoe and pulled out the heart Billy had given to Jacy. She looked at the beautiful diamond-like substance and could not figure out what it was or where it had come from. She put it back into the shoe and pushed it back under the bed. The things Jacy had said about her shoes now made more sense. But Lucille could not imagine where she had come upon such an unusual piece of jewelry.

She tiptoed out of the room because she did not want Jacy to know that she had found the item. She believed that her daughter would tell her what she wanted her to know. As she held the clothes close to her while she carried them to the laundry room, she could not help but notice the strong smell of citrus. It was a soothing and very pleasant smell.

"That's weird. I've never noticed Jacy wear perfume with this smell before. Where did her clothing absorb this pleasant odor?"

Macy was now awake and joined her daughter in the kitchen. Lucille brought the clothes to her mother and asked her to smell them.

Macy smelled the citrus odor and remarked, "Doesn't smell like the swamp to me. It smells clean, with a citrus scent."

"I agree," said Lucille. "But how?"

"Only Jacy knows," said Macy. "I'm sure she will be up soon."

Lucille also told her mother about the object she had found in Jacy's shoe.

"Well, maybe she took it with her when she left," said Macy.

Lucille answered, "Jacy always shows me her new jewelry, and I have never seen this piece. It's a heart, Mother. Something a man would give to a woman. I know there's an explanation. I just can't wait to hear it."

"She was lost in the swamp for days and comes back smelling good and with jewelry. No sense to that at all. It's a mystery," said Macy. "She's home and safe. That's all that matters right now."

The two women were quiet while they fixed breakfast, lost in their thoughts about what could have happened to Jacy.

When the alarm clock went off, the men got up to a brighter and less stressful day. But when they looked out the window, they could see that the media was still in their front yard.

"Hopefully Jacy will have answers for them today so they can go about their business," Murphy said.

As the men ate breakfast, they discussed their plans for the day. Pierre and Murphy were in agreement that they were not leaving the house until they had spoken with Jacy.

Lucille and Macy cleaned the kitchen and saved some breakfast for Jacy in the oven. As she walked past Jacy's room to go get dressed for the day, Macy peeked into the room and saw Jacy sitting on the side of her bed. She motioned to Lucille. Lucille joined her mother, and they watched Jacy as she sat on the bed and stared out the window in front of her. Lucille and Macy walked into the room and turned on the light. They each sat on one side of Jacy and put their arms around her.

"Good morning, Jacy," Lucille said. "How do you feel?"

Jacy looked at her mother and said, "Grandfather and Bubba got bit by water moccasins, Mom."

"Yes, they did, and you saved their lives."

"Roy saved them, Mom. Roy saved them," said Jacy.

"What happened to you while you were lost in the swamp, Jacy?" asked Lucille.

Macy got up and told Murphy and Pierre to join them in Jacy's room. The two men got up and walked into her bedroom. When they saw their daughter and granddaughter, they both hugged her and told her how worried they had been before she was found.

Jacy grabbed Pierre by the neck and said, "Grandfather, you are safe. How is Bubba doing?"

He answered, "He is fine, Jacy. He stayed in the hospital a day longer than I did, but we both had a quick recovery, thanks to you."

At that Jacy got a big smile on her face and squeezed her grandfather's hand as tight as she could.

The two men pulled chairs up so they could all ask Jacy questions and get information about what had happened to her.

Lucille once more asked Jacy, "What happened to you while you were lost in the swamp?"

"Well," she said, "I took a nap after Roy rescued Grandfather and Bubba. When I woke up, I could no longer see Roy's boat. He told me to stop and wait for him until he returned for me, but I thought I knew the route he took home. I traveled down a boat path for a couple of hours and got scared. It was very dark. So I pulled the anchor up and drifted until morning. I could see land a short distance away. It looked like a sandy beach. There were huge trees everywhere. It was beautiful, with a yellow light bordering the land. There were no reptiles in sight. I thought I was home, so I got out of the boat. The land felt so good beneath my feet that I just stood there for a few minutes. Then I started up a hill and must have fainted because I don't remember anything else. I must have found my way back to the boat and then my way home. That's all I remember."

"Why would you leave dry land to get back into the boat? You had been scared and lost in the swamp. Why didn't you go into the town and call someone?" her father asked.

"I don't know why," said Jacy.

"When you left the land, where did you go from there?" asked Murphy.

"I think I fell asleep and somehow drifted home."

The family looked at each other in shock. "You were gone a week—lost in the swamp," said Lucille. "You couldn't have just drifted, Jacy. You would have gotten caught up in mud bogs or stumps. Do you remember eating, drinking, fishing…anything?"

"No," she said. "I just slept."

"You slept for a week, Jacy?"

"I can't remember, Mom. I can't remember."

Macy told them what the doctor's report had said. It had said she was in good health.

"That means she had been eating and drinking," said Lucille. "She had not lost weight and was not dehydrated. Her skin and clothing were clean, and she had no mosquito bites. Maybe the only way we will ever get answers is to take Jacy to a psychiatrist. But we can decide that later. Maybe her memory will come back."

They all left the room to let Jacy shower and get ready to meet the media who were waiting for her in the front yard. The media had surrounded the house, each of them hoping he or she would get the first coverage of Jacy's return home. There were twice the number of people that morning than the morning before.

After she showered and blow-dried her hair, Jacy put on jeans and a long-sleeve shirt with buttons down the front. As she looked at herself in the mirror, she thought something had changed. She just kept staring at herself. She put her face close to the mirror, as if she were trying to see into another dimension.

"What is it?" she thought to herself. "Something is not the same. Somehow I'm different. I feel it."

Then she sat on the side of her bed and pulled out her shoes. She put her foot in one shoe and felt something in it. She took the shoe off, found the beautiful stone, and clutched it to her heart.

"What a gorgeous heart," she said. "But where did it come from?"

As she held the heart in her hands, a feeling of love and happiness overcame her. She felt wonderful.

She looked at the stone intensely as she placed it in her jewelry box.

"I must get a chain for it today and wear it forever."

She could hardly stand to walk away from it and could not get it off her mind. It had to be more than a precious stone.

Jacy ate her breakfast and then joined her family in the living room. They explained to her about the media outside and the many questions they were going to ask her. Pierre told Jacy to tell them what she had told them and to explain that she had temporarily lost some of her memory. It was not unusual for that to happen to someone who had been traumatized by an awful event.

When Jacy opened the front door, the media closed in on her. She answered all the questions she could and gave her explanation of what had happened to her while she was lost in the swamp. Everyone was taking pictures of her and calling her name so she would look their way. All she saw were bright lights flashing in her face. It felt familiar to her, like something that had happened before.

When she was done answering questions, she walked to her car and started the motor. She backed her car out but did not know where she was going. Life had taken on a different meaning now. Somehow she was different. She kept thinking of the heart and how she loved it. It seemed to be a connection to her inner self.

She drove around a while, looking at the scenery and trying to remember what had taken place over the last week. She ended up at her grandparents' store and walked in. Miss Susan was at the counter waiting for Macy to take over. No one else was there.

Miss Susan ran up to Jacy and hugged her. "Are you okay?" she asked.

"Yes," said Jacy. "I'm just having trouble with my memory."

Miss Susan looked into Jacy's eyes and said, "It was them, wasn't it, Jacy?"

"Who?" she asked.

"You know, the aliens that live around here. They're around us all the time. They monitor everything we do. They call on me often," she said.

Jacy looked at Miss Susan and saw that she really believed what she had said.

"You can't remember because they erased your memory. It works on everyone but me. I'm immune. You do believe me, don't you, Jacy?" asked Miss Susan.

"Maybe so," said Jacy. "Because I have no idea what happened to me."

"If it was them," said Miss Susan, "they will come to you often for different reasons. Watch the skies. There are small spaceships and very large ones. Their speed is as fast as light. They are there one second and gone the next, sometimes with you as a passenger. I'm going to keep a watchful eye on you, Jacy."

"Thank you, Miss Susan," said Jacy as she walked over to get a soda. "My grandmother will be here soon. Until then, I can take your place if you have something to do."

Miss Susan said she would stay because of the media. They had been coming in all morning, and she knew they would be bothersome if Jacy was behind the counter.

Jacy looked at Miss Susan and asked, "What are they building in the middle of town? As I drove around, I saw the new construction going on. It looks like a big project."

"I guess you have been gone a while. It's the new civic center the town has been planning for two years," said Miss Susan. "When it is completed, they are adding an open-air section with a stage for bands to perform. It will hold six thousand people."

"Wow," said Jacy, "that sounds wonderful. When will it be completed?"

"It will be completed by next October, according to the newspaper," Miss Susan answered.

Jacy sat down on one of the chairs that lined the wall of the store. She leaned back and said, "It's good to be home."

Then the door opened and her grandmother walked in. "Thank you, Miss Susan. You really helped me out of a jam."

"No problem, Mrs. Bellard. Call me anytime, night or day, if you ever need me."

Macy reached into the cash register to pay Susan before she left. Susan waved her hands at Macy. "This was an emergency. You owe me nothing." Then she turned and left the store.

"You look comfortable," Macy said to Jacy.

"Yes, ma'am," said Jacy as she closed her eyes.

Just then a customer walked into the store, and Jacy opened her eyes. It was a well-dressed young man in jeans, a white pullover shirt, and brown sport coat. He was about six feet tall with blond hair and green eyes. He had a slim build and was very good looking. Her first thought was that he was from the media and had come for more information on her disappearance. She sat up straight and looked away from him.

Macy put her hand out to the young man and said, "She is finally home."

He clutched Macy's hand and told her how happy he was for the family that their nightmare was finally over.

Macy looked at Jacy and said to the young man, "This is Jacy, my granddaughter."

Jacy smiled at them shyly. She was a little embarrassed.

The young man walked up to her with his hand held out and introduced himself. "Hi, Jacy," he said. "I'm Cameron Leger. I am very glad you are home safely."

Jacy shook his hand and looked questioningly at her grandmother. Macy came out from behind the counter to explain to Jacy who he was.

"Jacy, Cameron is the architect for the new construction of the civic center. He is from New Orleans and is renting the house next to mine. He has had supper with the family many times since you were gone."

"Oh," Jacy said. "Pleased to meet you, Cameron."

He said, "You have a very nice family, Jacy. I know you are very proud of them."

"Yes, I am," she said. "I love them very much."

"Well," he said," I've come to get my lunch." He then picked up a loaf of bread and some lunch meat and set it on the counter. He paid Macy and then turned to Jacy and told her that he hoped to see her again. Then he told Macy good-bye and left the store.

Jacy walked to the door and watched him get into a new black Mercedes.

"Well," she said, "he's certainly not walking. That car is beautiful."

"Jacy, that is one of the nicest single young men I have ever met. Every day you were missing, he came by to inquire about you. I'm going to invite him to supper tomorrow night, and I want you to come."

"Oh no, Grandmother," Jacy said. "You are not going to play matchmaker. He is an architect from the big city, and I'm a small-town girl. No match there, Grandmother. I am not interested."

"Please, Jacy. Can't you just be friends with him? He doesn't know anyone in town."

"With his looks, it won't take him long to meet someone," said Jacy.

"Tomorrow night, Jacy. You be there. I'm serving your favorite—shrimp Creole. Just be his friend, like the family is. Just friends, okay?" pleaded Macy.

"Okay, Grandmother. I'll be there. Just friends. Remember that."

Jacy told her grandmother she was going to the local mall to get a gold chain for the beautiful heart she had found in her shoe. She then walked to her car while Macy watched her through the screen door of the store.

When Jacy arrived at the mall, the locals surrounded her and told her how happy they were that she was all right. She thanked them and then escaped into the jewelry store. As she looked at the many chains through the glass, she realized that she had to decide on a length. Would she get a short, medium, or long chain? They were all so beautiful and shiny. She asked the lady behind the counter to show her several of the chains. It did not take her long to decide. She picked a beautiful, medium-length chain and paid the clerk. Now that she had the perfect chain, she could not wait to get home and put her heart around her neck. It was one piece of jewelry that she would wear always and not ever take off.

As she pulled into the driveway at home, she noticed her parents' vehicles were not there. That was a good thing. She needed to be alone for a while.

Jacy rushed into the house and went straight to her room. She opened her jewelry box and picked up the heart. It looked like an oversized diamond. She put the chain into the hole at the top of the heart and hung it around her neck. She opened the blinds in her room and let the sun shine in. The heart sparkled with all the beauty of a high-priced diamond. She could not stop looking at the necklace in the mirror. How lucky she was to have found such a beautiful piece of jewelry deep in the swamp.

It was now lunchtime, so Jacy went into the kitchen for a sandwich. As she sat down at the table to eat, she heard the door open. It was her mother and father. Jacy looked up at them when they walked into the kitchen. The necklace sparkled around her neck.

"My," said Lucille, "that is a beautiful necklace, Jacy. Where did you get it?" She had wanted to ask that questions since she had found the heart in Jacy's shoe.

"I don't know, Mother. I found it in the swamp."

"Where?" asked Lucille.

"I don't remember, Mother."

Murphy nudged Lucille and whispered, "Enough with the questions." Then he looked at Jacy. "Finish your sandwich, Jacy. Your necklace is pretty."

Lucille and Murphy walked into their bedroom and closed the door. Immediately, Lucille put her hands on top of her head and said, "Murphy, did you see the quality of that stone? It looks like a diamond, and she found it in the swamp? Something is very wrong with that story."

"I'm sure when her memory comes back she can tell you more, Lucille. Don't worry about it, and don't drill her about what happened," said Murphy.

Lucille turned and looked at Murphy. "I'm not sure if Susan's tales about the aliens are false. We have many missing pieces here."

"Please," said Murphy, "you're making way too much out of this. Calm down. And please don't drag Susan into this. She will make a mountain out of a molehill. Jacy will remember in time."

Jacy called out to her parents from the kitchen. She asked them to come out and talk to her. Her parents walked out of their room and into the kitchen. Jacy asked them to sit down at the table with her.

"First of all, I want to tell you how sorry I am for causing you so much worry and unhappiness in the time I was gone. I love you both very much and never want to see you in pain. But I'm home now, and it's time for you to get back to your own life. I want you to go back to Baton Rouge and pick up where you left off. I'm going to start college as soon as the next semester begins. I'm going to be an elementary school teacher. I think I'll like working with children."

"What?" asked Lucille. "A teacher? I would have never guessed you would want to work with children."

"Yes, Mother," said Jacy. "That's what I'm going to do."

"I think it's wonderful," said Murphy. "I think you will make a great teacher."

"I think you can accomplish anything you want, Jacy. If it's a teacher of children, I know you will be the best," said her mother.

"This is sort of a shock," said Murphy. "I guess you had a lot of time to think over the past week. I'm very glad, Jacy, that you want to further your education, and I want you to know I'm willing to pay all of your tuition, for however long it takes. I'll open you savings and checking accounts tomorrow to cover your expenses. You can live here, in this house, for as long as it takes to get your degree. The nearest college is fifteen miles away. You will also need a gas credit card."

"Thanks, Dad. I appreciate your help. But I plan on working part-time," said Jacy.

"That's good, Jacy. You can use that money for your personal use. We will get you fixed up tomorrow morning and return to Baton Rouge. Your mother and I want you to visit us as often as you can. We will try and visit you as often as possible. We are not that far away."

"I'm proud of you, Jacy," said Lucille. "You have made a very good decision."

"Thanks, Mom. I'm glad y'all are pleased."

Jacy then got up from the table and went into her room to lie down on her bed. She closed her eyes and clutched the heart around her neck. A wonderful feeling came over her body when she concentrated on the heart. She lay there and rested for thirty minutes. Then she decided it was time to visit her grandfather's wood shop to see what was going on there.

She called loudly, "See you later, Mom and Dad. I'm going to visit Grandfather."

Jacy and her grandfather had a close bond. She was interested in what he was now making in his workshop. She decided to walk instead of driving. The shop was only about a mile away.

When she stepped outside, it looked like rain. There was a cool breeze blowing, and the colorful foliage from the trees was drifting slowly to the ground as she watched. The sun was hidden behind dark clouds, and she could see lightning flashes in the far distance. Tiny droplets of rain hit her face and hair. She stopped and looked up at the sky as she put her hands in the air to let the rain bounce off of them.

As she walked, cars slowed down, and the drivers looked at her. Many of them motioned for her to get into their cars. She just shook her head no, and they drove on. Before long, the rain started to come down harder. The wind picked up, and she shivered from the cold. She was almost at her grandfather's shop when a black Mercedes stopped, and a man jumped out of the car. It was Cameron, the young man she had met earlier at her grandmother's store.

"Hi, Jacy," he said. He opened the door on the passenger's side of his car and gently pushed Jacy into the car. "You are soaking wet," he said. "I'm going to take you home to put some dry clothes on."

Jacy looked straight ahead and agreed with him as her body shook from the cold. He pulled into her driveway, and they jumped out of the car. They ran to the door as the rain pounded on them. Jacy reached into her pocket for her key. She opened the door, and Cameron followed her in. Her parents were in their bedroom, probably taking a nap. The house was very quiet.

Jacy told Cameron to take a seat, even though he already had. She excused herself and went into her bedroom to change clothes. After putting on something dry, she walked back into the living room where Cameron was sitting. He stood as she entered the room.

"I know you must feel warmer now, Jacy," he said.

"Yes, I do. Thank you for caring," she said.

He smiled at her and asked if he could drive her to wherever she had been headed.

She answered, "Yes. I was going to visit my grandfather's shop."

She grabbed an umbrella by the door and opened it. They both got under it and walked back to the car. The rain had not let up. It was pounding the windshield, and the wind blew hard.

"You picked a good time to visit," said Cameron.

"Good as any," answered Jacy.

As he pulled up to her grandfather's shop, she wondered how he knew where everyone lived.

"Would you like to come in?" Jacy asked as she got out of the car.

"No," he answered, "but I will see you tomorrow night at Mrs. Bellard's house for supper. Hope you'll be there."

"Thank you for the ride," Jacy said. "Yes, I will be there for supper."

He told her good-bye and drove off. Jacy opened the door and went into the shop. Pierre was stooped down, sanding a chair made from cypress. When he saw Jacy, he stood and gave her a big hug.

"Now," he said, "everything's perfect with my granddaughter here."

Jacy grabbed a piece of sandpaper, and they sanded the chair together.

"Grandfather," she said, "Cameron picked me up in the rain earlier as I was walking here. He took me home to change, waited for me, and then drove me here. He knew where I lived, and he knew where the shop was. How did he know?"

"Jacy, he's been here for two weeks. He is a very nice young man, but he knows no one in town. Your grandmother befriended him, and now he is like part of the family."

"He's nice, Grandfather, but I hope Grandmother doesn't think there is a love connection here."

"Oh," said Pierre, "you know Macy. She just wants to see you happy."

"I am happy. I'm very happy."

Pierre noticed the necklace around Jacy's neck. "I've never noticed you wearing that heart before."

She reached for the heart and answered, "I found it in the swamp."

"It's very pretty, and very unusual."

Jacy changed the subject. She did not like to discuss her necklace. She continued to help Pierre with the chair. They worked for three hours and then she told him she wanted to go home before it got too late. The weather had cleared up, but it was still very wet and dark outside.

"Let me take you home," said Pierre.

"Okay," said Jacy.

Pierre drove Jacy home in his truck. When they arrived at her home, he said, "See ya'll tomorrow night."

"Okay. I love you, Grandfather."

He drove off as Jacy walked into the house. Lucille was in the kitchen making supper.

"Is that you, Jacy?" she called out.

"Yes, Mom," she said as she entered the kitchen.

"Did you enjoy your visit with my dad?" she asked.

"Yes, ma'am. We had a good visit."

"I've been packing. Your father and I are ready to go. We will leave tomorrow, as planned, for Baton Rouge."

"Tomorrow morning, I'm registering for college," said Jacy proudly. "I'm going to watch TV for a while."

Jacy walked into the living room, plopped in her father's recliner, and picked up the remote to surf the channels. She liked watching old comedy TV shows like *The Andy Griffith Show* and *I Dream of Jeannie*. She found the cable station she wanted, and her favorite was on, Andy Griffith. Aunt Bee was walking down the street of the quaint town.

Jacy sat up straight in her chair and said out loud, "I've walked down a street like that. I know I have."

In the show, children were riding bicycles on the sidewalk, and people dressed casually were walking around the town.

"This feels real to me," Jacy said aloud. "I feel like I'm there with them, and it is a good feeling."

The show ended, and she dropped her head in her hands. "Is something wrong with me? Am I losing my mind?" she thought.

Just then, Lucille called for Jacy to come and eat their last supper together for a while. She got up and walked slowly to the kitchen where she sat down and said nothing.

"Why are you so quiet, Jacy?"

"I think I'm sad, Mother, but I can't figure out why."

"You'll be all right as soon as you start college. You will have no time to feel sad. Homework and the computer will take up all of your time."

"The computer," said Jacy. "I forgot all about it. Maybe I've got e-mail."

"Stay, Jacy. Eat before you get on the computer."

Murphy walked in and sat down. "Just like old times," he said as he looked at his only daughter.

After dinner, Jacy went into the office where they kept the computer. Lucille had taken an extra bedroom and converted it into an office. The room was where all the business issues were taken care of. Now it would be the space Jacy used for homework.

Jacy had no new e-mails. So she pulled up the college she wanted to attend and got all the information she needed to enroll for the fall. When she started to get tired, she went to the living room where Murphy and Lucille were watching TV. She sat down to spend some time with them. Tomorrow she would start a new life, one she was looking forward to.

After preparing for bed, she lay down, closed her eyes, and touched the heart hanging around her neck to make sure it was still there. As she fell asleep, dreams came to her. She dreamed of a young and beautiful dark-haired girl with dimples. She waved and called to Jacy, "You're my best friend." Then she was walking down a street in a quaint little town from the sixties with an older lady with salt-and-pepper hair. Children were riding bicycles all around them. She could only see the back of them, not their faces. As the soothing dream continued, she could now see a man walking in front of her with a bald head and black uniform. She could not see his face. The dreams continued all night long.

When morning came, Jacy got up feeling happy and ready for her long day. She went into her closet and took out slacks and a sweater to put on. She decided to leave her auburn hair down and to wear makeup. When she was finished dressing, she walked into the kitchen and poured herself a cup of coffee. She grabbed a piece of toast and kissed her mom and dad good-bye before she got into her car and headed for the college.

When Jacy arrived at the college, there were hundreds of people everywhere. The sight was a little frightening. Jacy had been out of school for three years. She parked her car and walked toward the entrance. Many of the students looked at Jacy, waved, and told her they were glad to see her home safely. She didn't know them but responded by saying thank you. She did not know how she would respond if someone asked her what had happened to her. The only answer she knew was, "I don't know." Her memory still had not come back to her.

When she reached the office for registering, there were at least fifty people filling out information papers. They all looked up and smiled at Jacy and then put their heads down and continued their business. Everyone knew her face. She was like a celebrity in the Yelgar area. She registered for a semester and left the campus as soon as she could.

Jacy was happy. She turned her radio on and sang with the music. Classes started in three days. She had a list of school supplies she needed and could not wait to get them. But her parents were leaving for Baton Rouge, and she needed to get home to have lunch with them first. As she arrived home and pulled into her driveway, a car pulled up behind her. It was a black Mercedes—Cameron. He jumped out of his car and opened Jacy's car door.

As she got out of the car, Cameron looked at her and said, "You look beautiful."

She said thanks and asked him what he needed.

"I just wanted to know what kind of wine you like, red or white? I'm going to bring a bottle tonight."

She answered, "I like red wine."

"Any certain brand?" he asked.

"No," she said, "anything will be fine."

He then closed her car door and said, "Got to get back to work."

As he backed out of the driveway, Jacy watched him drive away.

"That question could have been answered with a phone call," she said out loud, as if talking directly to him. "This guy is everywhere and very forward. I don't like it," she thought.

When Jacy got to the door, she saw a note her parents had left for her. They wanted her to meet them at a local restaurant for a salad. She turned and went back to her car and drove to meet her parents for lunch. They had a nice lunch, and her parents gave her the bank books for the accounts they set up for her. Her mother explained that she had to go by the bank and sign something and then they would give her the checkbooks for the account. There was enough in the accounts to take care of all of her tuition and books.

"I have called the electric company," said Lucille. "They are going to send me the bill every month. And here is a credit card for your gas. Now you are all set."

Jacy was pleased. "Thanks, Mom and Dad. I really appreciate this."

Murphy looked at Jacy and patted her hands. "We love you and want you to be happy."

"I promise you," said Jacy, "that I will give this 100 percent. I will be a teacher."

The family left the restaurant and headed home. Jacy's parents needed to load their luggage before leaving for Baton Rouge, but not before stopping by Lucille's parents' businesses to tell them good-bye.

Jacy helped her parents with the luggage and gave them each a big hug. After they left, Jacy went back into her house, lay down on the sofa, and closed her eyes to rest. It had been another tiring day.

After she felt rested, Jacy got up and went to her computer. This time she had mail. The message read, "You have my heart." There was no sender's name after the message. She read it again. "You have my heart." Could this be Cameron, or maybe someone pulling a joke on her? Why would they not give their name with the message? What good is the message if you do not know who it is from? She kept looking at the message and did not erase it from the computer.

It was now evening, and she decided to get ready to go to her grandparents for supper. Cameron was bringing the wine, so she thought about not taking anything. But she changed her mind and decided to stop on the way to get some Italian bread that her grandparents loved. She was ready for the evening and very hungry because of her small lunch.

She had to go a little out of the way from her grandparents' house to get the Italian bread. As she walked into the store, she glanced up at the dark sky. It was a cool night, and there were a few stars out. She thought she saw some red lights wink. She stopped and stared at the heavens. The lights had stopped. Maybe she had not seen light after all. It could also have been a passenger plane passing over the area.

She walked into the store and went straight to the bakery. It was her favorite place in the grocery store because of the smell of baked bread. She asked one of the bakers for a loaf of the freshest Italian bread they had. The baker went into the back and brought out a nice loaf of hot bread.

"This is right out of the oven, Jacy. Enjoy it."

"Thanks," she said and wondered how he knew her name. "I think everyone knows my face now," she thought. She paid for the bread and then was off to her grandparents' house. The smell in the car made her hungry. She was tempted to tear a piece off the end to taste it.

When she arrived at the house, she noticed the black Mercedes that Cameron drove had its parking lights on. The car was parked on the side of the street. She went to the door and rang the doorbell. Her grandfather came to the door and let her in. She carried the bread into the kitchen and handed it to her grandmother.

"That smells good," she said.

Just then Cameron came from the living room with a big smile on his face. "Would you like a glass of wine, Jacy?" he asked.

"I would love one," she answered.

He brought her a glass of wine, and Macy told Jacy to take their drinks out to the deck. "It's nice and cool outside. Just relax until supper is ready."

"All right, Grandmother, but call for me if you need help with anything," said Jacy.

They followed her grandmother's orders and went out to the deck.

"No one argues with Macy," Cameron said.

While they relaxed outside, Jacy looked up at the sky and thought she saw red lights winking again.

"Did you see that, Cameron?" she asked as she pointed to the sky.

"No," he said. "What did you see?"

"I thought I saw winking red lights."

"*Winking* red lights?" he asked. "I think you mean *blinking*, don't you?"

"No," she said. "I mean winking. Don't ask me why, but the word of choice, my choice, is winking."

"Okay," said Cameron, "winking it is. But I see nothing."

The two stared at the sky. "Isn't it beautiful?" Jacy asked. "The sky, isn't it beautiful? Couldn't you just get lost in it?"

"It's beautiful, Jacy, but can we talk about you for a while?" asked Cameron.

"What do you want to know?"

"How old are you?" he asked.

"I'm twenty-one, soon to be twenty-two. How old are you?" she asked.

He answered, "I'm twenty-six years old. I just turned twenty-six. I'm from New Orleans and have one brother and one sister. Both of my parents are alive. I'm here until probably next November, when the new civic center is completed. I'm the architect, as you probably know, and I'm overseeing the work on the civic center project."

Jacy nodded her head at him and said, "Well, you know my grandparents. You know my mother and father. I have no brothers or sisters, very few friends, and I'm starting college in three days. I'm going to be a teacher."

"That means you're going to be a very busy girl for the next few years," said Cameron. "I hope you have time to fit me in for the occasional dinner and dancing."

Jacy did not answer him. She got up from her seat and told Cameron she needed to go into the kitchen to help her grandmother set the table. He picked up the wine glasses and followed her into the kitchen.

"Back already?" asked Macy.

"Yes, ma'am. I came to set the table for you."

"Okay. You know where the dishes are."

Jacy set the table while Cameron went back into the living room with Pierre.

Macy put the food on the table so they could serve themselves. She whispered to Jacy, "He's nice, isn't he?"

Jacy grinned and said, "So-so, Grandmother. The shrimp Creole looks and smells delicious. You've made too much food."

"Not really. It's just rice, potato salad, corn, and iced tea to drink. That's just enough."

"Don't forget the fresh bread," said Jacy.

"What? No way. I will cut it up for the table now," answered Macy.

When the table was set, Macy called for the men to come to the table. It did not take them long. They came immediately. The smell of the food was sensational. The shrimp in the Creole were extra large. Four of the shrimp would certainly be a complete meal for Jacy, but the men could probably eat many more.

The men pulled out the chairs for the women as they all took a seat at the table. Pierre bowed his head and said the blessing before they started their meal.

Jacy looked at Cameron and said, "You're our guest. Serve yourself first."

"Are you sure?" he asked.

"Yes, very sure."

They passed the food to Cameron while Pierre started the conversation. He made sure it was not about Jacy's disappearance. He talked about the fishermen's catches. They were some of the best catches in two years. The shrimp, oysters, and crabs were plentiful. Everyone seemed to be making money.

Cameron then said to Pierre, "I don't mean to change the subject, but did you ever find anymore swamp cypress?"

"Very little," said Pierre. "My friends sometimes find knees and cypress driftwood. They cut it and deliver it to me for a small fee. I'm going to start using wood from the trees found in this area for my furniture needs. I have contacted many of my customers, and they are fine with the wood change as long as it is attractive and native to this area. But I think I have lost my best helper to college," he said jokingly and looked at Jacy.

"No, Grandfather. I will be around to help you, just not as often," she said.

Macy then jumped in and asked, "Are you going to work in the store while going to school?"

"Yes, Grandmother, but just part-time. After I get my schedule, I'll give you the times I'll be available."

"Good," Macy said. "But remember that school and homework come first."

"I'll remember," said Jacy.

Everyone finished their meals and complimented Macy on the wonderful food.

"Glad everyone enjoyed it," Macy said. She told them all to go in the living room. "I will bring dessert and coffee in to you as soon as I clear the table."

Jacy asked, "What's for dessert, Grandmother?"

"Pecan pie. Another of your favorites, Jacy."

"Grandmother, you are spoiling me, as always," said Jacy.

The men walked into the living room, and Jacy stayed to help Macy clean the table and prepare the desserts for everyone.

While Macy sliced the pie and placed the pieces on saucers, Jacy poured the coffee into cups and placed sugar and cream on a tray. Macy put the pie on the tray, and they were ready to serve. Jacy carried the tray into the living room with the dessert and coffee. The men were watching a boxing match on a sports cable station, but eyed the pie and took a break, even though they were very interested in the fight. The main event fight was a boxer from Louisiana against a boxer from Florida.

Macy put the tray on the coffee table and handed out the pie. She gave them each a fork, and everyone fixed their own coffee. The boxing match was in the third round. They all sat back and finished watching the match. The boxer from Louisiana won, and everyone cheered.

Jacy said to her grandparents, "This evening was great. I have really enjoyed it, and the food was out of this world. But I have had a long day, and I'm very tired. It was good seeing you again, Cameron, but I'm out of here."

"You're welcome, Jacy," said Macy. "I'm sure we will be seeing a lot of you. Stop by anytime."

"Bye, everyone." Jacy opened the door and headed out to her car.

Cameron gave his thanks to the Bellard's and followed Jacy out the door. She ran to get into her car. Cameron knocked on her window and asked if he could follow her home. Jacy rolled her window down and told him that she would be fine. He said okay and that he would see her later.

On her drive home, Jacy noticed that Cameron had followed her anyway. She pulled into her driveway, and he kept driving. "This guy is very persistent. This could be a problem, since he lives next door to my grandparents."

Jacy went into the house, put on her nightshirt, and went straight to bed. She hoped to have wonderful dreams like the ones she'd had the night before, but that night she had no dreams that she could remember.

Jacy spent the next day buying school supplies, doing her banking, and preparing for her first day of school. She went to the supermarket and bought food that she could prepare quickly and plenty of fruit. For some reason she could not even walk through the meat department. She subconsciously bypassed it completely.

That evening, she was finally ready for the next day—the day she would start college.

The next morning, Jacy jumped from the bed and got ready for her first day of school. This was the beginning of her future. All she could think about was being a teacher of children. She would definitely fulfill this goal. The name Mark came to mind. She had no idea why. She knew no one named Mark—at least, no one she could remember.

Back at the Tavie colony, it was morning, and everything was the same as when Jacy had left— except for Samuel, Billy, Cindy, and Lavern. Their lives would not be the same until they were with their loved one again. Billy reported to the laboratory as usual, Cindy attended school as usual, and Lavern and Samuel returned to their regular duties. Life went on, but not without a bit of sadness. Although Billy, Cindy, Lavern, and Samuel could predict the future of others, their own futures sometimes were foggy from emotions.

Billy would soon start to travel with the protectors. Would they allow him a visit every once in a while with Jacy? It was doubtful that Philip would allow it as she would not remember Billy anyway. But just seeing her in person would be good for Billy. Time would tell. He was sure that when it was right, he would be reunited with his love. Philip had his reasons for sending her back, and there was nothing anyone could do. He was the ruler of the colony. No one questioned his decisions.

It was about twelve thirty, and Billy walked to the room full of screens where he had introduced Jacy to Zen and Qua. He sat down and pressed a button that turned one of the screens. This screen was focused on the college. He moved the control through the college campus. There—he saw Jacy walking to her car. She had an hour break and did not have to be back until one thirty. Billy had a big smile on his face as he watched her drive away. He kept the car in sight as she pulled into a fast food restaurant. When she got out of her car to go into the restaurant, two young men smiled at Jacy and told her hello. She responded to them, and they turned and watched her walk into the restaurant.

Billy put his hand under his chin and placed his elbow on his knee. His human emotions were once more taking over. It was jealousy. He took a deep breath and shook his head as he thought, "Why am I doing this to myself? There is nothing I can do. The good thing is that she didn't look back. But how long will it take before she does?"

He waited a while and watched Jacy drive back to the campus. Time was up; he had to go back to work. He could have stayed and watched her all day, but it was not allowed. He could only spend two hours a day tuning in on Jacy. He would come back later in the evening and watch as she worked in her grandmother's store.

Jacy's first day of college was over. It was three thirty, and she was on her way to her grandparents' store to help out. When she arrived, Macy asked how her first day of school had gone.

"Good, Grandmother, real good. I'm happy with my decision."

Customers came in for groceries as they headed home from work. Jacy got behind the counter to check out customers while Macy got bait for the fishermen who were preparing for the next day's work. For the next two hours, customers did not stop coming in. Business was very good.

Finally, the store cleared out, and Macy and Jacy got to take a break to relax and talk about their day.

At the same time in the colony, Billy was also relaxed while he tuned in on Jacy for one hour. He knew she would be in the store, so he decided to put his focus there. She was sitting with her grandmother. He bent over and touched the screen. It was the next best thing to touching Jacy. He watched the two women for about fifteen minutes as they relaxed and talked. Then the door opened, and for the first time Billy saw Cameron as he walked in. He told the women to keep their seats, and he sat down beside Jacy. Cameron asked Jacy about college, and she told him the same thing she had told her grandmother. Macy purposely got up and sat behind the counter so Jacy and Cameron could talk.

Cameron put his hand on Jacy's and asked what time she got off work. Jacy got up from the chair, and Billy saw her necklace. He was pleased as he saw this. He thought, "She has not totally forgotten about me as long as she wears that necklace."

Jacy answered Cameron's question. "I get off at eight o'clock tonight."

"Would you like to go for a hamburger or something?"

"No," she said. "I have some homework tonight."

Macy then jumped in and said to Jacy, "You can leave early if you want to."

"No, Grandmother, I will not leave you by yourself," she replied as she glared at her.

"Okay," said Macy. "Whatever."

Cameron then got up and walked to the door. "I'll see you tomorrow evening." He left the store.

"Grandmother," said Jacy, "don't do that again."

"What, Jacy?" asked Macy.

"You know what. Don't make it so I'll have to go out with Cameron."

"Sorry, I'll keep my mouth shut from now on. I promise," she said as she held her right hand up.

"He's a nice guy, but I'm not ready for a relationship," said Jacy. "Not now."

Billy sat and listened to all of the confusion and shook his head. How much longer would it be before Jacy did go out with Cameron? The future was once more foggy in his head. He could not see their future. He knew that as long as she wore the necklace she could feel the love in his heart for her. As he continued to watch Jacy, he noticed that she grabbed the necklace and held it in her hand for comfort. This brought Billy comfort, too. He turned the screen off. His hour was up for the day. He left the room with his head down.

Jacy helped Macy close the store. On her way home she stopped to think about how Cameron was complicating her life. She had to tell him without hurting his feelings that she did not want to date him. As she walked into her house, the phone rang. It was her parents. They were anxious to know how she had enjoyed her first day in college. Once more, she assured them it was all good and that she was happy.

Jacy took her books out and did the small amount of homework that she had been assigned. Tired from the day's activities, she showered and went straight to bed. She went to sleep quickly, and the dreams began. This time there was a pretty little girl smiling and waving at her. She had dark hair and eyes with big dimples. Jacy got a big smile on her face as she watched her skip through the town that she saw over and over in her dreams. Tonight she definitely had sweet dreams. She did not want them to end.

The wonderful dreams of the Tavie colony continued almost every night for over two months. It was now December, and Jacy was still enjoying school and not dating Cameron. He came by the store almost every night and tried to convince her to go out with him. Billy still watched in hopes of being reunited with Jacy soon. "Absence makes the heart grow stronger," Billy thought. That old saying certainly applied to his heart.

Christmas was right around the corner, and Jacy had been very busy with school, shopping, and work. She was now on Christmas vacation and was going to put up her tree and decorate it with lights of many colors. She had decided that she wanted red, yellow, blue, and green lights and that she would keep the red lights blinking and leave the others still. When she was finished with her tree, she turned her ceiling light off and sat down to look at the tree in all its beauty. It reminded her of the beautiful lights she had seen in the sky when they were searching for cypress deep in the swamp.

She wrapped some presents in pretty foil. It was silver and gold paper with red bows. Then she placed them under the tree. The lights from the tree bounced off the paper to enhance the tree's beauty even more. "Wow!" she said out loud. "This feels good."

Macy stopped by for a visit with her granddaughter while Susan tended the store. She walked in and looked at Jacy's tree.

"Your tree is pretty, Jacy, but where is your garland and the Christmas decorations?"

"I'm not using them this year," she answered. "They would clutter the tree, and I would not be able to see the lights."

Macy rolled her eyes and said, "It's your tree. Let's make a pot of coffee."

They went into the kitchen.

"Have you ever remembered any happenings from your disappearance in the swamp?"

"No," said Jacy, "but I am having these dreams, Grandmother, dreams that are so vivid I feel like I'm there."

"Are they frightening?" asked Macy.

"The streets are brick, and there are small businesses lining them on both sides. It is a very quaint small town. There are no cars, just people riding bicycles and walking around. It's the kind of place anyone would love to visit. It's like going back in time."

"How often do you have these dreams?" asked Macy.

"Almost every night," Jacy answered.

"Maybe it's the TV shows you're watching before going to bed at night. It sounds a little like Mayberry," said Macy.

"You're probably right. I love that show, and I do watch it before going to bed, but not always," said Jacy. "I'm not complaining. These dreams are good. I just wonder why I have the same ones so often."

Macy watched Jacy from across the table. Then she looked down at her coffee cup.

"You're different, Jacy. Since your return from the swamp, you've changed. You're more focused on life, and I think you have matured. You're not the same young woman that left. How is that possible? Who changed you?"

Jacy looked up and said to her grandmother, "I look at life completely different. I know now what I want out of my life, and I will achieve it. Don't ask me why, but I know there's more to life that meets the eye. There's much to learn about our world, Grandmother. Wonderful things. I feel it."

"See," said Macy, "there you go again, talking weird. If there is more to learn about our world, Jacy, I hope you acquire this knowledge and let me in on it. It sounds very interesting, but I have to go back to work. Will you come by the store later and have a soda with me?"

"Yes," said Jacy. "Later this evening."

It was Billy's twenty-sixth birthday, and he was to begin traveling with the protectors. He had been waiting for this day for a long time. In one hour he would be in the main ship protecting the planet Earth. He put his uniform on and walked out into an open space of the colony. As he stood there, the huge ship appeared and beamed him up. He found himself on the main deck of the ship in front of Philip.

"Welcome, Billy," said Philip. "Zen will show you to your living quarters."

Billy followed Zen to a lower level of the spaceship and the room he would call home for a while.

"Look around," said Zen. "Everything you will need is here. Your connection to Earth is your computer found in that cabinet." He pointed to a piece of furniture next to the bed.

Billy opened the cabinet door and took the computer out. He looked at it and remarked, "It's very small."

"Yes," said Zen, "it's the size of a cellular phone. You can tune it in on Jacy as often as you want."

Billy looked up in shock. No one had mentioned her name since she had left. Zen then turned and walked out of the room. Billy knew that he could not remove the computer from the room without Zen's permission. He could only use it when he was off duty.

The light in the room began to blink. It was Philip calling for him. He walked into the hall and stepped into a beam that took him to the main deck. He walked up to Philip and took a seat next to him. Philip pushed a button. A large panel of metal rolled back, and a windshield appeared. Through the clear windshield, he could see the universe in all of its beauty. The ship stood still and then picked up power very slowly.

Philip explained to Billy that they were in search of a ship from the planet Mitz. The Mitz were looking for a dumping ground for their evil inhabitants. They were peaceful people unless they were pushed.

The men of Mitz were very tall, about six and a half to seven feet tall, and the women were all at least six foot. Their bodies were big and muscular. Their skin was dark gray, and their hair was straight and black. Their eyes were slanted up and dark. Their ears and mouths were like humans'. Their hands and feet were partially webbed. They each had black freckles on their faces that uniquely identified them. They could be a great danger to the planet Earth. Their people were survivors. They would probably drop their unwanted on a high mountain, in the middle of a desert, or maybe in a swamp area. The Mitz were very intelligent and could adapt quickly.

The Mitz ship was shaped like a bullet and hard to spot. Philip tried to contact them. He wanted no trouble, but they could not dump their people on planet Earth. Finally, a face appeared on a screen from the Mitz ship. Philip turned to speak with the leader. He had met him before but did not know how he would react to his demands now. Philip explained that they could not drop off their hostile rejects on planet Earth.

The Mitz leader's answered, "Or what?"

"We will destroy them and your ship too when you enter Earth's atmosphere."

"We will retreat," said the Mitz leader. "We want no trouble." Then he disappeared from the screen.

Philip looked at Billy and said, "They will retreat, but we must now watch them until they return to their planet."

Billy continued to watch the universe go by. He saw other ships pass. Some moved slowly while others moved very fast.

"How long do you think you'll have to watch them?"

Philip answered, "As long as it takes. There will be two smaller crafts released, and they will follow them, keeping in contact with us in the main ship."

All was well for now. The ship returned to Earth and disappeared in the swamp. It had been an exciting day for Billy. If only he could contact Jacy to share his excitement with her.

Billy returned to his living quarters, lay on his bed, and picked up the small computer. He tuned in and saw Jacy having a soda with her grandmother.

He said out loud, "I love you, Jacy. I love you."

At the same time as he said those words, Jacy put down her soda and said to her grandmother, "Did you hear that?"

"Hear what?" asked Macy.

"Someone is speaking to me." Jacy grabbed the heart hanging around her neck and listened for more.

Billy continued to tell her he loved her.

"I hear it again," she said.

Billy smiled as he watched her reaction to his words. "She's doing it. She's tuned in on me. That's a good girl, Jacy. Keep concentrating."

Macy said to Jacy, "I'm going to make you an appointment with a psychiatrist tomorrow morning. You are troubled. You need help."

"No," said Jacy. "I will not go. I am not troubled. I believe someone is trying to contact me through my mind."

"Jacy," said Macy, "you're saying things that are not normal."

"Maybe it's normal for me," said Jacy.

"Since when, Jacy? Since when? You were lost in the swamp. What happened to you out there? Something very strange is going on. I'm getting frightened for you. I think I should call your parents."

"Please don't, Grandmother. I promise nothing is wrong with me. Please trust me. I'm fine. Don't concern my parents. They have been through enough."

"I'm going to keep a close watch on you, Jacy. If there's something wrong, I want you to confide in me. I'm always here for you."

"I know that," said Jacy, "and I will if need be."

Jacy returned home and poured a glass of tea. The she went out to the back porch to stare into the heavens. Another day had gone by, and life was good. As Billy retired for the night, he thought the same thing.

The next morning, Jacy was up and ready for the day when she heard her phone ring. It was Cameron. He wanted her to ride to Baton Rouge with him. He had some business to take care of. He offered to drop her off at a mall so that she could Christmas shop while he was busy. Afterward, they would go out to dinner.

Jacy had no other plans for the day, so she accepted his invitation. "When are you leaving?" asked Jacy.

"In one hour," he said with excitement in his voice. Finally, he could be alone with Jacy.

As she hung up the phone, Jacy thought about how she only liked Cameron as a good friend. She hoped their little trip would not give him the wrong idea. It would be good for Jacy to get out of town for the day and catch up on her Christmas shopping.

Jacy hurriedly got dressed in a red pantsuit. She put on her makeup and decided to wear her hair down. As she passed the mirror, she could not help but glance toward it. The red color of her suit was reflecting off her necklace. She took out her Christmas list as she waited for Cameron. When he drove up, she did not wait for him to come to the door; she walked out to meet him, and he opened the car door for her. Smiling, he thanked her for keeping him company on the trip.

"Thanks for inviting me."

Cameron tried to converse with Jacy by asking her about school. She answered his questions and then turned the conversation to the construction of the new civic center. He explained to her how it would look when it was completed.

When he mentioned the fountains that would sit in front of the project, Jacy said, "Fountains … I love fountains." Then she leaned back in her seat, and they just listened to the radio.

As they entered Baton Rouge, Cameron explained his meeting schedule to Jacy. The meeting started at eleven thirty and would end at four. He told her to get a sandwich for lunch and that they would eat at a nice restaurant that night. He would meet her at the entrance to the mall at four thirty.

"I'll be there," she said as he got out and opened the car door for her.

"Oh, Jacy," he said, "you look beautiful."

She stopped and thanked him and then walked into the mall.

The mall was full of Christmas shoppers and decorated for the season—complete with a Santa Claus and his elves. When she walked past the line of children waiting to take a picture with Santa, she stopped to watch the little ones as they sat on his lap and told him what they wanted for Christmas. They touched his beard, laughed out loud, and talked with their hands as they explained the special toys to him. Santa saw Jacy watching and waved to her. She waved back and walked away to start her shopping.

At the entrance to the first large department store, she was met by a saleslady with a perfume sample of a new scent. She then went to the nearby cosmetic counter. There were hundreds of different perfumes and colognes. Some of the fragrances were sold in a set with powder and lotion. Macy and Lucille loved perfumes. She purchased a set for both of them in new scent.

Then the saleslady asked Jacy if she needed any cologne for men. She thought a while and Cameron came to mind. Should she get him a gift? He was a friend.

"Maybe," said Jacy. "Can you help me pick a scent?"

"Yes, ma'am," said the saleslady. She put about eight bottles of cologne on the counter. "These are my favorites." She sprayed a piece of paper with the different scents to let Jacy smell them.

"Is this for your boyfriend?" the saleslady asked.

"No," said Jacy, "just a friend." After she had smelled all the different scents, she decided on one.

"I'll take this one," said Jacy.

"Good choice," said the saleslady. "Ma'am, we have a free wrapping. Would you like it?"

"Yes," said Jacy as she paid for the purchases. "I will pick them up on my way out."

"They'll be ready. Thank you," said the saleslady.

Jacy continued to walk through the store, looking for ideas for those on her list who were hard to buy for. She soon found herself in the toy department. Jacy always donated toys to the underprivileged children in Yelgar. She looked at all the different toys in amazement. The dolls could talk, walk, cry, and crawl. The toys for boys, such as cars and trucks, could move by remote control. They would be perfect for the children's toy drive. She could only purchase what she could carry around, so she decided on two baby dolls and two of the remote-controlled cars. They would make four children very happy for Christmas.

Cameron had told Jacy to get a sandwich for lunch, but instead she got a soft pretzel and a soda. She had to stand in line for ten minutes, but she enjoyed the pretzel. She was getting tired, so she sat on a bench to kill time and watched all the shoppers walk by. She wondered what her parents were doing. She could call them, but they would definitely want to see her. That was not a good idea. How would she explain being with Cameron? They would automatically think she was dating him.

After a while, Jacy continued her shopping and bought two more gifts. Cameron would soon be at the entrance of the mall, so she walked that way. It had been a tiring but very productive day. As she reached the door, she noticed Cameron's car waiting.

When he saw her, he got out of the car and helped her put her packages in the trunk.

"How about a glass of wine, Jacy?"

"That would be nice," said Jacy.

"Traffic is bad, but it shouldn't take long to find a good spot." Cameron knew the area and took back streets to try to stay out of the main drag. They laughed as he darted in and out of traffic. "Hold on, we are almost there, Jacy," said Cameron.

"Take your time. I'm in no hurry," she answered.

Finally, they pulled into a valet line in front of a gorgeous restaurant.

"How nice," said Jacy.

"I think it's the best place to eat in Baton Rouge," said Cameron.

They entered the restaurant and walked into the bar area for a drink before dinner. An older man was playing the piano and singing softly. It was a very romantic setting that made Jacy very uneasy. They sat at a corner table and ordered their drinks. Cameron pulled his chair close to her.

"This is not good," she thought and sat very still.

Cameron tilted his head and looked into her eyes. He did not say anything. He just stared at her as his lips moved closer to hers.

The waitress appeared with their drinks and set them down on the table. Cameron sat up straight and asked Jacy if she was hungry.

"Very," she answered.

"They have excellent seafood here."

She thought, "That was a quick change of subject. Just in time."

Jacy drank her wine slowly and hoped that their table would be ready soon.

"How about those Saints?" asked Cameron.

Jacy giggled and answered, "They're winners."

The hostess then came to seat them for dinner.

Billy had been busy all day and had no time to tune in on Jacy. Philip had made sure of it. There was so much to learn. It would take him months, even at a fast pace. Billy would learn to navigate the smaller ships and the main ship and how to fly small airplanes. Because he looked human, he would also be called on to make visits to the surrounding cities when necessary. There were many unwanted visitors walking among the humans, mostly in big cities. Billy was to find them and then contact the ship. They called those who did this job a *sweeper*. He was to find the undesirables and get rid of them.

Many of these aliens meant no harm to Earth and were here just there to learn and study humans, but others were vicious, murdering aliens who had come for evil deeds. No matter the reason, they must all leave and return to their own planets. Billy, along with many other Tavies stationed on Earth, was there to protect.

Jacy and Cameron had finished their dinner and were on their way back to Yelgar. Both of them were tired from the long day and looked forward to getting home. When they arrived at Jacy's house, Cameron helped her with the packages as he walked her to the door. She opened the door, and he took the packages inside.

"Oh," he said, "I see you've started decorating your Christmas tree."

"I've finished decorating my tree," she said. Jacy plugged in the lights. "Don't you like it?"

"It's different," he said. Cameron stood by the door, hoping Jacy would ask him to stay a while.

Instead, she walked up to him, gave him a peck on the cheek, and said, "Thanks for everything. It's been fun."

"Okay," he said. "See you." Then he walked out the door.

Jacy plopped in the recliner and said, "I'm glad that's over with."

Billy returned to his living quarters. He'd had a very long day that had gone on into part of the night. It was almost eleven, and he was thinking of only one thing. He wanted to tune in on Jacy. He found her on his small computer, sitting in the recliner. He tried to see what her day had been like but could not. The fog was denser than ever.

Once more, he said, "I love you, Jacy."

He closed his eyes and said it again, "I love you, Jacy."

Jacy sat up straight and looked around.

He had gotten through. They were connected.

Jacy looked around the room and smiled. She reached for the heart around her neck and fell asleep in the recliner as she watched the lights on her tree.

Jacy had a dream that night of a handsome, dark-haired man. This was the dream Billy had prayed she would have. She had made the connection she needed for Billy to be with her. His spirit could now go to hers. She dreamed of the time she had spent with him in the colony. Their spirits were together once again. She would not remember the dream completely when she woke up. It would only be in pieces. Her subconscious could only take over in her dreams.

Billy's visit with Jacy was good. He had promised her he would see her in her dreams, and now it had happened. It would have to do for now, until they could be reunited.

Billy had thought he would be traveling with the scientists and doctors, but instead, he would be sweeping the undesirables from other planets. This was a big change in jobs, but he could do it. Philip stayed close to Billy. It was almost too close. It made Billy think he was protecting him from something. That, of course, was impossible. Philip was all business. He had no time to focus on just one individual.

Billy lay on his bed and wondered whether there could be uninvited guests in Yelgar. He decided to ask Philip when he saw him the next day and went to sleep.

When Billy asked Philip, his answer was, "Probably not. The undesirables tend to settle in large cities where they can move around easily."

Billy thought, "Too bad. It would be really good to just look into Jacy's eyes again, and maybe even touch her hand."

If only he looked completely human like his two brothers. Then he could have lived in her world and been with Jacy. But would she have accepted Billy in her world? He concentrated to get the answer to this question, but again, nothing came to him. There were too many emotions moving around in his head. This was not good. Even though he was more human than any Tavie in the colony, he was still expected to fight off human emotions. The Tavies teach, "Don't show emotions; bury them." If only he could.

Today, Billy was to learn to fly a small airplane. He would take lessons for one day, and he would be a pilot with a Louisiana license to fly tomorrow. He had inherited amazing learning abilities from the Tavies, along with the hands.

Flying an airplane was very different from the spaceships. The plane moved very slowly, and he could actually see through the window and down to the ground from the plane. Billy liked flying the airplane and could not wait to go solo. His first flight would be to a large city in Louisiana.

Philip was close to everyone in the colony. He knew their weaknesses as well as their strengths. He knew Billy could only mingle with the humans for a short time—no more than eight hours at a time. If he stayed longer, Billy would defy him and use his powers for his own interests. Humans craved the attention of other humans. There were only a few exceptions, and Billy was not one of them.

Billy had been allowed to visit the city where his parents lived many times before, but he had only stayed at a distance. He could only visit them in the winter because he needed gloves to cover his hands. He had been completely under control during those visits, but that was before he had met Jacy. Things were different now.

It was three days until Christmas. Jacy had all of her shopping done, and her parents were coming home tomorrow for Christmas Eve. Macy had been coming by to help her get the house ready. The family was going to gather there this holiday. The weather was expected to be in the thirties, with freezing rain the next week.

Jacy had raised the blinds and opened the curtains that morning, and now she was building a blazing fire in the fireplace. The smell of freshly brewed coffee mixed with the smell of oak burning was wonderful way to wake up.

She sat on the sofa and finished wrapping her gifts for the family. When she was done, she placed them under the tree. She was finished with her Christmas obligations, except for the cooking. Macy was coming over today to do their baking. On Christmas Eve, they would prepare the dressing and then she would bake the ham and turkey Christmas morning.

Jacy was excited that her family, even though it was small, was happy and healthy and that they would spend another Christmas together.

The doorbell rang. It was Macy, and Jacy could see through the window that She had her arms full of Christmas gifts. She opened the door and helped her grandmother place them under the tree.

Macy was in a very good mood and had a big smile on her face. "Guess what?" she asked.

"What?" asked Jacy.

"This year we are having guests for dinner."

"We are? Who?"

"Bubba, Susan, and Cameron are coming."

"Why?" Jacy asked. "Don't they have family?"

"Yes, but their families are going out of town. It will be fun. You can play the piano, and we'll sing Christmas carols. We'll open gifts and enjoy each other's company. We always have way too much food anyway, Jacy."

"I'm glad you told me ahead of time, Grandmother. I will go out to get gifts for Bubba and Miss Susan."

"What about Cameron?" asked Macy.

"I have a gift for him already," Jacy answered.

"Well, that was nice of you, Jacy. Thinking of Cameron on this wonderful holiday."

"He's a friend, and that's all. A friend, just like Bubba is to me," said Jacy. "And Miss Susan is like family. She is always there for us anytime we call on her. This will be a good excuse to buy her something really nice."

"I'm going to start the baking, and you hurry out and get your gifts."

"Okay," said Jacy. She pulled on sweatpants and a sweatshirt, grabbed her coat, and headed out the door. "I won't be long, Grandmother."

When she walked outside, she noted that it was typical Louisiana Christmas weather. Frozen raindrops peppered Jacy's head and face as she walked to her car. She had not parked her car in the carport because it was full of boxes her parents had stored there when they left for Baton Rouge. Anyway, Jacy liked being exposed to the elements.

Jacy was gone for an hour and a half. She did her shopping and returned home to help her grandmother. The house smelled so good. Macy was already baking the pecan pies. Jacy washed the dishes as Macy peeled apples for another pie.

"I miss Mom," Jacy said. "She's always been with us when we do the baking."

"I miss her too, Jacy. But she will be with us tomorrow on Christmas Eve."

While Jacy had been out shopping, Macy had hung mistletoe in the doorway and decorated the fireplace mantle with pine needles and pinecones. Jacy had not noticed this when she walked in. The heat from the fireplace mixed with the smell of the pine needles and filled the house with a fresh pine smell. It smelled like Christmas.

The two continued their baking into the evening and went to bed very early so they would be rested for the next day.

While Jacy planned her holiday, Billy was about to go out on a mission. He was to fly into New Orleans. Strange things were happening to people who worked on the railroads at night. Many of them had gone missing for days, and when they were finally found, they had no memory of what had happened to them. They all also had two needle-like marks on the backs of their ears, as though they had been branded.

Philip explained to Billy that the aliens responsible would only come out after midnight because they could not be exposed to sunlight. He must fly into the town and take a cab to the location where they would be lurking. Philip handed Billy a tiny communicator and told him to signal when he sensed the aliens. Billy agreed and returned to the colony to climb aboard the plane.

After he left the colony's surrounding security light, Billy contacted air control and cleared his way into New Orleans. He was dressed all in black—pants, shirt, boots, short leather jacket, and leather gloves—except for his purple LSU baseball cap. A pilot wing pin adorned the lapel of his jacket. If he was to be a pilot, he must dress like one.

He landed the plane at the airport and assured the attendant that he would return for his plane before daylight. It was ten o'clock. By the time the cab arrived at his location, everything should almost be in order, and the hunt would be on. If the railroad workers spotted him on the tracks, they would only see a blur. His communicator was putting off waves that would confuse the aliens so they could not sense his presence.

Billy paid the cab driver. The location had been chosen to keep down suspicions by the locals. He turned on his communicator and walked toward the railroad tracks. Glancing at the sky, he could see their small Tavie spaceship in the distance—ready to pounce on the enemy. He walked around the area for a while and then spotted a man walking toward him. He stepped aside and watched. As the man got closer, his image changed. He was an alien on the prowl. Humans could not see the alien's true features until it was too late.

The alien was hideous. His skin was white but transparent. The veins of his face and head could be seen beneath the surface. His head was oversized, and he was bald except for a strip of white hair that stood straight up on top of his head. His eyes bulged and had red veins running through them. His mouth was large and protruded several inches from his face. His nose was wide and flat, and his large ears jutted out from the sides of his head. His legs were stocky and slightly bent at the knees. He had a heavy upper body and short stubby fingers. The temperature was freezing with light rain. He was dressed in something that looked like a light jogging suit. Around his waist he wore something that looked like a tool belt. It had many objects hanging from it.

Billy hid and watched as he passed by. The alien was looking side to side while moving his head very fast. Billy followed him to see if maybe there were more of them in the area. The aliens' spaceship was probably close by and undetected. The Tavies' spaceship was completely out of sight. As Billy continued to watch the alien, he noticed two more men walking toward him from different directions. As they got closer, their images also changed. They were aliens too. All three of them looked the same. They were all dressed alike and had belts hanging around their waists. They looked side to side as they approached each other. When they met, they spoke in a strange language and continued walking together. Billy followed close behind them.

The aliens were following the train tracks. Billy could not understand why there were no people in sight, but he continued to follow the aliens. From a distance, Billy heard clanging from the frozen darkness. He knew then there were men working on the tracks and that the aliens were about to abduct them. Billy concentrated and sensed there were six men. They were fixing some damaged tracks ahead. He really wanted to see how the aliens would abduct the men, but his orders were to contact the ship.

As he took the communicator out of his pocket, he sensed another ship close by. He looked to see another ship lurking in the sky above. It had no lights on. He had to communicate with his ship fast or he would be the next victim. He pushed the button, and his ship was there in seconds. The alien ship retreated and disappeared. Billy watched as the Tavie spaceship hovered over the aliens and beamed them up. The intruders would be delivered to Philip. Philip would find out why they were on Earth and where they had come from. He would interrogate them thoroughly. If they were evil, they would be destroyed.

Billy continued to watch the sky to see if the aliens' ship returned. The only ship he saw was one of their own. It was standing guard over him until he returned safely. He could sense the Tavies onboard. They told him to go back to the colony. His job was over, so he walked back to the train station and called a cab. The cab picked him up and delivered him back to the airport. He climbed aboard his plane and headed back to the colony where his people would be waiting for him. He had done a very good thing that day. He had helped rid the world of evil.

As Billy flew home, he thought about how the aliens had left one of their own to be captured. "Why did they not fight? Our ships were ready for a fight. Now they are exposed. The Tavies will know everything there is to know about their planet and their people. And if they are found to be evil, which is probably the case, Philip and his allies will hunt their ships down and destroy them because of their intrusion on Earth and its people. If they had gotten away with hurting our people, other worlds would consider us weak and try their own takeovers. Only the strong survive in the universe."

Billy landed his plane in the colony at their small airport and was beamed up to a small spacecraft and then taken to the main ship. He made his way to the main deck and saw that a bright red light was on. This meant that they should be on alert. Philip walked back to his chair, sat down, and nodded to Billy.

The chase was on. The Tavies must destroy the alien intruders. Twenty small ships were released from the main ship. Their task was to keep the main vessel up-to-date on what was happening in the universe.

The aliens were from the planet Octe, and they were evil. Their intentions were to study the humans and then to infiltrate their towns and take over. The marks behind the ears of their victims were where they had placed control devices. They had not been on Earth long. New Orleans was their first quest.

Octe was located far outside of our solar system. It was a very cold planet with little sunlight. That was the reason the Octe could only come out at night. The aliens the Tavies had taken had been destroyed, and as soon as the Octe ships were located, they would be too.

Philip contacted his allies from the other planets for all the information he could get on this new enemy. Suddenly the red light began to blink again, which meant that one of the smaller ships had spotted an Octe vessel. Within seconds, the small Tavie ships surrounded the enemy ship, and it was destroyed. The entire event took about two minutes.

Philip's contacts assured him that the rest of the Octe ships had retreated back to their planet. As long as they stayed there, the Tavie ships would not bother them. But if they came close to the planet Earth, they would be destroyed without mercy.

The red light went out, and the Tavie mother ship landed once more in the calm swamp of Louisiana. All was well for now.

It was almost daybreak, and the Tavies had not slept. Many of them were tired and went down to their living quarters for rest. Billy sat down and relived the events of the night. He thought about how many generations of Tavies had been protecting Earth. Through the years, they had changed from pure-blooded Tavies to part-human Tavies. Without the Tavies, Earth would have surely fallen prey to hostile aliens. Billy stared at his surroundings a while and then got up and went to his quarters. He was tired, so he cleaned up and lay on his bed, hoping to go to sleep.

There were no Christmas celebrations on the Tavie ship. In the colony, one tree was decorated in the center of town. Colored lights and mirrored stars hung from the branches, and it had a large star on top. On Christmas morning, only children were given presents as they gathered around the tree. Christmas carols played, and the Tavies sang along. Sometimes visitors from other colonies brought food from their states or country.

This year, the Australian colonists were visiting. They had visited many times before and had a lot in common with the people of Louisiana. The Australian colonists enjoyed their stay in Louisiana. They loved the Louisiana seafood. Their diet was the same as the Louisianans'; it was just prepared differently. This year the Australian colony had brought many different types of seafood that were not available in the swamp area. Everyone would watch the children open their gifts and then they would all enjoy a huge Christmas seafood dinner.

Billy would miss the festivities this year because he had obligations, but he could tune in on Jacy and watch as she celebrated Christmas with her family. Seeing her happy would bring joy to his heart. Billy finally fell asleep as the sun peeked out from behind the clouds and brought with it Christmas Eve.

Jacy woke up and was excited that her parents were coming home. Together again, the women of the family would cook up some good food to celebrate Christmas. The men would meet with their friends and indulge in a little Christmas spirit and fishing tales. Then they would congregate at the store for a gumbo lunch.

The weather was still cold with off-and-on freezing rain, but inside it smelled really good from the baked goods and the pine scent from the fireplace. Smell to Cajuns was one of the things that helped to set their moods. If the smell was good food cooking, they were instantly happy. Cajuns did not eat to live; they lived to eat.

The doorbell rang, and Lucille and Murphy came in with armloads of gifts. Jacy rushed to help them. They put their gifts under the tree, and Lucille stood back and looked at it.

"Jacy, get your ornaments. I will help you hang them on the tree."

"Why, Mother? I like it the way it is."

Murphy looked at the tree and agreed with Jacy. "I like it, too—just like it is."

Lucille put her hands up in the air and said, "Okay, I'm outvoted."

They all hugged and got on with their visit.

"Mom, did you know we are having guests this Christmas?"

"Yes," she said. "Your grandmother called me. What do you think about it, Jacy? Is it okay with you?"

"I'm okay with it, Mother, as long as no one tries to make a love connection with me and Cameron."

Lucille said, "Sit down, Jacy. I have a question for you."

Jacy sat down. Lucille looked at her and said, "I'm your mother, and I love you. What is wrong with Cameron? He's smart, handsome, very nice, and he likes you. What is the problem? You won't ever give him a chance. Why don't you date him and then maybe you will see in him what everyone else sees.

"You act like there's someone else in your life. Are you in love, Jacy? I sense something going on that I'm not aware o£ Do you have secrets? Tell me, Jacy. I only want the best for you."

Jacy dropped her head and grabbed the heart around her neck. Tears fell from her eyes as she looked at her mother and said, "All the things you said about Cameron are true, Mother, but I don't have any feelings for him at all. It's almost like I've given my heart to another, and I'm waiting for him."

"Why do you always grab that heart for security? There is something going on with that heart and the way you cling to it. Why don't you ever take it off? You didn't find it in the swamp, Jacy. I think it was given to you by someone. Wasn't it? Someone you love very much. Am I right, Jacy? Answer me."

"I can't remember, Mother. I just can't remember."

Lucille picked the heart up in her hand and took a closer look at it.

"Jacy, if a man did give you this exquisite gift, believe me, he will be coming for you soon. This is definitely a gift of true love." Then she dropped the heart.

"Jacy, I'm going to tell you something no one else knows. Miss Susan and I are best friends, and all the wild things she said about aliens are not all false. I know there are things that happen in that swamp that are unexplainable. I have witnessed some of them.

I'm not going to say anything more, except I'm with you, Jacy. There will be no more said about Cameron from me. I love you, and we're going to have a very Merry Christmas."

The mother-daughter talk made Jacy feel a lot better. But what did her mother mean when she said Miss Susan was right about certain things and happenings in the swamp? They had been best friends for always. If Miss Susan was telling the truth, her mother must have witnessed some of the strange things she had talked about.

Macy arrived and was very happy to see her daughter and gave her a big hug.

"Let's get busy," said Lucille.

They set the table with spiked homemade eggnog and the cookies and candy that they had made during the week for their friends that would drop in on Christmas Eve. It was a tradition that had been carried on for generations. Friends began arriving after lunch and continued coming into the night, each bringing with them some kind of sweet treat. It was almost lunch, so the women grabbed a sandwich and continued with their Christmas preparations.

The men would soon return so they could help meet the guests as they arrived. The large dining table was ready. Jacy lit some Christmas candles surrounded by fresh holly in the center of the table.

The doorbell rang, and Pierre opened the door. It was Roy.

"Come in," said Pierre, "and a very Merry Christmas to you."

"Merry Christmas back at you," said Roy. "Doris will come by soon. She is still on duty at the hospital."

Jacy walked into the room to see who had arrived. She walked up to Roy and gave him a big hug.

"You know you're my hero. You definitely saved the day, not to mention two men's lives. Thank you, Roy, and thanks to Doris. She is an angel."

He replied, "Thank her in person. She will be here shortly. And you are welcome, but I just drove the boat. Doris did the doctoring."

"What a team you and Doris are," said Jacy. "Godsent."

The doorbell continuously rang as friends and neighbors kept coming and going. Laughter and happiness filled the home that not so long ago had been filled with gloom because of Jacy's disappearance. Carolers gathered outside the door, bundled up in coats, scarves, and hats while holding umbrellas. They sang beautiful Christmas songs. Macy went outside and invited them in for hot apple cider served with a cinnamon stick and cookies. They stood in the front of the fire and enjoyed their refreshments. Then they thanked Macy and headed out to the next house.

It was evening, and the temperature outside was getting colder. Ice was forming everywhere. Driving was getting dangerous as the wind picked up and the freezing rain came down harder. Everyone was leaving and going home for the night so they could prepare for Christmas morning.

Jacy slipped off to call it a night. As she lay in bed under her favorite quilt, she could hear the freezing rain hitting the window panes. It was a soothing sound that eventually put her to sleep. In her dreams, she saw the same little girl that she had dreamed of so many times before, except this time the little girl was not smiling and skipping through the streets. She was sitting on a bench with a very sad face. This troubled Jacy. The dream made her very sad, and she suddenly woke up crying. Wiping her eyes, she sat straight up in her bed and looked around, as if she had expected to be somewhere else.

"Please don't be sad," she said out loud.

Then she lay back down and finally fell back to sleep. This time she had no memorable dreams.

On Christmas morning, Jacy jumped out of bed to get ready for the most wonderful day of the year. She could smell the turkey and ham baking in the oven. Her mother had already started preparations for Christmas dinner, which they ate at two o'clock every year. After dinner, everyone would help with dishes and clean the table and then all the desserts would be set out. They would then help themselves to dessert whenever they wanted. Her mouth watered thinking about it.

This year there would be three extra guests, but that was no problem as the table seated eight people. Hopefully with the extra guests there would not be a lot of leftovers, although they did taste good the following week in turkey and ham salad.

Jacy walked into the kitchen where her mother was cooking and said, "Merry Christmas, Mom."

"Merry Christmas to you, my precious daughter," said Lucille. She grabbed Jacy and hugged her closely.

"What can I do, Mother?" Jacy asked.

"You can start setting the table with our Christmas dishes, and don't forget the Christmas candles for the centerpiece."

Jacy did as her mother told her and added red wine glasses to pace settings. The table looked beautiful. As she stood back and looked at it, she was very pleased. The whole table was decorated in white, red, and green.

Macy and Pierre arrived at eleven o'clock so Macy could help Lucille with the last-minute cooking. Pierre and Murphy kept the fire blazing in the fireplace while they enjoyed eggnog and watched *It's a Wonderful Life* on TV. Today the Bellards and Heberts had a wonderful life, Jacy mused.

At one o'clock, the guests began to arrive. Bubba was first, and then Miss Susan, and finally Cameron—all with an armful of gifts. Jacy opened two bottles of wine, one white and one red. She sat the wine on the table and told the guests to enjoy a glass before dinner. They each poured what they wanted in the red wine glasses and mingled.

Bubba found Jacy and thanked her for all she had done for him on the boat in the swamp. She hugged Bubba and told him how glad she was that he had survived and that he should thank Doris because it was really her who had saved his life.

Cameron walked in just as Jacy hugged Bubba. He walked up to her and said, "Why don't you ever hug me like that?"

She then hugged Cameron and said, "Merry Christmas."

Macy walked in as Jacy hugged Cameron. She glanced up and said, "There's mistletoe hanging in the doorway." Then she laughed.

"Ha ha, very funny, Grandmother," said Jacy. "She's just not going to give up," she thought.

Dinner was ready, and the food was on the table. Everyone found a seat. Cameron sat next to Jacy with Bubba on the other side of her. Lucille looked at Jacy and smiled. Jacy looked back at her mother and shook her head. Pierre said the prayer, and they passed the food around.

Cameron, thinking Bubba might be his competition for Jacy's affection, started asking him questions. "What do you do? How long have you known the family? Are you from here? Did you go to school with Jacy?"

Bubba answered his questions without looking up from his plate one time. He was getting irritated with Cameron.

Miss Susan interrupted the questions by saying how wonderful the food was, how much she appreciated being invited, and how much she missed her friends. She then directed her conversation to Lucille and asked her how she liked living in Baton Rouge.

Lucille answered, "Well, it's not home, but it's okay. And I miss you too, Susan. You need to meet me in Baton Rouge for a few days so we can do some shopping. It will be fun. I will also take you to some great restaurants."

"I'll be there," said Susan. "Just tell me when."

Back in the colony, a Christmas celebration was going on. Everyone was singing Christmas carols, and the children were enjoying their gifts and playing around the Christmas tree—that is, everyone but Cindy. She was sitting on Lavern's lap with her head on her chest. Cindy had been sad since Jacy left the colony. Carol went over to Cindy and asked her to take a walk with her to the tree to sing Christmas carols with her and the other children. Cindy agreed and got off Lavern's lap.

As they walked toward the tree, Carol bent down and whispered in Cindy's ear, "Jacy wants you to be happy until she returns. She wants you to laugh and play with the other children. If she knew you were sad, she would be very sad. Will you be my good friend, Cindy, until we see Jacy again?"

Cindy looked at Carol, smiled, and nodded her head yes. Carol stood up and continued to walk toward the tree. Cindy began to skip. Carol knew she had said the right thing to Cindy. She was happy again—at least, for now.

Lavern was really not in the Christmas spirit either, but seeing Cindy happy, even for a little while, had uplifted her. Samuel brought a group of small children to his mother so they could sing to her. This made Lavern happy. Samuel knew that every Christmas his mother missed being with her son Murphy and now her granddaughter, Jacy. Despite that, Samuel knew Lavern would never leave Cindy for any reason. Christmas was a time to be with your loved ones, and she was with Murphy and Jacy in spirit.

Lavern watched the children but could not help but notice how Mark helped the children with their food and led them in songs. He was staying busy, as usual. Samuel had made sure Mark had no sadness that day by taking control of his mind. Mark could not concentrate on the loss of his family, but the next day Samuel would not have time to help him. He was a very busy man in the colony.

Billy, who was back at the ship, wanted to take a break from work, so he went to his room so he could check in on Jacy. What he really wanted was to board his plane and fly into Yelgar to visit with her. He was getting restless and not being able to tune in on Jacy mentally made it worse. If he could find a way, he would see her and suffer the consequences with Philip later.

The only problem with Billy's plan was that Philip was always a step ahead of him. Philip knew Billy was ready to do anything to see Jacy. He had to think of a way to help Billy before there were major problems. Maybe he would let Billy make contact with Jacy for a short visit. The time would eventually come for the two to be reunited, if everything stayed the same and Jacy did not give her love to another man.

Philip called Billy mentally to report to him. Billy answered Philip's call by slowly walking toward him, knowing that Philip was aware of everything he had been thinking if he had tuned in on him.

"I hope I'm not in trouble," thought Billy.

Philip looked at Billy and said, "You're not yet, Billy, but you're having some thoughts that could get you into serious trouble."

"I'm sorry, Philip. But not knowing what she's doing or thinking is driving me crazy."

"Billy, you were taught to control these emotions. Why don't you?"

"I try sometimes," said Billy.

"No, you don't. You're focusing on your human side. You're forgetting your training," said Philip. "I know you're trying to work out a scheme to get to Jacy. There's no need to. I'm going to fix it so you can fly to Yelgar on New Year's Eve. There will be a band in the park, and everyone in town will be there. You will see Jacy and maybe have conversation with her—hopefully a short conversation. She will be very confused when she sees you. You can be cordial, but no mind control. It's just a visit. Do you understand this, Billy?"

"Yes, sir. I will do as you say, Philip. Thank you."

"I'm not so sure," said Philip, "but I'm letting you go anyway. I will be watching you."

Philip had to keep Billy out of his room for a few hours. He did not want him to see what was going on in Yelgar. Cameron was with Jacy a lot, and Billy might get jealous and respond by getting mean. He could be a danger to Cameron. He had put a block on Billy's mental contact with Jacy so he did not know what was going on, and this was very frustrating to Billy.

Philip assigned Billy to a job in the laboratory, helping the doctors to make right the harm that had been done to the men working on the railroad. They had to find the men and heal them. Billy would travel in a smaller ship with Zen and Qua and leave immediately for New Orleans. The job would probably take at least four hours, just long enough for Jacy to complete her Christmas with her family and friends.

Back in Yelgar, everyone had finished their dinner and gathered around the Christmas tree with their wine glasses. Macy asked Jacy to play some Christmas carols on the piano. Jacy was a very good pianist. She had been playing since she was five years old. Everyone wanted Jacy to play, so she took her wine to the piano, which sat in a small room opposite the living room, and she played "Jingle Bells." Some of them sang, and some just listened to the music. She continued playing Christmas carols as everyone relaxed and enjoyed the mood.

Macy went to the Christmas tree and asked Jacy to stop playing so they could open presents. Jacy got up, picked up her wine, and took a seat as Macy gave out her gifts to everyone. They opened them and then Lucille got up and gave out her gifts. They all thanked the two women for the lovely gifts. Lucille then asked Jacy to give out the other gifts under the tree. As Jacy gave out the other gifts, she noticed that Cameron had given her a gift in a very small box.

She thought, "I hope it's is not jewelry."

After she handed out the gifts, she took her seat and opened her gifts, leaving the small one for last. She paused and walked around to see if everyone had liked the gifts she had chosen. She had given Lucille, Macy, and Miss Susan perfume and powder sets. For her grandfather, she had chosen a waterproof watch he could wear while working. Bubba got a new compass, and Cameron had received cologne. The women loved their perfume and raved about how clean it smelled.

"It has a citrus smell about it," said Miss Susan.

Jacy's grandfather and Bubba thanked Jacy for their gifts.

Cameron opened his cologne and sniffed it. "I like this fragrance, Jacy. Thank you," he said. "Now open yours from me."

Jacy went back to her seat and picked up the tiny box while everyone's eyes watched her. She opened the tiny box very slowly. She got the paper off and saw that it was the kind of box that jewelry came in.

"Oh, brother," she thought. "What do I have here?"

When she took the top off the small box, she saw a pair of diamond earrings.

"Oh, Cameron, I can't take this gift," she said. "They are beautiful but way too much."

"Yes, you can," he said. "They will look very nice on you. You've got to take them; it's Christmas. You can't give a Christmas gift back."

Jacy looked at her mother with a what-should-I-do look on her face. Lucille shrugged her shoulders and smiled at Jacy.

She said, "They're gorgeous earrings, Cameron. You have good taste."

"Thank you, Mrs. Hebert," he answered.

Macy said, "Put them on, Jacy. Right now. We want to see how they look."

"Okay, Grandmother."

She out the small hoops she was wearing off and replaced them with the diamond earrings.

"You're more gorgeous than ever," said Cameron. Everyone else agreed.

Miss Susan remarked, "They go nicely with that unique stone you have around your neck. That stone looks like it's from another world, Jacy. I've never seen anything like it on Earth."

Murphy shook his head and said, "Let's concentrate on Earth tonight, not outer space, Susan."

"All right," Miss Susan said. "I'll shut up, but …" She left the rest of her sentence unspoken.

It was getting late, and the weather was still cold and rainy. Everyone was getting tired and ready to go home. It had been a long but enjoyable day and night. The guests left one at a time. First Miss Susan, then Bubba, and last was Cameron. Cameron had hung around with the hope that he might get to be alone with Jacy. But it had not worked out that way.

After the guests were gone, Lucille and Macy began cleaning up while Jacy cleared the table and put the leftover desserts in the refrigerator. As she passed the kitchen window above the sink, she glanced out and saw lights in the sky—colored lights.

She yelled, "Wait!" And then she ran out the back door and onto the porch.

The lights were steady, except for the red ones that blinked. Tears filled her eyes as she watched the lights.

The lights were Zen and Qua giving Billy a very special Christmas gift. Jacy appeared on their monitor, and Billy touched her face with his hand.

"I'll see you in a week, Jacy," he said to the monitor. "Merry Christmas, my angel."

Billy, Zen, and Qua just stared at the monitor as Jacy stared up at the small craft.

Lucille walked out on the porch and asked Jacy, "What are you looking at?"

Jacy pointed to the lights in the sky, and Lucille looked up.

"What is that?" she asked.

"I'm not sure," said Jacy, "but I get a good feeling looking at it."

Then the lights disappeared into the night. Jacy dropped her head and walked back into the house with her mother following.

Lucille told Macy, "You would not believe what I just witnessed."

"I'll believe anything after these last few months," said Macy,

"Believe this, Mother," she said. "Do you see the lights on Jacy's tree?"

"Yes," said Macy.

"Well, I just saw the same ones in the sky, complete with the blinking red lights," said Lucille.

"You're kidding," said Macy. "What in the world could it have been?"

"In the *world*," repeated Lucille. "That's the key word. Maybe they are not from this world."

"Stop it," said Macy. "Don't say those kinds of things, Lucille. That's crazy talk."

"Well, you explain it, Mother," said Lucille. "Do you have any explanation?"

"Let me think," said Macy. "It could have been a balloon or an airplane. It's Christmas. Someone could be spreading the Christmas spirit from the air."

"Not acceptable, Mother," said Lucille. "I've heard that explanation before. You should have seen the look on Jacy's face while she stared at those lights. It was like she was hypnotized.

"Mother, Jacy's miserable, and I can't help her until I know why. I can't talk to Murphy. He thinks I'm too emotional and that I should stay out of her business. Please keep a close eye on her when I return to Baton Rouge and call me every day to let me know how she's doing."

"I'll call you, Lucille. Don't worry. Jacy is going to be all right," said Macy.

"Tomorrow's a new day," continued Macy. "We are going home now. It's been another wonderful Christmas with my family and friends. And I love you, Lucille. I'll see you tomorrow. Bye." With that, she and Pierre left.

Lucille went into the living room where Murphy was watching TV. She sat on a chair in front of the fireplace and watched the fire dance on the log and make crackling noises. Then she looked at Jacy's Christmas tree.

"You're awfully quiet tonight, Lucille," said Murphy.

"I'm just tired," she answered. She wished she could tell him what had just happened with the lights, but she knew he would shrug it off as nothing. "I'm going to bed. Good night."

"Good night, Lucille. And Merry Christmas," he answered.

On her way to bed, Lucille opened the door to Jacy's room and looked at her daughter while she slept. It was something she had done since Jacy's childhood. But she was not a child anymore. She was an adult with adult problems—problems she would have to solve herself.

It was the day after Christmas and time to return all the Christmas presents that did not fit or were not to the receiver's taste. The malls would be filled with people looking for after-Christmas sales.

Jacy never returned gifts. She kept all of them. And she definitely would not be going to the mall today, but her mother and grandmother would be there. Lucille and Macy were bargain shoppers, something they had done together every year for as long as Jacy could remember.

Jacy decided to go to Pierre's workshop to work with him all day long. He had two employees working with him, but he could always use one more. When Jacy walked in the door, Pierre was pleasantly surprised.

"Come on in, Jacy. I always need a good hand like you," he said.

Working with her grandfather was a good way to get her mind off any unwanted thoughts.

"What do you want me to do today, Grandfather?" she asked.

Pierre showed her some unfinished furniture he had just put together.

"You can stain and varnish this furniture any color you want."

"I will be very glad to," she said and then got busy with her paintbrush. "I've missed this."

"I've missed your excellent work and, of course, your company," said Pierre. "But you're going to make a great teacher. You can always come by and spend time here at the shop with me. Think school first, Jacy."

"I can't wait to be a teacher," said Jacy. "Working with children will be fun and rewarding. I will think school first."

The two continued to working on the furniture into the evening, only taking short breaks for food and refreshments.

The holidays were exhausting, and this year's festivities were especially so. It was almost the New Year, and there would be another celebration. This one would be held in the local park for the people of Yelgar. The adults would gather in one section to bring in the New Year with music and dancing while the children enjoyed a fireworks display in another section. Most families enjoyed the fireworks with their children and then took them home to a sitter so that the adults could return to the entertainment. The townspeople brought ice chests with beer and soda, whatever their tastes were. Everyone in town would be there. Families and friends would gather in their lawn chairs to relive the past year.

The New Year celebration was very relaxing. There was no work involved, and no dishes to wash.

The partygoers could just sit and dance and drink. And rain was no problem. There would be small canvas tents all over, and some people would bring their large umbrellas. The band's area was the only place with a roof so their performance would not be hindered. The show would go on.

The weather for the New Year's celebration called for clear and cold conditions with no rain in the forecast, but weather conditions could change at any time in Louisiana. Jacy enjoyed this event every year because all of her old schoolmates would attend, and they could catch up on what the others had been doing since graduation. It was kind of like a mini class reunion every year instead of every ten years.

It was December 30, and Jacy wanted to help her grandmother with the store. She stocked shelves most of the day because Macy could not stoop down to restock the bottom shelves. It made her back hurt. So Jacy, being the wonderful granddaughter she was, came to her rescue. It was a busy day. The customers began to come in early. They were all talking about the following day's New Year's Eve party. Everyone bought beer, sodas, chips, peanuts, and popcorn.

The band that was going to perform was very good. They played rock 'n' roll and country music and entertained the old and young alike. Whenever they performed, there was a sell-out crowd. Those who planned to go to performance often sent one person from their group early to claim their spot. They would set out some chairs and wait for the party to start.

Murphy and Lucille had been headed home to Baton Rouge but had changed their minds. They loved the band that was playing New Year's Eve. Any excuse was a good one to prolong their stay.

Murphy was going out into the swamp with friends to fish and trap while Lucille hung out with her best friend Miss Susan and shopped.

Jacy was just living day to day, not expecting much out of life. Since her return from the swamp, she has not had one day of true happiness. Everyone around her constantly tried to make her smile or get a little giggle from her by telling her jokes. In return, she gave them a phony smile and tried to be nice, knowing what her loved ones were doing.

The door opened, and Cameron entered the store.

"Hi, Mrs. Bellard. How are you today?"

Jacy heard his voice as she was stooped down to stock a lower shelf and put her head low so he could not see her. Hiding between the shelves did not do any good.

Macy shouted to Cameron while he was in the back of the store getting milk, "Jacy's on aisle six stocking shelves!"

Jacy stood up quickly and gave mean eyes to her grandmother. Then she turned and smiled at Cameron.

"How are you?" she asked.

He replied, "A lot better after seeing your pretty face, Jacy."

She thought, "I know he uses those same lines over and over again on all the women."

Cameron walked up to Jacy and said, "Save me a place next to you at the park. I will be there tomorrow night. We can dance the night away."

Jacy just smiled at him and went back to work.

After he had left and she heard the door close behind him, she jumped up and yelled to her grandmother, "I don't want to dance the night away with him! Now he will be there sitting next to me all night."

Macy came from behind the counter and said, "I thought you would want to say hi to Cameron. He is your friend."

"Grandmother, I was hiding from him for a reason. I didn't want to go to the New Year's Eve party with him. I want to mingle with my friends I haven't seen in a while."

"Sorry," said Macy. "I'll know better next time. You are very touchy lately. No matter what I say or do you get mad at me, Jacy."

Jacy walked to her grandmother and hugged her tight.

"I know you mean no harm, Grandmother, but please let me hide from Cameron if I want. Don't try and push us together. It's not working for me. Maybe in time a romance will develop between us, but now is not the time, okay?"

"Okay," said Macy, and she put out her hand. "Friends?"

Jacy took her hand and answered, "Friends till the end."

Jacy was not looking forward to the New Year, knowing that she would have to kiss whomever she was dancing with at midnight. Maybe at ten till she could go to the restroom or go buy nachos. She was already scheming ways to escape from Cameron. He was jealous and rude to every man that talked to or came around her. He questioned them and belittled them in front of Jacy. This made her very uncomfortable, but there was nothing she could do about it. He did it in a way that was inconspicuous. He was a very intimidating person.

Jacy thought, "Perfect life. Is there such a thing? Who has a perfect life, and exactly what is the correct definition of the word *perfect*?"

Jacy's life was in turmoil, but she still never expected or wanted to live a perfect life because she wanted to deal with everything thrown at her today, tomorrow, and forever. Cameron was just a friend that was trying to control her. It would never work. Jacy was putting up with him because her family liked him so much. She must find another friend to date so Cameron would not take their relationship seriously. She had not gone out to area dance clubs in months. To start the year off right, she would call her friends and party with them every once in a while. Maybe she would meet young, nice men to date.

Jacy would be twenty-two on January 10. Many people would think it was time for her to find the right guy for a serious relationship—her mother and grandmother in particular. But no one was going to rush her. She was stubborn and would know when the right guy came around. Right now, she enjoyed being an independent woman.

Macy turned the radio on to a local mixed-music station. Christmas music was still being played until the New Year came in. Customers coming and going sang and moved to the music as they walked through the store. They were getting into a party mood for the New Year.

"Well," said Jacy, "another year gone by, Grandmother. Can you believe it?"

"Yes, I can," said Macy, "and what a roller coaster it has been. I thought I had lost my only granddaughter. What a nightmare this family went through. The only good thing that came out of it was that you left with childlike ways and returned a woman with a direction in life. Thank God you were unharmed. The swamp is, as you know, very unpredictable. I can't think of a scarier place at night, and you were alone out there, Jacy. The thought of it gives me the creeps. I'm glad you can't remember the experience. It had to have been so bad that you mentally blocked it out of your mind."

Jacy looked at her grandmother and said, "I think whatever happened to me out there was meant to be, and I would not change a thing. One day, I know I'll remember. It will all come back to me.

"But enough talk about the past year, I'm looking forward to a new year, and I plan to live my life to the fullest."

"What time do you want to close New Year's Eve, Jacy?" asked her grandmother.

"Let's close at six. Everyone should have everything they will need by then."

Macy then made a sign that said "Closing at 6 p.m. on New Year's Eve" and put it on the door for everyone to see.

"The band starts playing at eight. We will have plenty of time to get dressed and drive to the park," said Jacy.

"Don't worry about bringing lawn chairs," said Macy. "I'll bring some extra ones. I've got the beer and wine coolers covered, too. Just bring yourself."

The store was filled with customers, so Macy and Jacy returned to work. They kept busy until closing time. Then Macy locked the door and turned off the lights. Jacy was very tired. She just wanted to go home and soak her sore muscles in a hot bubble bath. Standing and stooping while stocking the shelves had worn her out.

Billy desperately tried to contact Jacy mentally to no avail. wondered if she had maybe found someone else and had strong feelings for him. But he would not have to wonder anymore after tomorrow night. He would come face to face with her, and his questions would finally have answers. He would probe her mind to see just where she stood. Could he handle it if the answers were not the answers he hoped for, and could Philip keep control of him once he was reunited with Jacy? Soon their future would be determined. Of all the places on Earth and in the universe where Billy could be, he only desired to visit one small town in Louisiana.

Morning arrived on New Year's Eve. Jacy jumped out of bed and had breakfast with her parents before going to work. Everyone was in a good mood and enjoyed being together once more. Lucille told Jacy that she and Murphy would meet her at the park later that night. The men would go early to hold the spot for family and friends to congregate.

"Put your dancing shoes on, Jacy. We are sitting close to the dance section."

Jacy smiled at her mother but did not say anything.

As she walked out the door for work, she called to her parents, "See you tonight."

The weather was great, although clear and cold. There was a slight smell of hickory smoke in the air. Most of the locals had fired up their barbecue pits and smokers for family visits today. Barbecuing was a New Year's Eve and New Year's Day tradition in Louisiana. Lucille and Murphy would be with friends on the wharf where they had a large barbecue. Lucille would bring Jacy and Macy a plate for lunch, complete with potato salad and baked beans, and they would wait patiently for it.

Time seemed to pass slowly on the last day of the year. Not knowing what the New Year had in store was a little scary. Everyone in Yelgar was spending this last day of the year with family and friends. They all hoped for a prosperous and healthy New Year.

Billy stood on the deck with Philip and watched the monitors of all that was going on in the universe. But all he could think about was being with Jacy once again that night. He wondered when Philip would give him his orders. The plan was that he would dress in his pilot clothes once more and fly to Yelgar, keeping the communicator in an inside pocket of his leather jacket so Philip could guide him through the night. The communicator looked exactly like a small folding cell phone. It rang and received text messages; it also vibrated and gave off an electric shock. He would not go anywhere without it. If it were to fall into the hands of earthlings, it would convert into a cell phone and disappear shortly thereafter.

Zen and Qua stood next to Billy and helped navigate the ship. They occasionally looked his way. They had befriended Billy during Jacy's visit and were excited for him because they knew how much Jacy meant to him. Their faces showed no expression, but their thoughts wished him the best. Billy knew Philip would send them in their small ship to follow him while he flew the plane into Yelgar. Of course, they would wait patiently and stay completely out of sight.

Billy would only have a short time to rekindle the flame of love that he and Jacy shared. It had happened so quickly in the colony, but this time it had to hold its own in the world of humanity. If it was real love, it would hold up anywhere. But this time he had competition. Cameron would try to control her time if he was around. Billy would not have much of a chance—or would he?

The clock approached six o'clock at the store. Macy and Jacy were ready to close up, go home, and get ready for the celebration. As soon as it was time, they both left and headed home.

When Jacy got home, she filled her bathtub with bubble bath and soaked for ten minutes. Then she washed her hair and dried and curled it. She took time to put her makeup on perfectly. She was going to see all her old classmates and wanted to look nice. As she went to her closet to look for something special to wear on the cold night, she noticed a long-sleeve turtleneck and pulled out a pair of her favorite jeans to go with it. This ensemble would look good with her brown fringed leather jacket with boots that matched. When she had finished dressing, she looked in the mirror and saw that the heart around her neck had a gorgeous glow. She grabbed a pair of large hoop earrings and was ready except for combing her long auburn hair. She wanted to let it hang down tonight. It was only seven thirty. The park was not far from home, so she decided to watch TV for thirty minutes and then go off to the park.

Finally, Philip signaled Billy to report to him on deck. He suddenly felt very nervous. He had lost contact with Jacy and did not know how she would react to him. The fear of rejection was fogging his mind. It was definitely a human trait. Every human on Earth naturally feared rejection. He slowly put his clothes on and combed his hair. He wore his hair a little longer now and hoped Jacy would like it. He was clean-shaven and had used the citrus-smelling aftershave that Jacy seemed to like. He looked good. When he arrived on deck for his orders, some of the crew made loud sniffing noises and smiled. Already nervous, he just ignored them.

Philip was sitting a table waiting for him.

"Billy," said Philip, "are you ready to make a delivery to Yelgar airport?"

"A delivery?" asked Billy. "Yes, of course."

"Okay," said Philip. "You are delivering some medical supplies to a lady that will be waiting for you with a sign that says 'Medical.'"

"That's easy enough," said Billy.

"Good," said Philip. "From there you are on your own to find a ride to the park where Jacy is right now. The celebration is about one and a half miles from the airport. Good luck, and I will keep contact with you through your communicator."

Billy then went with Zen and Qua. They took him to the plane, which was already loaded with the medical supplies he was to deliver. He climbed aboard the plane and started the engine to let it warm up. He glanced at his watch. It was ten o'clock. He was supposed to arrive in Yelgar at ten thirty, so he must wait until ten fifteen for takeoff.

As his plane left the ground, he took a deep breath and said, "God, let this night end well." As he flew over the swamp area, he saw the lights of the Yelgar airport and headed in that direction. A few minutes later, he had arrived and landed the plane. He picked up the small package of medical supplies, got off the plane, and walked to the airport entrance. Just like Philip had said, there was a lady holding a sign that said "Medical."

Billy walked up to the lady and said to her, "I have your delivery."

She lowered her sign, took the supplies, and thanked him. Billy then walked to the ticket counter and asked directions to the park. The lady he had given the supplies to overheard the question and jumped in abruptly, "I'm going there now. Would you like a ride?"

"Yes," he said. "I would be very grateful to you."

"No problem," she said, and he followed her to her car.

Billy sat next to her in the front seat and smiled, thinking how lucky he was that she was going in the same direction.

She looked over at him and introduced herself, "My name is Susan. What's yours?"

"Billy," he answered. "I'm so glad to make your acquaintance." He raised his brow. He knew this lady. She was Miss Susan, Jacy's friend. Philip had planned this, that sly fox. She would lead him right to Jacy.

Miss Susan said to Billy, "Would you like to sit with me and my friends at the park? They are all nice people, and we would enjoy your company."

Billy answered, "Are you sure I won't be intruding?"

"Very sure," said Miss Susan.

"Okay," he said. "Thank you, Miss Susan."

She turned quickly gave him an odd look. "Oh no," he thought, "she senses something." But she did not say anything else to him as she parked the car.

They got out, and she popped the trunk of the car and handed him a folding chair.

"Follow me," said Susan as they walked into the park entrance.

It was eleven fifteen, and the park was full of happy people dancing to the very loud music. As Billy walked through the crowd, every female from three to eighty years old could not take their eyes off him. He was the females' definition of eye candy. Looking at him was a treat. Getting closer to Jacy's group, Billy took off his baseball cap and nervously ran his gloved fingers through his hair.

"So many humans in one place," Billy thought. "How many of these people have the look but are not fully human?"

Then Miss Susan said, "Don't get lost, slow poke."

Billy thought Miss Susan was a good example of both Tavie and human and a very thoughtful, wonderful person. She was a real credit to the world.

As they approached Jacy's family and friends, Miss Susan announced she had brought a friend with her to welcome in the New Year. She introduced Billy to the men.

The men lifted their hands to Billy and said, "Welcome," and, "Glad to meet you." He responded by lifting his hand and saying thank you.

The men were sitting on one side of the group while the women sat on the other—except for Cameron. He sat next to Jacy. They were sitting on the end so they would have easy access to the dance floor. Billy's back was to Jacy as Miss Susan introduced him. As he turned, his eyes were immediately drawn to Jacy's face. She looked up, and their eyes locked. Miss Susan started to introduce Billy to the women, but his eyes were still on Jacy.

"Billy," said Miss Susan.

"Oh," he said, "I'm sorry. I just had my mind on something else. So pleased to meet all of you, and once more, thanks for having me."

Then he turned to Jacy and held out his gloved hand.

"My name is William Joseph Hooper, ma'am. But please call me Billy."

Jacy stared back at him, grabbed his hand, and answered, "I'm Jacy Hebert. Glad to make your acquaintance, Billy."

Cameron then stood up and said, "I'm Cameron Leger, Jacy's boyfriend."

Jacy turned to Billy and said, "Yes, Cameron is a boy, and he is my friend."

Billy smiled at her and set his chair behind Cameron so he could have a perfect view of Jacy as he listened to the music.

Jacy looked straight ahead but tried to glance at Billy out of the corner of her eye. She was very nervous, and her stomach was churning. This young man had lit a fire in Jacy's heart. She could not ever remember having a reaction like this after just meeting a handsome man.

Billy leaned back in his chair and tried to relax and enjoy being near Jacy, but he could not help but probe her mind. She was, as Philip had said, confused in her thoughts but happy at the same time. Everything was good so far.

Cameron noticed the attraction Jacy had for Billy and became very uncomfortable. It was obvious.

He turned around, focused on Billy, and began his usual line of questioning.

"I know you have a pilot's license. Do you have any degrees?"

Billy did not answer.

Cameron turned back around and faced the band. He then turned and faced Billy again.

"Where are you from?"

Billy looked at him and said loudly, "The planet Earth."

Jacy heard this smart remark and giggled to herself.

"What about the degrees? Got any?" asked Cameron.

"You mean besides this third degree you're giving me right now?" asked Billy.

Cameron turned back around. Billy was not playing the put-down game Cameron usually played with Jacy's other friends.

Billy already resented Cameron, and his actions were definitely adding fuel to the fire.

Cameron put his arm around the back of Jacy's chair and looked back at Billy. He was trying to show Billy that Jacy was his girl.

Jacy did not move. She just sat really still and wished Cameron was not there.

Billy then touched Jacy on the shoulder, and she turned around. He handed her a card with his name and e-mail address on it.

"If you ever need to be somewhere in a hurry, please contact me. I'll fly you there free of charge."

Jacy took the card and placed it in the side of her boot.

"Thank you, Billy," she said. "I may do that."

Cameron was furious. There was nothing he could say to Billy to put him down in front of Jacy. He would not cooperate.

Out of pure meanness, Cameron turned to Billy and said, "Why don't you take your gloves off and stay a while."

Billy just stared at him. He was mad—very mad. Jealousy had finally taken its toll. He noticed Cameron's car keys on top of the ice chest that contained the drinks. Billy had taken enough. He knew that he could get into trouble, but he had to do something. He concentrated on Cameron's key remote with his mind and made the alarm go off on his Mercedes Benz. It was so loud that it drowned out the music.

Soon the announcer called out, "Please, would the owner of the black Mercedes please go to your car and turn off your security system."

Cameron looked at Billy as he stood up and picked up his keys.

Billy looked back at him and said, "I'll keep my gloves on and stay a while."

Cameron rushed out the entrance to turn the alarm off on his car. When he reached his car, he had a problem; no matter what he did, the alarm would not go off. A security guard came by and tried to help him. They even disconnected the alarm system, but it still sounded off.

The security guard shook his head and said, "I've never seen anything like this. I'm sorry, sir, but you must take this car off the premises immediately until you can shut off your security system."

Cameron hit the steering wheel and drove his car off the parking lot with the alarm still blaring.

Billy knew Cameron would be gone as long as he wanted, and he sensed that Jacy was now more relaxed. Jacy turned and looked at Billy, as if to say, "What did you do?" He just looked back at her, leaned to the side of his chair, and gave her a sexy one-sided smile.

He then looked at the singer on stage, and the singer stopped midsong and said, "I want to sing this song now."

It was a song Billy had mentally placed in his mind. It was his favorite love song, and he wanted to dance with Jacy to it.

Billy got up and looked down at Jacy.

"Will you dance with me," he asked, holding out his hand.

She took his hand and stood up. "Yes, I would love to."

The singer began to sing as Jacy put her arms around Billy's neck, and he placed his arms around her waist. They were very close as they listened to the words, "Honey, you don't know what it's like to love the way I love you." The song was moving for two people in love, even if one did not know that she was. Jacy touched her cheek to Billy's, and they both closed their eyes. He pulled her close. She rolled her cheek onto his lips, and her heart skipped a beat. Their chemistry was unmistakable.

Lucille, Macy, Miss Susan, and the other women in the group watched but did not say a word to each other. Everyone in the crowd around them watched quietly, except for Murphy and the men in their group. They drank their beer and talked and had not noticed the two of them dancing. The singer extended the song a few verses. He was also watching them dance. Then, without a pause, the band went into another song that was much faster.

Billy and Jacy pulled away from each other reluctantly and danced to the new beat. Billy stood in one place, moving his feet and body to the music, but Jacy turned it on. She moved seductively in front of Billy, moving her hips in close to him as well as every other body part, but she kept her eyes on Billy's face the whole time.

Now the entire group of family and friends had their eyes on the two dancers.

"What is going on?" Lucille asked Macy. "I've never seen Jacy dance like that before. What is she doing?"

Macy and Miss Susan fanned their faces with their hands and said nothing. Lucille looked at Murphy. When he saw her look at him, he looked at the sky, telephone lines, the lights, anything but his daughter and her dance partner. Pierre and the other men did the same. They would glance at the couple from the corner of their eyes and guzzle their beer as if nothing was going on.

Billy watched Jacy move around him and cocked his head to one side as he smiled. He knew everything that was going on in her mind. She was acting out her feelings. The song stopped. It was midnight. A recording of "Auld Lang Syne" came over the speaker, and the announcer said, "It's twelve o'clock. Kiss your partner."

Jacy took Billy's face in her hands and kissed him passionately as he pulled her close to him and they embraced.

Lucille said, "I've never seen Jacy so forward with a man in my life."

Everyone was watching Jacy. Lucille looked back at the men. They raised their eyebrows and looked back at her, confused. The women in the group could not take their eyes off the couple. Lucille could not get any of the women to talk to her, including her mother. They continued to fan their faces with their hands.

Billy's shoulders suddenly slumped. He had received an electric shock from his communicator. Things were getting out of control. It was time for Billy leave. He pulled back from Jacy and took out his communicator. The text read "Mission accomplished. Go to your plane and return home." He closed his communicator and walked Jacy back to her chair.

Billy kissed and squeezed Jacy's hand tightly. He explained that he had to go but would see her again, hopefully soon. He waved to everyone and told them he had enjoyed meeting them. They waved back at him, and he left.

As he left the park, he looked up at the sky and said, "Thanks, guys." He then mentally turned Cameron's security system off so he could return to the park.

Billy walked back to the airport. He felt that he could use the exercise, and it was very close. As he walked, he had time to think about what a wonderful night it had been and how beautiful Jacy had looked. When he reached the airport, he climbed aboard his plane and returned home.

Jacy sat still in her chair and thought to herself, "What just happened?"

No one in the group said anything. Then Lucille asked, "Jacy, did you have fun?"

Jacy turned to her mother and answered, "The best time of my life."

Macy nudged Jacy's arm and said, "You go, girl."

"Mother," said Lucille, "don't encourage her aggressive behavior with men."

Macy turned to her daughter and said, "Jacy is not an aggressive person. This was a meant-to-be meeting. She felt comfortable with that young man. And who wouldn't? He is gorgeous. I wish he would come back. We liked looking at him."

"Yes," said the other women, agreeing with Macy.

Jacy laughed at her grandmother. "Thanks, and I hope he comes back too—real soon."

"I'm not sure you can control yourself with that man," said Lucille. "You could be heading for trouble."

"Trouble," said Macy. "There should be more trouble like him in the world. The word would take on a different meaning."

Lucille shook her head. She knew she could not win this argument with her mother.

Jacy said nothing. She just listened to her mother and grandmother as they discussed the evening's happenings. She glanced at Miss Susan. She was shaking her head while looking back at her.

"What?" asked Jacy.

Miss Susan answered, "That man loves you, Jacy. I feel like it was set up somehow. I was meant to deliver him to you." She then looked up at the sky and shook her finger. "Somehow I know they were involved."

Jacy smiled at Miss Susan and said, "Whoever set it up, please tell them thank you from me."

At that, Murphy decided to change the subject by commenting on how wonderful the band had been.

The night had been one to remember. Jacy thought about how it had kind of been like the Cinderella story, except Cinderella was a man. Jacy wondered if she would ever see him again. Instead of a glass slipper, she had the card he had given to her. But she was hesitant to contact him—at least, not so soon.

Cameron's car alarm had finally stopped, and he returned to the park. He rushed in so he could welcome in the New Year with Jacy, even though it was a bit late.

He walked up to her and said, "Happy New Year."

She looked up at him and said, "Ditto."

He knew by the look on her face that something had happened between her and Billy. As he sat down next to Jacy, she yawned and put her hand over her mouth.

"Wow, I'm so tired. I think I'll go home now and get some rest."

"So soon?" he asked. "It's not even twelve thirty."

"Well," said Jacy, "I got up early, and now I am tired."

Jacy told everyone good night and got up to go home. Cameron walked her to her car. When Jacy moved to get in, Cameron grabbed her by the waist and spun her around. He looked into her eyes and said, "We are starting this year off with a kiss." Then he pulled her close to him.

"Let me go," Jacy protested, and she moved his hands from around her waist.

"What is wrong with you, Jacy? Why don't you like me?"

"My heart belongs to another, Cameron. I'm sorry."

"Who?" he asked. "You don't date anyone else. Where is he? Is he an imaginary boyfriend?"

"Oh no," she said, "he's very real."

"Please tell me it's not that William Joseph Hooper call me Billy guy. You know nothing about that man. Where's he from? What kind of person is he?"

Jacy said nothing. She just stared into space.

"Beware of strangers, Jacy. It's a crazy world." Then he turned and drove away.

When Jacy returned home and walked into her bedroom, she looked into the mirror and pictured Billy standing next to her. The thought of him gave her goose bumps. Maybe her mother was right. She might lose control with him. Then she thought, "What the heck. It's a chance worth taking."

She got undressed and put on her nightclothes. She lay in her bed and read the card he had given to her. It was just a name and an e-mail address, but that was enough. The card even smelled like Billy. She kept putting it up to her nose and pictured his face in her mind. She could see his dark eyes and great smile, with those straight white teeth, and remembered that he had smelled so good. Thoughts of Billy gradually helped her to sleep.

Billy had to report back to the main ship and do some explaining. What would Philip say about his mind games with Cameron? He was not looking forward to it. Tavies did not disobey.

When he arrived at the colony, Zen and Qua quickly picked him up and delivered him to the main ship where Philip was waiting for him. Billy walked to Philip's side and took a seat. Philip turned and looked at him for awhile. He finally asked, "Did you have fun?"

Billy answered him hesitantly, "Yes. Thank you for making it possible."

Philip then asked, "Did you feel superior to the people around you?"

"I didn't think about it," said Billy.

"Did you feel superior to Cameron?" he asked. "Was he in your way, Billy?"

"He was rude to me," said Billy.

"Why couldn't you handle him without using the special abilities you have learned in the colony?"

"It just happened. I didn't think it would hurt anything, and it was a way to spend the little time I had with Jacy."

"You couldn't think of another way?"

"Not really," said Billy.

"Maybe you should have handled it like the humans around you would have."

"I don't know how the humans would have handled it, Philip."

"Exactly," said Philip. "That is the reason, Billy, why you will never be able to live in Jacy's world. What you did is wrong, and now you see why Tavies stay in the colony. Jacy is no threat to us when she comes here, but you are a threat to anyone that crosses you when you are in her world."

Billy banged his head with his hand "What? You are telling me that we have no future together?"

"I'm telling you," said Philip, "to think about what you've done. Tell me if you think I'm right."

Billy shook his head. "No, I think there is a way I can see Jacy. What I did to Cameron's car alarm was wrong, but I did not cause any pain to him."

"Did it cross your mind, Billy?"

"Not really, Philip. I meant no harm."

"You meant no harm," said Philip. "What if he would have gotten in a wreck while driving around with his car alarm blaring?"

"He didn't," said Billy.

"No, because he was under our watchful eyes. He was the underdog there, Billy. He was no match for you and never will be. It's a good thing Jacy doesn't have any feelings for the man. You could have caused trouble in their relationship."

"She loves me, Philip. I know it," said Billy.

"I agree," said Philip. "But this is not a traditional relationship, and I think you should go to your quarters and think about everything we have discussed."

Billy got up and said to Philip, "I'll think about everything we've discussed, but nothing will change. I love Jacy, and she loves me. There will be a way we can get together. I know it."

Billy went to his quarters and thought about everything Philip had said as he unsnapped the band at the wrist of his leather gloves that held them securely on his hands. As he took them off, he looked down at his hands and moved his fingers around. He was different from the humans. Philip did make sense in a lot of things he had said, but nothing was ever going to stop Billy from seeing Jacy. He lay down on his bed and went to sleep, not knowing what the year had in store for him and Jacy.

When day broke on January 1, Jacy jumped from her bed and said out loud, "God, it's good to be alive."

She dressed for the day and went into the kitchen where Lucille and Murphy were sitting at the table drinking coffee. She said good morning to her parents and kissed each of them on the cheek.

Murphy said to Jacy, "Why are you in such a good mood today?"

Lucille looked at him and said, "Need you ask?" Then her eyes widened. "I think Jacy met a new friend."

Jacy poured a cup of coffee. "I hope so, Mother. I sure hope so."

"Well, it's good to see you happy," said Murphy.

Then Lucille said, "Jacy, we will be leaving this afternoon for Baton Rouge. We have to take care of business."

"Okay, Mother. I will be fine, but of course I will miss y'all."

"Promise to call me often, and let me know what's going on in your life," said Lucille.

"Yes, Mother. I'll call you often and let you know if Billy calls me." They all smiled at each other.

"You mean *when* he calls you," said Lucille. The three then just sat and enjoyed being together.

After a while Jacy got up and began to sing an old Cajun song that described life on the bayou. She stopped and said to her parents, "Call Grandmother and invite them for lunch. I'm going to make chicken and sausage filé gumbo."

"You are?" said Lucille.

"Yes," said Jacy. "You pack and leave the cooking to me."

"That sounds wonderful," said Murphy. "This is gumbo weather. It is very cold today."

Lucille called Macy as Jacy had asked and invited her and Pierre to lunch.

"Sure," said Macy. "Jacy's cooking all by herself?"

"Yes, Mother. She's in there preparing everything right now. Wait till you see her. She is beaming."

"I bet I can guess why," said Macy.

"Your guess would be the same as mine and definitely right."

Jacy was very happy, but Billy did not share the same feelings. He was not sure what the day would bring for him. He had never disobeyed orders before and did not know anyone from the colony that had. There were a few men that had been taken away from the colony and never seen again, but he had no idea why or what had happened to them. No one ever questioned the leaders.

He looked at his watch. It was time to report to Philip.

Billy sat quietly next to Philip as he watched the universe go by. He was waiting for his orders for the day.

Philip turned to Billy and said, "Today, Billy, you will take a trip with Zen and Qua."

"Where am I going?" he asked.

"You will see when you get there."

Billy got up and followed Zen and Qua to the small spaceship. They all boarded and took off shortly after. Billy sat in the ship with many things going through his mind. One of the things was that he was afraid of being banished from the colony.

Zen and Qua said nothing, as usual. They just looked straight ahead while navigating the small ship. Why would no one tell him anything? It must be a harsh punishment he was about to receive. Was Philip going to keep him away from Jacy forever?

The small ship landed, and the three exited from the craft as the door opened.

Billy looked around and asked Zen, "Where are we?"

"Take a good look, Billy. You know where we are."

Billy remembered seeing the buildings in pictures of Tavus.

"I'm being banished to the planet Tavus," said Billy.

Zen said to Billy, "We are following orders, and they were to deliver you here."

Zen and Qua walked Billy to the door of a pyramid-shaped building.

"We're not in Egypt are we?"

"'No, you were right with your first guess. This is the planet Tavus."

The door opened and many Tavies of pure blood in brown robes met them. The Tavies looked at each other but did not say a word. They were communicating mentally. Billy could not understand anything they were saying to each other. The speed of their minds was way beyond anything Billy had ever experienced.

One of the Tavies pointed at Billy, and he involuntarily began to walk toward one of the rooms in the building.

"How did he do that?" thought Billy. He opened the door and was astonished to see a room with humidifiers coming from the ceiling. Maybe he could not survive the environment of this planet without them. He would probably be confined to this room forever. Things were going from bad to worse. He ran to the door to open it, but the door had disappeared. The room was only four walls now and Billy. He had no communicator—no nothing.

Billy sat on a piece of furniture that slightly resembled a bed. It was a large shelf connected to the wall with a mat made of a strange substance on top of it. The mat felt like it was full of gel. It moved when he did. He tried desperately to communicate with Zen or Qua mentally, but nothing happened. Then he tried his other special abilities, but they were null and void here.

He went into the bathroom. Instead of a commode, there was a circular white pipe that attached to the floor. The top was the size of a dinner plate. The base was the same size from the top to the bottom, and it was about twenty inches high. There was no way to flush it, so it must flush automatically. The shower was a six foot high enclosed box that you stepped into. The water came through a hose from the top and bottom of the shower. It could be picked up and used wherever.

In the main room, there was a closet with clothing in it, uniforms in many colors, like the one he had on. A small shelf at the same height as the bed served as a nightstand. There was nothing on it. There was nothing else in the room. The light came from several golden bubbles floating around the room, just like in the underground facility in the colony, but they were much smaller.

Billy could not help but wonder, "How am I going to survive here and for how long?"

He was worried about the food. "That's a Cajun for you," he thought. He knew the Tavies were vegetarians. Most of the planet was unlivable, so very little could grow there. They probably received much of their food from Earth.

He knew he should be scared, but instead, he found everything interesting. He was just a little concerned about the door disappearing. It had to be mind control. Doors could not just disappear.

What would he do, just sit and look at four walls? It was morning on Earth. What time was it here? There was nothing to do but lay on his gel bed and think of Jacy and how he could get back to Earth. He had plenty of time to think. This was his punishment for disobeying. He could deal with it. Philip was a just man. No one questioned his decisions.

Suddenly, the door reappeared. He walked to the door and opened it. He was being summoned. His mind was no longer his. Someone had taken control of it. He kept walking until he reached a long narrow room. Inside was a long table where nineteen Tavies were seated, and there was one empty chair for him. In front of each person was a plate with a one-inch slice of something that looked like tofu and whole kernel corn. Next to the plate was a utensil that looked somewhat like a fork. It had prongs at the end of the long handle, but they were curved slightly and closer together than normal. To drink, there was a small cup about four inches high and three inches wide with a purple liquid inside. Next to the plate was a white paper napkin.

Billy took a seat and put his hands in his lap. The Tavies were of all ages. Some of them looked to be about his own age, and there were both women and men. The women wore outfits similar to the men's, except they were more colorful. The women's bodies were much like those of Earth, except that none of them were overweight. On their heads they wore hats to match their outfits. The hats looked like the beanie hats worn by earthlings. Their jaw lines were not as pointy as the males, and their lips were a bit larger. They were pretty.

All eyes were on Billy. He knew they were scanning his mind. No one spoke. Older men in robes sat at each end of the table. They picked up their forks and began to eat. Everyone else followed, showing respect to their elders. Billy just sat and watched.

The young woman next to Billy looked toward him and said, "Eat," with her mind. She kept looking at his hands as he ate his food. His hands were proof that he had ancestors on the planet.

While eating, everyone held mental conversations. Billy could not understand anything they were saying, so he concentrated on his food. The tofu looked and tasted like seafood gumbo, the corn tasted like corn, and the purple liquid tasted like blackberry wine with very little alcohol in it. It was all very good.

One of the older men at the end of the table stood up and spoke directly to Billy. "My name is Zaia, and I welcome you to Tavus as our guest."

Billy rolled his eyes and thought, "'Guest'? What a relief."

"Would you like us to speak to you instead of mentally communicating?

"Yes, please," said Billy. "We speak mostly where I came from."

At that remark, the young people around the table asked him about the colony he was from. He explained that he was considered a Cajun from Louisiana. He told them how many Cajuns spoke Cajun French as a second language and about the food and music of the colony and of the reptiles and mammals that lived around the colony in the swamp. They were really interested. Apparently many had visited colonies on Earth before, but no one had ever been on the bayou.

Billy thought the woman next to him might be flirting. She smiled at him and blinked her large dark eyes. Then she leaned over and rubbed her shoulder against his. It was making Billy very uncomfortable. The young man sitting on the other side of the table watched them and glared at Billy. Then Billy was sure she was flirting. Eyes don't lie. He tried to ignore her while he talked with the group.

Suddenly Billy felt both feet go to sleep. He pounded them on the floor to wake them up. The guy in front of him had a smirk on his face. Finally, his feet woke up, but then he got a crick in his neck. He could not move it. The guy in front of him still had the same smirk on his face. He rubbed his neck until he could move it again. He was helpless against him. His powers were nothing compared to the Tavies'. He tried to scoot his chair away from the girl, but it was stuck to the floor.

The young Tavies were so interested in Billy's colony that they were unaware of what was going on. Billy glanced at the guy in front of him and wondered what he was going to do next. It was obvious that the girl flirting with Billy was his love interest, and he was jealous.

Billy thought, "I think I've been in this type of love triangle before, except I was sitting in the power seat."

The Tavie man stared at Billy from across the table, and Billy nodded his head yes, indicating that he had gotten the message. The man then joined in on the conversation, and Billy felt no more pain.

For the first time in Billy's life, he had felt the emotion of fear and the fear of being alone. In the colony, he'd had a few scary moments, but he had others, his own kind, around him to help. He felt more comfortable around humans than Tavies, although the Tavies had treated him very well. Any of the colonists, part-human and part-Tavie would probably have felt the same way he did on this planet. The Tavies had far more intelligence and mental abilities way beyond anyone of Billy's acquaintances in the colony. Zen and Qua, Billy's friends, had to have the same intelligence and mental abilities, but they refrained from using them in the colony.

Lunch was over, and everyone got up from the table to leave. The girl who had sat next to him looked at him as she walked away. He turned his head and looked at Zaia, trying not to even glance at the female. He'd had enough pain from her boyfriend. Zaia looked at the doorway of the narrow room, and Billy turned to see Zen and Qua walk in. Billy breathed deeply when he saw them.

The two Tavies motioned Billy to come to them. Billy moved quickly to join his friends.

Zen said to Billy, "Time to go back to work."

"Yes, sir," Billy replied. "I'm ready."

Billy thanked Zaia for the hospitality and bowed. Zaia nodded to him. Then Billy walked to the ship and boarded with Zen and Qua. He sat down in his seat, put his head back, and thanked God that he was going home.

He looked at the two Tavies navigating the ship and said to them, "Never have I ever been so glad to see someone in my whole life. Thanks again, guys."

The two Tavies looked at Billy and nodded. Nodding must be the Tavie "you're welcome" Billy decided.

In his short time on Tavus, Billy had learned a lot about his ancestors. One thing he had learned was that humans were very lucky that the Tavies were protecting the earth. He could not imagine any other planet in the universe with the intelligence of these aliens.

Billy was soon home safely and back in the main ship. As they entered the room where Philip was sitting, Billy looked at Philip and mentally said to him, "I understand now. Everything you said to me makes sense. Sorry, Philip, I won't make that mistake again."

Philip responded, "You never know how someone feels until you have been put into the same situation. Respect the people around you, Billy. You don't have to like them. Just respect them."

Billy returned to his quarters to unwind and tried to tune in on Jacy. His trip had been very stressful. As he lay back on his comfortable bed, he felt the love coming from Jacy to him and could not help but smile. She was alone. Her parents had gone back to Baton Rouge, and she was relaxing and thinking about Billy. Jacy's thoughts were coming in loud and clear for the first time since she had left the colony. Philip was allowing him to mentally communicate with her completely at last. Things were looking up once more.

Jacy enjoyed the quietness in the big house she had shared with her parents over the holidays. Now they were gone, and things would go back to normal. She would return to college and work with her grandmother in the evenings. But Jacy now also had something to look forward to. His name was William Joseph Hooper, but she would call him Billy. She would wait patiently until he contacted her; she knew he would. He had offered her a free plane trip. Maybe she would take him up on it.

Billy was happy. He hoped he would be allowed to see Jacy again soon because he was deeply in love. He would work hard and follow orders to prove to Philip he would not make any more mistakes.

It was the second week in February, and soon another celebration would take place in Louisiana. It was probably the biggest celebration next to Christmas—Mardi Gras. Every Cajun considered it a legal holiday. Schools, banks, and businesses closed so everyone could attend the many parades. In the small towns of Louisiana, people lined the streets, many barbecuing for family and friends, as they waited for the parades to start. The main street was cut off to traffic so everyone could visit with their friends and the children could play. There were loud bands playing in different sections of the city, and everyone danced.

Each year for Mardi Gras, Jacy and some of her girlfriends drove to Lake Charles, Louisiana, where the people were nice and the food was outstanding. The crawfish were in season, and Lake Charles had the best, whether boiled or in jambalaya or etouffee. Jacy and her friends always bought a strawberry king cake with cream cheese filling when they got into town. Whoever found the hidden baby in her piece had to drive home the next day.

This year only two of Jacy's friends could go to the parade with her. It was time to pull out the old Mardi Gras purple, green, and gold T-shirt and light-up beads and to practice the "Mardi Gras Mambo." It would be a good time in Lake Charles on Fat Tuesday.

Denise and Sharon, her longtime friends, picked Jacy up in the morning. They sang songs and relived happenings from the past on their short drive to Lake Charles. Upon their arrival, they went straight to the small deli with the best king cakes in town and purchased one. They would cut into the cake later when they got a room for the night.

After they found a room and put their luggage away, they headed for the street and waited for the parades to start. There had been parades and Mardi Gras balls going on over the past weekend, but the best parades were yet to come. Today was the merchants' parade. The merchants in town lined up their floats for free advertising while throwing beads, candy, and T-shirts to everyone lining the streets, but later that night would be the parade everyone looked forward to all year—the Krewe of Krewes parades.

The krewes were groups of people that picked out a theme for their krewe and wore costumes to represent it. The costumes were extreme. They were sequined, glittered, feathered, and made from the most expensive fabric the krewes could buy. With the costumes, they wore headdresses that were also feathered and glittered to perfection. The krewes all dressed according to their themes and threw beads, cups, candy, and krewe doubloons as their floats rolled by. The men and women of the krewes spent a lot of money on the costumes, and they were greatly appreciated by the spectators on the streets. Everyone was in awe when they passed.

The girls walked up the street and looked for family or friends to talk to before the merchants' parade began. They walked up and down the street until the police began to clear the streets for the floats. Everyone waited patiently. Finally, the first float arrived with Zydeco music blaring. The merchants threw goodies from the float, and people in the crowd screamed, "Throw me something, mister," as candy and beads came down in showers. Jacy and her friends jumped and stretched as they tried to catch the beads and laughed at each other while doing it. After the parade, the girls divided the beads they had caught so that they each had the same amount.

All the walking and jumping had caused the girls to work up an appetite. Sharon had family in Lake Charles who barbecued every year, so they headed in their direction. Jacy had never met Sharon's family before. When her two male cousins walked out to meet the girls, Jacy stopped dead in her tracks and stared at them. Sharon and Denise stopped also, but did not realize anything was wrong. Sharon introduced her cousins.

"Jacy and Denise, these are my cousins, Jeff and Robert Hooper."

The men looked just like Billy, and they shared the same last name. It had shocked Jacy. Could it be a coincidence?

Sharon's aunt and uncle welcomed the girls and set about trying to make them feel comfortable. They brought out folding chairs and made them each a plate of barbecue. Jacy had lost her appetite. She wanted to question them but thought it might be out of line.

She turned to Sharon and asked, "Do your aunt and uncle have another son named William Joseph Hooper?"

Mrs. Hooper overheard the question and answered, "No. But if I would have had another son, that is the name we would have given him, and we would have called him Billy." She smiled at Jacy and asked, "Do you know someone with that name?"

"Yes, ma'am, I do, and I just wondered if he was your kin."

Mrs. Hooper then pulled her chair close to Jacy and never left her side while the girls visited.

As the girls left, Sharon said, "Aunt Liz sure took a liking to you, Jacy. She asked me to bring you with me next time I come down."

"How are you kin to them, Sharon?" asked Jacy.

"Aunt Liz is my mom's sister. That's why we don't have the same last names. Something happened to you when we were walking up," said Sharon. "What was it?"

"Your cousins, Sharon, they bear a striking resemblance to a man I know, a man I'm very interested in romantically, and they have the same last name."

"What are the odds in that?" said Denise.

Sharon said, "Maybe they are distant kin and don't know each other."

"Maybe so," said Jacy." But I'll tell you, I really like your family. They feel special to me."

"Well," said Sharon, "we have that in common, Jacy. They're special to me too."

Denise looked at her friends and said, "Enough bonding. I don't want to miss the Krewe of Krewes parade. Let's find us a good place to stand."

As Jacy walked with her friends, she tried to make sense of what had just happened to her. Then the Krewe of Krewes parade started. The floats decorated with lights that twinkled in the night took her mind off the Hooper family for a while. The crowd went wild again, jumping for beads and anything else they could catch. In this parade, the beads were bigger, longer, and more plentiful. Jacy could not take her eyes off the gorgeous costumes worn by the krewes. They were exquisite.

When they returned home the next day, the girls were tired and in much need of rest. Jacy sat in the backseat by herself and thought of Billy. She thought about how he hadn't let Cameron intimidate him and how he had looked at her. She remembered his face against hers as they danced, and the best memory of all, the kiss they had shared before he left.

"You're home, Jacy!" Denise shouted.

Jacy opened her eyes. "Already?"

She got her luggage, told her friends good-bye, and thanked them for the ride. "Call me," she said as she walked to her door.

Jacy walked to her bedroom and was unpacking her suitcase when she noticed the business card Billy had given to her on the dresser. She picked it up and stared at the e-mail address.

"Should I?" she thought. "He said to contact him if I needed him. Where do I need to go? I need a destination. I can't call him for a free plane ride to nowhere—or maybe I can. I have never been on a small plane before. It would be a first time. I could tell him that. I'm going to do it."

She grabbed the heart around her neck for courage and headed to the computer room. She pulled the shelf out that held the keyboard and stopped.

"Should I call Grandmother and ask what she thinks of this idea? No, I'm going to keep it to myself, just in case he does not respond to my e-mail."

Jacy identified herself in the message and then requested that he pick her up the next day after lunch for her first airplane ride with him. She gave no destination. Then she leaned back in her chair and read the message over and over and said out loud, "I don't know. What if he thinks I'm forward?" Then she accidentally clicked and the e-mail was off. "Oh my God! I did it, and I can't take it back now."

Jacy stood up and moved her feet up and down while shaking her hands. "I can't believe I did that," she kept saying. "I've got to get out of here now." She grabbed her purse and went to meet her grandmother at the store.

"Hi, Jacy," said Macy. "Did you enjoy Mardi Gras in Lake Charles?"

"Yes, ma'am. I had a good time but as usual ate way too much."

"I don't think that should be a worry to you," said Macy.

"I got you some beads," said Jacy. She removed some beads from her neck and put them over her grandmother's head.

"Thanks for thinking about me, sweetie."

Jacy wanted to tell her grandmother what she had done but was afraid of what her response would be. Her mother definitely would not have agreed with her decision to contact Billy, but what was done was done. It was too late for opinions now.

"Will you be here tomorrow for work, Jacy?" asked Macy.

Jacy stopped and thought, "I forgot to tell him where to pick me up on the e-mail. I left no address for him. Well, that was a stupid thing for me to do, but I was so nervous." Then she said out loud, "Yes, Grandmother. I'll be here."

Billy could not pick her up if he had no address, and she could not e-mail him again. That was out. She felt embarrassed.

"We haven't been too busy," said Macy. "If you have other plans, you don't have to come in."

"No, Grandmother. I'll be here."

Philip was sitting in front of the monitor when Jacy's e-mail came across the screen. He looked at the message, and his human compassion kicked in. He knew this was a very complicated relationship, but Billy was not the only one in the colony that loved and yearned to see Jacy. His son and her uncle Samuel, Cindy, and her grandmother Lavern waited patiently for her return—hoping there would be a return. With Billy in control of himself now, maybe this was a good time for her to visit her loved ones in the colony.

Philip summoned Billy to report to him. Billy hurriedly responded to his command.

Philip said, "Billy, it's time Jacy returns for a visit."

"Really, Philip? She's coming here?" asked Billy.

"Yes," said Philip. "You will fly your plane to Yelgar tomorrow, walk to her grandmother's store, and tell her you received her e-mail and are there to take her for the ride she asked for. Understood?"

"Yes, sir," said Billy excitedly. "Yes, sir."

"Now go to Lavern, Cindy, and Samuel and tell them to prepare for Jacy's visit tomorrow," said Philip.

"I'm on my way," said Billy.

Billy patiently waited for Zen and Qua to return him to the colony. He saw them boarding their small ship and ran to meet them. He went aboard the ship with them, and they beamed him down to the colony.

It was afternoon in the colony. Cindy was still in school, so Billy looked for Samuel and Lavern. He soon saw them walking down the street. He stopped them, and Samuel smiled. He knew what Billy was about to say, but Lavern could not read his mind.

"Jacy is coming for a visit tomorrow, Lavern. She is returning to the colony. I am to pick her up at one o'clock in Yelgar."

"Good," said Lavern excitedly. "Goody, goody, goody. I'll see my granddaughter again."

Mark was standing close enough to the group to hear the conversation and could not help but join in.

"Let me tell Cindy," he said. "Please let me go and tell her. Cindy and I must plan a welcome to show Jacy how much Cindy loves her."

Samuel agreed with Mark. "Go, Mark. Go and tell Cindy the good news. Her heart will be filled with joy."

Mark went to Cindy in the facility below ground. He called her out of class, and she ran to him.

"Jacy's coming tomorrow!" she screamed. "Mark, I love her. She's my friend."

Mark picked Cindy up. Her small body was shaking with happiness. Mark and Cindy had to plan a welcome for Jacy.

Lavern and Samuel very excitedly spread the good news throughout the colony so everyone could be there to meet Jacy on her return. Carol had news to share with Jacy. She had followed her advice about Louis, and now they were dating. Her life was happy thanks to Jacy's speech on self-confidence.

Jacy's stay at the colony had touched many hearts, and now she was returning for a visit. It was another reason to celebrate in Cajun Country. A loved one returning home for a visit was as good a reason as any. Billy would stay in the colony the rest of the day and spend the night. It felt good to him to be back with his friends in the colony.

Billy went back to the laboratory where he had spent so much of his time and looked at the beautiful babies coming into the world. Wendy, the baby Jacy had seen in the lab, was now living with her parents in the colony. Hopefully her parents would bring her to greet Jacy. Jacy loved Wendy, Miss Susan's child.

Night had arrived, and Jacy had no idea what was going on in the colony. She believed Billy would not know where to find her because she had not put an address on the e-mail she had sent. The next day would just be another day in Yelgar for her. She would get up and go to work. It was still Mardi Gras holiday, so there was no college.

In the morning Jacy got ready for her long day at the store. Macy would have fresh coffee and doughnuts waiting for her when she arrived, so she was out the door quickly.

"Hi, Grandmother. I'm here," said Jacy. "What do you want me to do?"

"Have coffee and doughnuts before you do anything," Macy answered.

As the customers started to come in, Jacy and Macy went to work.

Billy was dressed and waiting for his okay from Philip to board the plane and head for Yelgar. It was almost noon, so the order should be coming soon. Billy paced back and forth on the pavement; he was very ready to go. Zen and Qua's small ship rose up to hover above him. That was his signal to go. He boarded the plane once more and headed toward Yelgar.

Once he arrived, he had twenty minutes to walk to the store to get Jacy. He thought about jogging but did not want to get sweaty. Instead, he walked at a fast pace. Many cars passed him as he walked on the side of the road. Some of the drivers waved as they passed.

Macy was behind the counter and happened to be looking out of the curtained window when she saw Billy coming.

"Jacy!" she called. "Hurry and come here. I think I see the young man you met at the park on New Year's Eve."

"What?" said Jacy as she ran to the window. "It's him, Grandmother! It's him! What am I going to do?"

"What are you going to do?" said Macy as she peeked out the window. "Look at him, Jacy. He walks so proudly with his shoulders back, head up, and chest out. He has all the confidence of a marine going into battle. I like him. He's a keeper."

Jacy talked out loud to herself, "How did he know where to find me?"

Macy heard her and remarked, "Well, that would not be too hard to do. Everyone in Yelgar knows you work here. All he would have to do is ask someone."

"Grandmother, I e-mailed him to come to take me on a plane ride."

"You e-mailed him, so I guess you're going to take that plane ride today," said Macy.

"How do I look, Grandmother?" asked Jacy.

She answered, "You look good, as always. Calm down, Jacy. He's almost here."

"What do I say to him?" asked Jacy.

"Say hello, Jacy. Shake his hand. Tell him thanks for responding to your e-mail."

The door opened, and Jacy stood in shock.

Macy walked up to Billy and said, "It's good to see you again." Then she asked him to take a seat.

Jacy finally unfroze and said, "Hi, Billy."

He motioned for her to sit by him. She walked over and took the seat next to him.

He said, "I got your e-mail and was so glad to hear from you. I would be honored to take you anywhere you want to go."

Jacy looked at his handsome face as he spoke to her and chills ran down her body. "Oh no, not again," she thought. She was afraid to speak because she could not keep a chain of thought when he was around. She was afraid only gibberish would come out of her mouth.

Macy knew Jacy was very nervous, so she started a conversation with Billy until Jacy could calm down. Macy told him that Jacy was her granddaughter and how special she was to her and her grandfather. Then she talked about the weather. She was running out of things to talk about, but she did not want to make him uncomfortable with questions.

When she finally had control of her emotions, Jacy stood up and asked Billy if he wanted something to drink before they left.

"No thank you, Jacy," he said. "I'm ready to go if you are."

"I'm ready," she said as she grabbed her purse from behind the counter. She hugged her grandmother and whispered thanks in her ear.

"Have a good time," said Macy as the two walked out the door.

Jacy walked to her car and said to Billy, "Let's drive to the airport instead of walking."

"Whatever makes you happy."

They said very little to each other as she drove to the airport. Then they got out of the car and boarded the airplane. Billy helped Jacy put on her seatbelt. She looked down at his gloved hands while he buckled it. He touched her nose when he was through.

Billy started the engine, and they were ready for takeoff. Jacy looked straight ahead and thought, "I never told him where I wanted to go. Who cares? Just sitting here next to him is good enough."

Once in the air, Billy looked at Jacy and said, "How about a ride over the swamp?"

"I would like that," said Jacy. He reached over and grabbed her hand. As she looked out the side window, she could see the boats scattered through the swamp. She then looked out the windshield and saw the bright light bordering the colony.

She pointed at it and said, "I've seen that light before."

"I know you have, Jacy," he answered.

As the small plane entered the light, Jacy screamed, "Billy! Billy, I love you!" She bounced up and down in her seat, even though she was still buckled in. "Uncle Samuel, Grandmother, Cindy. Oh my God. I want to see them. Hurry! Land the plane."

After Billy landed the plane and they got out, Zen and Qua were there to pick them up in a beam of light and deliver them to town where everyone was waiting for them.

Jacy and Billy stepped out of the beam, and to her surprise Cindy was standing right in front of her. Samuel was on one side of her, and Lavern was on the other. A young man in jeans and a T-shirt stood on a bandstand and played guitar with a small band behind him. Mark and seven other children stood behind Cindy.

The young man on the bandstand sang, and Cindy and the other children began to dance, keeping in step with each other. The children kept in beat by swinging back and forth. Then they pointed at the heavens and touched their hearts as they pointed at Jacy. Cindy laughed out loud and stared at Jacy, her hair swinging as she moved.

Jacy's eyes teared up, and soon she was crying large teardrops that streamed down her face. They were tears of joy as she looked around at her family that she loved so much. The tears kept coming while she watched the children perform. She knew she was the one that had been blessed by the grace of God.

As she watched the children, she noticed Mark had on a cowboy hat and that he moved to the music as the children danced. She knew he had to have been the coordinator of the event. As the song ended, he raised his hands to the heavens and looked upward as he sang, "I'd be lost but for the grace of God."

When the song stopped, Cindy ran up to Jacy and kissed her face and hugged her. Jacy picked her up and told her how happy she was to be in the colony again. Then Lavern came up and hugged Jacy and Cindy, holding them tight. Samuel just stood next to her and smiled.

"Oh no," Jacy said, "you're going to hug me." She gave Samuel a big hug while she held Cindy.

Mark came up to Jacy and said, "Glad to have you back."

"Thank you, Mark. And thanks for the children's performance. I loved it."

"And you're welcome," he said.

Billy said, "Let's dance, Jacy." Jacy put Cindy down and watched her run off to play with the other children. The two held each other tightly as everyone watched.

After spending time with her loved ones, Jacy and Billy took a walk to be alone. There was much to be said between them. Billy started the conversation by telling Jacy of his travels with the protectors. He told her he was no longer based in the colony but lived on the main ship. Then he went on to tell her about his punishment from Philip after what he had done to Cameron and how scared he had been during his visit to Tavus. He had thought he would never see her again.

Jacy smiled as she remembered his trip to Yelgar on New Year's Eve.

"I knew deep down inside," said Jacy. "when I looked into your eyes, Billy, that I loved you. Not Cameron or anyone else could have taken my mind off you."

"He was trying," said Billy. "He said he was your boyfriend, and he asked me all those personal questions that were none of his business."

Jacy smiled and agreed. "It was funny how you handled him, especially when his car alarm went off. I knew you had something to do with it somehow."

"Well it wasn't funny to Philip, and I'll think hard next time before I act on jealousy."

"What next time, Billy? What does our future hold?" asked Jacy.

"Our future is not in our hands, Jacy. You know that. We will love each other and hope we can continue our relationship in both worlds. I believe one day we'll be together. We've come this far, and our love has remained strong."

Jacy grabbed the heart around her neck and looked at Billy. "Now I know why this means so much to me. I've never taken it off."

"Seeing you with that token of love from me hanging around your neck got me through a lot of very sad and lonesome times while I missed you," said Billy.

"Many times while watching you on my communicator, I wanted to tune in on your subconscious so you could communicate with me. I was really tempted. But the minute I would have done it, Philip would have intervened and taken my communicator away. As a matter of fact, he sometimes cut off my contact with you for days just because I had thought about it. There are no secrets in this colony."

"I felt like someone was trying to communicate with me mentally several times. Now I know it was you, Billy. I heard you, Billy. I heard you say you loved me. My grandmother thought I was losing my mind because I was responding to the voice in my head," said Jacy.

"It was me, and I was glad when I could see that you heard me. It gave me hope that somehow you remembered our love that we share," said Billy.

Jacy and Billy sat down on a bench by the water. He put his arm around her and kissed her passionately, something he had yearned to do for a very long time. Jacy hugged him tightly, enjoying the moment.

Then Billy pulled back and looked into Jacy's eyes. "You have to go back tonight."

Jacy replied, "I know Philip won't let me stay. It's probably for the best. I wouldn't want to put my family through the misery of another disappearance."

They got up from the bench and continued to walk without speaking to each other. Jacy had never been in this area of the colony before. They must have walked at least three miles. She could see what looked like large barns in the distance. She had not seen any livestock on the island and wondered what the buildings could be. She didn't ask Billy. It looked like he was in deep concentration.

Getting a little tired from the walk, Jacy dropped to her knees and wrote Billy's name in the sand with her finger. She then lay on the ground with her arm behind her head, and Billy joined her.

"What are we doing?" asked Billy.

"Looking at the great beyond," said Jacy, "and how wonderful it is. Where is Tavus?"

Billy pointed at the western sky. "Around there," he said. They both lay quietly and stared into the universe.

Jacy turned her head to the side and saw something that made her sit up and grab for Billy.

"What is it? Billy asked.

Jacy pointed at a creature and screamed, "It's Bigfoot!"

The creature made a whistling noise and ran away from them.

"Calm down, Jacy. He's harmless. He lives here."

Billy looked toward the creature, and it turned and walked back to them. Jacy held Billy's hand very tightly as the creature approached. He was at least eight feet tall and had long, chocolate-colored hair on his head. His humanlike face was covered with what looked like whisker stubble, and the rest of his human-looking body was covered with long hair the same color as the hair on his head. His body had no alien features. His face and body looked human except that they were covered with hair, and he had very big feet.

The creature stood in front of Billy. They were mentally communicating.

"Why doesn't he talk?" asked Jacy.

"They don't talk like we do. They whistle to each other and speak to us mentally."

The creature looked at Jacy, whistled, and walked off.

Billy pulled on Jacy's hand as he followed the creature.

"I'm going to show you where they live."

"Is it safe?" asked Jacy.

Billy laughed. "Yes, it's safe."

They were getting closer to the barns that Jacy had seen earlier. As they reached the structures, Jacy could see at least fifty of the creatures all around. The creatures looked in their direction, and some came closer. There were groups of men, women, and children. It was apparent that they were families.

"The creatures are called Raspas," said Billy. They are from a small planet called Raspard. They are harmless, passive creatures unless provoked. Their planet was attracting many other aliens because of its location. Millions of Raspas were being killed as their world was invaded. They had no means of defending themselves, so our ships moved them off their planet and placed them in our colonies on Earth.

"These creatures have never evolved. They are somewhat like cavemen. They will always be the way they are now. They need protection, as they cannot protect themselves."

"How long have they lived in your colonies, Billy?"

"Well, how long have people on Earth been spotting Big Foot, Sasquatch, and the Abominable Snowman?"

"A long time," said Jacy.

"They have been on Earth even longer than that, Jacy. Many, many years."

Billy took Jacy into a large barn where a family was eating raw fish with their large hands. Billy told Jacy that the Raspas were like animals and did not eat cooked food. Unlike the Tavies, they could eat meat and ate birds and small animals from the swamp. Billy pointed at a large garden that was in the process of being planted and told Jacy that the townspeople planted seasonal gardens for them. This kept them from wandering too far in search of food and from being spotted by humans.

Billy explained, "They know if they are spotted by a human that they are to go back through the light of the colony immediately. For sure, the hunt would be on for Big Foot by the townspeople.

"We had such an episode during the Civil War, in 1864. I read about it in the library. The Confederate soldiers were being pushed deep into the swamp by the Union soldiers. The swamp was a safe haven for the Confederate soldiers. The Union soldiers would not follow them because they knew they had no chance of survival. The Confederates would regroup in the swamp before returning to battle.

"Some of the worn-out Confederate soldiers would linger for months in the swamp, trapping and fishing for survival. One evening, just as the sun started going down, four men in a pirogue found a patch of dry land and decided to make a fire and stay a while. They climbed out of their boat and tied it to a stump. As they sat down and started building their fire, a family of Raspas stood up. The men were in shock at the sight of the huge hairy beings. Three of the men just sat still, but the fourth one picked up his musket.

"The Raspas ran away from them. The man with the rifle aimed it at the female Raspa and pulled the trigger. The other men tried to stop him from firing the gun. The Raspas were not trying to hurt them; they were leaving. They were too late. The female Raspa fell to the ground. The other Raspas stopped and turned around. The male Raspa whistled a blood-curdling shrieking noise as the children kneeled by their hurt mother.

"The man with the musket tried to reload as the other three men sat still in shock. The male Raspa walked up to the man and took his musket out of his hands as the man tried to crawl away from him. The

Raspa broke the musket into two parts and threw it into the swamp. He then picked up the man and threw him in the same direction. He broke a lot of his bones when he hit the trees. The male Raspa looked at the other three men but did not harm them as they had not tried to harm him or his family.

"The female Raspa was still alive. The male picked her up, and the family walked quickly back to the colony. A doctor was summoned, and her life was saved.

"The four men left quickly. They climbed back into the boat and picked up their friend's crumpled body from the middle of the swamp. The shooter was in quite a bit of pain for many months while his broken bones mended. The men told their story to anyone that would listen, but most people thought it was unbelievable. After too much moonshine, people could imagine anything.

"Since that incident, they don't wander too far into the swamp," said Billy. "They are still spotted every once in a while, but they manage to get out of sight as quickly as possible. Some humans, though not all, will kill anything that looks different from them. That is why Tavies and Raspas keep their distance.

"Many years ago, the Indian tribes that lived in these swamp areas actually befriended the Raspas. They called them 'Sasquatch.' They didn't visit with each other or have powwows; they just respected each other's space. If the Indians saw them feeding in an area, they would go around them. They looked at the Raspas as a dominating race of people because of their size.

"Close to the Tavie colonies high in the mountains live the Raspas that humans call the

"Abominable Snowman." They have thick white hair on their bodies to blend in with their environment. Most of them stay close to the colonies for food because it is hard to obtain in the freezing temperatures, but as always, many wander away from their protected home. Most of the colonies are located high in the mountains where there is not a lot of human activities. But the Raspas are still spotted by hunting and trapping parties.

"Many of these humans try to convince themselves that Raspas are kin to polar bears, but because of the Raspas' upright position when they walk and their facial features, many humans are not convinced.

"Scientists and actual Bigfoot hunters have spent many years studying and trying to understand more about this being. The secrecy is still necessary to keep them safe, but one day all questions about the large hairy creature will be answered. Bigfoot will be introduced to the world."

"Those barns are huge," said Jacy.

"Yes," said Billy. "They were built to protect them from the elements, like winter rains and bad lightning storms. They prefer sleeping on the ground under the stars. Each family cuddles up at night when they sleep.

"The Raspas choose a mate at about eighteen years old and live with that mate their entire lives. They never have more than two offspring. Their lifetime is about one hundred years."

"Do they ever go into the colony where the people live?" asked Jacy.

"No," said Billy. "They mostly go into the swamp area that's protected by the surrounding light, which keeps dangerous reptiles from coming close to the colony for about a mile out. Sometimes the older Raspas looking for food wander deep into the swamp but manage to always come back unharmed. If a full-grown Raspa slapped an alligator, the alligator would die instantly. Their strength is amazing, probably fifty times stronger than the strongest man."

Billy pointed at the swamp area and said, "Notice anything different out there?"

"I see very few stumps and trees," said Jacy.

"Exactly," said Billy. "That's because when a fish or turtle the Raspa is after for lunch hides in the roots, they pull the tree or stump up to get it. Can you imagine pulling a tree up by the roots?"

"No. That is some strength," said Jacy.

Two of the Raspa children walked up to Jacy. One held a giant bullfrog. Jacy took a step back as the small child handed the frog to her. She took the frog and petted the small child on the head. Being a bayou woman, Jacy was not squeamish about holding the frog. The child just stood and looked at Jacy.

Billy said, "She's waiting for you to eat it."

"Yuck," said Jacy. "I won't do it. But thanks anyway."

Billy took the frog from Jacy and mentally told the children that Jacy was not hungry. Then he released the frog. The children whistled as they watched the frog hop away and then returned to their group.

"Billy," said Jacy as they walked away from the Raspas, "I have learned something new every day that I have been in this colony."

"You have much more to learn, Jacy. I have answers for all of your unanswered questions," said Billy. "All the strange things that have happened on earth that no human has an answer for, we know all the answers, and so will you as soon as the time is right."

"If you say so, Billy," said Jacy as they walked back into town.

Cindy was waiting for Jacy at the entrance of the town and ran toward her as they approached. Jacy picked her up and kissed her on the cheek as she sat on a bench next to Billy.

Cindy looked into Jacy's eyes and asked, "Are you still my best friend?"

"Yes, ma'am," said Jacy. "I will always be your best friend, Cindy. I love you, little girl."

"Do you love Billy?" asked Cindy.

"Yes, but in a different way," said Jacy. "He's my boyfriend, my handsome prince, like in the Cinderella movie."

Cindy smiled at Billy and said, "I will have a handsome prince one day."

Billy looked at Jacy and then answered, "I'm sure your handsome prince is waiting for you.

Both Jacy and Billy knew that when Cindy became an adult her powers would be triple what they were now. It would take a man with equal powers to be her prince. Only a pure-blooded Tavie could even come close.

Jacy, Billy, and Cindy walked back into town where Lavern and Samuel were waiting.

Jacy looked at them and said, "I'm so happy to see y'all again. If only…"

Jacy stopped in midsentence as sadness covered her face. She put her head down.

Lavern grabbed her hand and said, "Let's just enjoy your stay, Jacy. Come with us. Big Ben has prepared supper."

They entered the restaurant, and Big Ben met them at the door.

"Welcome, Jacy," he said as he showed them to their table.

Carol was sitting at the table already. Next to her sat a young man with human looks. Carol stood up and welcomed Jacy back and then introduced her to her boyfriend, Louis.

Jacy winked at Carol and told Louis she was pleased to meet him. Mark was sitting next to Carol, and beside him was the couple that Jacy had met in the laboratory with baby Wendy.

"Hello, everyone," Jacy said. Then she walked over to hold the baby, Miss Susan's baby.

Baby Wendy was precious. She was sitting up now and got excited when she saw Jacy. She clapped her hands and touched Jacy's face as she jabbered words of excitement.

Jacy gave the baby back to her parents and took her seat at the table. Billy sat on one side of her, and Cindy sat on the other. Lavern and Samuel were seated next to them. Jacy sat still while she looked at the friends and family around the table that she held so close to her heart. Beings from two worlds had come together, sharing love and respect for each other.

Big Ben and a waitress brought out the appetizers—oysters wrapped and grilled with spinach and large shrimp baked on a thick slice of tomato. The waitress filled the water glasses as everyone enjoyed the company and food. A cup of seafood gumbo followed the appetizers, complete with filé and rice.

"No salad today," said Big Ben. "We are going to the main course."

The waitress set large plates on the table as Big Ben brought out big bowls of shrimp jambalaya, crawfish bisque, catfish court bouillon, and rice. The food was delicious, and everyone complimented the cook.

When supper was over, Jacy stood and thanked Big Ben for all the time and effort he had put into cooking the wonderful meal.

"It was delicious," she said. "In my world, to show my appreciation, I would leave you a big tip."

Big Ben smiled at Jacy and said no tip was necessary as he knew she had no money. But Jacy knew that money was not important in the colonies. Everyone had everything they needed to live a good life.

Everyone left the restaurant, and Jacy and Billy were alone once more. They sat on a bench in the middle of town and talked about things past.

"I met your family, Billy," said Jacy. "They live in Lake Charles, where I go to Mardi Gras every year. I liked them. They are very nice, and your brothers look like you, very handsome."

"Thanks," said Billy. "They are very nice, and I'm glad you met them. I sometimes watch them and wonder what life with them would have been like. My brothers are good Christians, hard-working men, and I'm proud of them. But they have their lives, and I have mine."

Suddenly a thick fog rolled over the island. It rose above the roofs of the houses and blocked out the sky.

Jacy said, "I've seen fog roll in before, but never this fast."

"It's camouflage," said Billy. "This area is being investigated by your people. There have been many sightings of spaceships in the swamp area—more than usual. There are high-tech planes that fly around taking pictures of the swamp as we speak. And they have swamp buggies and airboats all over looking for anything unusual. It's dusk now; their favorite time of the day to investigate."

"Why do the spaceships let themselves be seen?" asked Jacy.

"Earth needs to know we are here, Jacy. Our ships will always be seen and have always been since the beginning of our time on earth. Humans know we are here; they just can't find us. You may think humans are frightened by these sightings, but most aren't," said Billy.

"What would happen if they did find you and if the plane got a picture of the colony?" asked Jacy.

"Their instruments are incapacitated when they approach the colony. If they stumbled into the colony uninvited, they would be escorted out unharmed. They would forget everything they saw as they exited the light. No problem," said Billy. "Every colony in the world is pursued by humans. We know every move they are going to make before they make it, so it's never going to happen.

"Humans and Tavies meet often. Our best allies of protection are humans. They don't really want to find the colonies. They are just doing the jobs expected of them. Miss Susan, for instance, with her far-fetched tales of encounters with aliens, protected me and my secret while I was at the New Year's Eve celebration. She knew I was not human. She felt it. I could tell in the car when I was talking to her. But she said nothing and led me to you. Our love for each other was apparent to her. She knows, Jacy. Just believe me, she knows.

"When the investigators see the fog, they will not enter it. Fog is a killer in the swamp. You can't see a foot in front of you. Remaining still is the only way to survive it," said Billy.

Jacy looked in disbelief at the thick soupy fog. It didn't seem to bother any of the colonists. They continued on with their regular activities. The fog stayed in the perimeter surrounding the colony. They could hear the searchers in the swamp and sky. They were all around, but none entered the thick fog.

Billy pulled Jacy close to him and kissed her.

"I wish I could hold you forever and never let you go. You make me happy, Jacy, an emotion I didn't know I had. When you're not around, all I do is think of you and wonder how and when I will see you again. My life will never be the same as it was before meeting you. I have needs now, something I never had before. My need is you. I need you completely, as a man needs a woman. I would do anything for you."

Jacy hugged Billy and said, "I love you completely and will love you forever. Nothing will ever change my feelings for you. Please try and contact me more often, Billy. I really miss you. I dread going home because I don't know how long it will be before I see you again."

The two leaned their shoulders against each other and remained quiet. It should have been dark, especially with the fog cutting off the light from the moon and stars, but a yellow beam of light shone from one end of the colony to the other, providing a soft, dim light.

Jacy looked up at the dimmed light and jokingly asked, "Is this your back-up generator?" Billy nodded his head yes and smiled.

Suddenly Billy stood up and looked straight ahead. Jacy knew he was having a conversation with someone mentally. She just sat quietly so she wouldn't interfere with his concentration. Watching his facial expressions, she could tell that whatever they were discussing was pleasing to him. Then he looked down at her, grabbed her hands, and pulled her up.

"What is it?" asked Jacy.

"Jacy," said Billy, "good news. Philip just informed me that in May, when you are out of college for the summer, you will be welcome to stay in the colony for as long as you want and visit other colonies in the world with us."

"Really?" said Jacy. "I can't wait. Are you sure he said for as long as I want?"

"Yes, Jacy, meaning your summer vacation time. Of course you will have to convince your parents and grandparents that you are going on a vacation so they will not worry."

"I can do that," said Jacy.

"Good," said Billy as he picked Jacy up off the ground and sat her back down in excitement.

"You're very strong," said Jacy. "I'm impressed. I should tell my grandmother and Cindy the good news."

"No need. They know," said Billy. "I can feel their excitement."

"Billy," said Jacy, "does this mean I can't see you for the next two months?"

"Two months will go by very quickly, Jacy. You have your studies and helping your grandmother with the store.

"Your life will return to normal when you get home, with a few exceptions. You will plan a trip for the summer and inform your family. When the time comes, I will call you on the phone to meet me in a location. You will drive there, and we will pick you up in a small spaceship. Your car will be brought to the island until you are ready to return home."

"I'll inform my family as soon as I return home that I'm taking a summer vacation with you, Billy. They may not like the idea, thinking I barely know you. They'll just have to trust me. I'm of age to do as I want, and I want to be with you," said Jacy.

"Jacy," said Billy, "if you get lonely, touch your necklace. Our love for each other will fill your mind, and your sadness will go away. That necklace is our communicator. Never take it off."

"I've had a wonderful time, Billy. I'm so happy when I'm here."

Cindy approached once more with her arms out for Jacy to hold her. Jacy hugged her tightly and told her she must return home but would see her again soon.

In a soft voice, Cindy said, "I want to go home with you."

Jacy just held her. She wished that was possible, but she knew it was completely out of the question.

She answered Cindy with the only thing that came to mind, "Lavern and Samuel would be very sad if you left them. They love you very much. Would you want to make them sad?"

"I'll stay," said Cindy. "Lavern would cry for me."

"Just remember, Cindy, I will be back," Jacy assured her.

Billy touched Cindy on the head and told her it was bedtime. She must go home. Cindy hugged

Jacy's neck and jumped off her lap, waving good-bye as she skipped home.

The fog was clearing, and Jacy and Billy saw a small ship lingering above them.

Jacy said, "I guess it's time to go."

"Yes," said Billy. "We will be taken back to the plane."

As he held her hand, a beam of light took them up to the ship. Zen and Qua were the navigators. Jacy was happy to see the Tavies she had met and befriended in the colony.

Once delivered to the plane, Billy and Jacy boarded. He started the motor, and the two buckled their seatbelts without speaking. They knew that when they went through the light their relationship would be very different when they emerged. Billy placed his hand on Jacy's head and told her he was placing a memory of the trip in her mind. She would remember flying around the swamp and the surrounding towns.

As the plane took off, Jacy closed her eyes, and they went through the light. When they came out, she turned to Billy and shyly said, "This has been a wonderful, scenic trip. My first plane ride has been very enjoyable. Thanks so much, Billy."

Billy looked Jacy in the eyes and spoke from his heart, "I'm crazy about you, Jacy. You're all I think about. Would you please spend the summer with me? I'm not asking for a commitment. Just think about it. I will fly you state to state and maybe country to country. Please say yes."

Jacy sat upright and answered, "You're special to me in every way. Yes, I will spend the summer with you."

Billy landed the plane at the Yelgar airport and walked Jacy to her car, holding her hand. She opened the car door and started to get in, but Billy turned her around and kissed her—a kiss to be remembered.

"I'll keep in touch," said Billy. Then he turned and walked away.

Billy climbed aboard the plane and sensed that something wrong. It was something with his family, his human family. His older brother Jeff was a crop duster. He was in trouble—bad trouble. Billy closed his eyes and could see his brother lying outside a plane crash, half alive. He took off from the airport, and instead of heading back to the colony, he climbed to dangerous heights, knowing Zen and Qua would rescue him.

When the spaceship retrieved the small plane, Billy pleaded with the Tavies to take him to his brother. Zen and Qua knew it was against the rules. But rules were made to be broken, even if there were consequences.

Zen said to Billy, "We will deliver you to the crash site, but then you are on your own. We will pick you up when you have completed your mission. Do not have any close contact with any human but your brother. We will have you on the monitor at all times."

"Good luck, Billy," said Qua.

When they reached the crash site, Billy was beamed down. Billy could feel what his brother felt, and he knew he was in trouble. His brother had been crop dusting a field in a nearby small town. The field had many trees nearby. As he looked back toward the crop to make sure the pesticides were being released, he had flown his plane into a tree and crashed. He had been thrown from the plane. His body was limp, and he was bleeding all over. He had been lying hurt for at least three hours. He was partially conscious and barely alive. Billy knelt down by his brother and checked to make sure his neck was not broken. He could have healed Jeff on the spot, but that would not be acceptable in either world.

After checking for broken bones and finding none, Billy picked his brother up and threw him over his shoulder using all the strength he had plus extra from his mind. He started walking down a dirt road, heading toward the nearest hospital in Lake Charles. His walk became a steady trot, but he tried not to shake his brother's hurt body too much.

Billy saw lights behind him. It was an old man in a beat-up rickety pickup truck. The old man stopped and motioned for Billy to climb on the back. Billy laid his brother on the truck bed and jumped on. Jeff barely opened his eyes as Billy looked down at him. Jeff tried to speak but could not. He was in and out of consciousness.

"Hi, Jeff," said Billy. "You are going to be all right. I'm going to make sure of it. We are almost to the hospital." Then he touched his brother's face for the first time in his life.

The old man stopped in front of the hospital's emergency room, and Billy picked his brother up once more from the bed of the truck to bring him inside. He yelled thank you to the old man, and the old man drove away. Billy held his brother in his arms as he stood in the hospital emergency room and waited for someone to help him. Two nurses came through the double doors with a gurney. Billy held and stared at his brother.

One of the nurses said, "You can lay him down. You must be tired. He looks heavy."

Billy looked at her and answered, "He ain't heavy; he's my brother!"

Jeff had come to once more, and he heard Billy's remark. Billy put Jeff down carefully, hugged his broken body, and left the hospital. The nurses tried to stop him to get information, but when he walked out the door, he was beamed up by Zen and Qua.

"Where did he go?" the nurses asked each other. "He just totally disappeared into the darkness."

As Jeff was rushed into emergency surgery, Billy was brought back to the colony once more for disobeying the rules. This time, Billy did not care what happened to him. The wonderful feeling of touching and being able to help his brother was overwhelming. But Zen and Qua could face consequences because of his actions. Billy did not want that.

Back on the main ship, Billy, Zen, and Qua made their way to the main deck. As they entered, no one acknowledged them. Philip was looking at the screen before him.

Then he turned his chair and said, "It's time to get to work. I think we have some trouble with unfriendly aliens in England."

Billy took a deep breath and waited for his orders. Zen and Qua took over their jobs of navigating the ship. All three men were very quiet. Philip summoned Billy, and he reported to him with his head down.

Philip said, "What you did for your brother was good. You did it out of love, and this is not the first time a Tavie has helped a family member in need. It's all forgiven. You are human, Billy. That's a fact. Now get in uniform, and let's do our job of protecting your kind."

Billy sighed with relief and headed toward his living quarters to get in uniform. While in his room, he focused his monitor on the emergency room where he had left his brother. The doctors were working on him, and they were in agreement that he would be all right—thanks to his brother who had brought him to the hospital just in time. Jeff had internal bleeding. If he had lain bleeding one more hour, he would have died. Billy had saved his brother's life. It made him feel closer to his family and more a part of it.

Jeff was married and had one child. His wife and parents were contacted and told of the accident. They all rushed to the hospital, except for Jeff's brother Robert. He was out of town on business and would not return for a week.

Jeff's doctor assured the family that he would have a quick recovery thanks to his brother delivering him to the hospital in time. The family all looked at each other and told the doctor that his only brother was out of town, so that was not possible. The doctor then told the family that he was sorry. The nurses must have misunderstood the young man that had brought him in. Then he excused himself and went back to his duties.

Jeff's mother and father took his four-year-old son Logan home with them for the night so his wife Megan could spend the night at the hospital with her husband. She wanted to be next to him when he woke from his deep sleep.

When morning came, Jeff opened his eyes and turned his head toward his wife.

Megan kissed him on the cheek and said, "Welcome back."

Jeff said, "It's good to be back. Where is he?"

"Who?" asked Megan.

"The young man that saved my life. The man that brought me to the hospital."

There was a knock at the door before Megan could answer him. It was Jeff's parents and son. As they approached the bed, Jeff kept talking about the man that had saved his life.

He looked at his parents and asked, "Is there something you're hiding from me?"

"Like what, Jeff?" asked his father.

"Like a younger brother," said Jeff.

"What are you talking about, son?" asked his father.

"The man that brought me to the hospital told the nurses he was my brother. 'He ain't heavy; he's my brother.' That's what he said. He held me close to him until the nurses brought out a gurney. We had a connection; I could feel it. I crashed and was thrown into a wooded area. It would have taken days to find me. I would be dead now, but somehow he found me. He just walked up. He had no car or means of transportation. How did he know?"

The room got quiet. No one could think of anything to say.

Tears came to Jeff's eyes. "I don't think I'll ever see him again. I'll never be able to thank him."

Logan climbed on the bed next to his father and hugged him. As Jeff looked into his son's eyes, he thanked God he was alive. Then the family all bowed their heads.

Time crept by slowly as Jacy marked each day off her calendar. She had returned to her life in Yelgar, working with her grandmother in the evenings and going to school during the day. She tried to keep her mind off Billy.

Jacy was waiting for the right time to tell her grandmother her plans for the summer with Billy. It was the first of May now, so she must tell her soon. Dreading her grandmother's reactions was bad, but telling her mother Lucille would be a lot worse. Maybe she would let her grandmother tell her mother.

Jacy sat in her car and thought about how she was going to break the news of her trip to her grandmother. She had to tell her today. She would be out of school in two weeks. She opened her car door very slowly and stepped out, still in deep thought. As she walked to the door, Macy opened it for her. Jacy looked surprised and stunned.

"What's wrong?" asked Macy. "You look like you've seen a ghost."

"Nothing's wrong," said Jacy. "I just need to tell you something. Something I'm dreading."

"What could be that bad?" asked Macy.

"It's not bad," said Jacy. "It's just something I think you will have a problem with."

"Tell me," said Macy. Then she sat down in a rocking chair next to the door.

Jacy sat down and turned to her grandmother. She looked her in the eyes and asked, "Do you remember Billy? I met him at the park, and later he took me on a plane ride into the swamp."

"Are you kidding?" asked Macy. "What woman could forget that handsome man?" She laughed.

"It's not funny, Grandmother. This is serious."

"Okay," said Macy, "out with it. But please tell me you're not pregnant."

"No," said Jacy. "That's ridiculous."

"It happens," said Macy as she dramatically wiped her forehead and shook her hand.

"Here it goes," said Jacy. "I'm spending the summer with Billy."

Macy looked at Jacy and put her hands out with her palms up. "What's so bad about that? We will be glad to have him around this summer."

"No," said Jacy, "you've misunderstood me, Grandmother. I'm going to go with him. We will be flying and making visits to all the states. I will be gone all summer."

Macy looked at Jacy once more and asked, "You're not serious, are you? Have you lost your mind? You've only met this man twice in your life, and now you're going to take off into the wild blue yonder with him? I don't think so. Your mother would have a heart attack if she knew you were even thinking of doing such a thing."

"Don't do this, Grandmother. Please don't make it hard on me. Billy is good, and I think I love him."

"You 'think,' Jacy?" asked Macy. "I agree he is a very nice young man, but we do not know anything about him. Nothing. What if he's a criminal?"

"He's not," said Jacy. "I would know. I'm going. I've always listened to you, Grandmother, but this time you're going to have to trust my instincts."

Macy walked over to the phone and picked up the receiver. She dialed Lucille's phone number.

"Here," she said as she handed the phone to Jacy. "Tell your mother. She has a right to know."

Lucille answered the phone, and Jacy said, "Hello, Mother. How are you?" She and her mother made small talk for a few minutes and then Jacy finally said, "I'm going out of town with Billy this summer—all summer."

Lucille was quiet, and Jacy froze. After a while, Lucille asked, "Did I hear you right? You're leaving town with a man you hardly know? Have you been drinking? You must reconsider this, Jacy."

"No," said Jacy. "I'm going and looking forward to it."

"I'm leaving today," said Lucille, "and driving to Yelgar."

"No, Mother, it won't do any good. No one is going to stop me. I'm going. My mind is made up. I will keep in touch with y'all so you won't worry."

Lucille once more got quiet, and Jacy gave the phone to her grandmother. Macy and Lucille talked a while as Jacy returned to her rocking chair with her head down. She looked at the floor. She felt bad. She didn't want to hurt her loved ones. But it was her life, and she would make her own decisions from this day on.

Macy returned to her chair, shaking her head in disbelief. "I hope you are planning on some kind of birth control, Jacy."

"What?" said Jacy. "You think I'm going to be having sex with Billy."

"Yes," said Macy. "I'm sure there will be that special moment where it is bound to happen. Two young people attracted to each other and spending every minute together for months. I'm old, Jacy, but not stupid. We all have God-given urges toward the men we love. How else could we procreate?"

Jacy said, "If it will make you happy, I will get on some kind of birth control."

"Thank you," said Macy. "I will have less worry."

"Everything is going to be fine," said Jacy. "Please don't be mad at me. I love you very much." She hugged her grandmother.

"You will need help in the store while I'm gone," said Jacy. "I thought about it, and I'm sure Miss Susan will be glad to help you. You can't stock shelves yourself. Would you like me to ask her?"

"No," said Macy. "I'll ask her. She's never turned any of us down when we are in need. Susan is a good friend to this family."

Customers began coming into the store, and the women went back to work as usual, glancing at each other throughout the day but not speaking. When night fell, the store closed, and Jacy said good night to her grandmother and went home.

Two more weeks and she would be with Billy again. Her heart fluttered just thinking about it. College finals were coming up, so Jacy would have to spend most of her time studying. "That should pass the time quickly," she thought.

The days passed quickly, and Jacy had not heard from Billy yet. Could he have changed his mind? She would be out of college in three days. It seemed like he should have called by now. All she could do was wait.

It was the last day of school. School was finally over for the year. When Jacy returned home, she heard the phone ring. She picked up the receiver and heard a voice that put a huge smile on her face. It was Billy. He was calling to give her instructions on where and when they were to meet.

After giving her the instructions, he said, "I can't wait to see you, Jacy. You are always on my mind."

"I'll be there, Billy," said Jacy. "I've missed you too. See you tomorrow."

Jacy began to pack everything she might need for her trip. Then she called her grandmother and told her that she was to meet Billy early the next morning.

Macy could hear the excitement in her voice and could not say anything negative to her granddaughter.

"I'll call your mother," said Macy. "You go and have a good time. Keep in touch."

Billy had told Jacy to drive to a catfish farm about ten miles from where she lived. Jacy thought that was a strange place for them to meet, but she knew Billy must have his reasons. She was to meet him there at seven in the morning.

Sleep did not come easy that night for Billy or Jacy. Morning could not come fast enough. She lay in bed picturing his handsome face, a face she had not seen for months. Finally, she fell fast asleep.

The alarm sounded at five thirty. Jacy jumped out of bed and into the shower. She got ready quickly but still wanted to look her best. She checked everything in the house before leaving, grabbed the luggage and her purse, and walked out the door, locking it behind her.

She was running a little early as she threw her luggage in the trunk of the car. She wanted to have plenty of time to get to their meeting location. What Jacy did not know was that Billy, Zen, and Qua were already waiting for her. She got in the car, turned the radio on, and headed toward the catfish farm. The farm was located in a wooded area down eight miles of dirt roads. She turned onto the dirt road, and she immediately lost her radio signal. She tried to adjust it, but nothing helped. She decided to turn it off. Then her car began to sputter and came to a stop.

Jacy put her head on the steering wheel and fell limp. The small space ship that had been waiting for her took her and the car up into the ship with a beam of light.

When they arrived at the colony, Jacy and her car were beamed down to a spot away from town. Then Billy was beamed down to her. Her head still lay on the steering wheel. Billy opened the door and picked her up in his arms. He held her close to him and touched his face to hers.

Then he called her name, "Jacy, wake up."

She opened her eyes, and excitement filled her body as she grabbed Billy around the neck and kissed him. "I've missed you, Billy," she said.

"I've missed you too, Jacy." He set her down.

"How did I get here?" she asked.

"Zen and Qua helped this time. You were brought here in a spaceship," said Billy.

"What part of the island are we on now?" asked Jacy.

"A secluded part," said Billy as he moved closer to her.

"You mean we are alone? Really alone," said Jacy. "Uncle Samuel and Philip can't sense us?"

"Secluded here means out of sight, but never out of mind. Yes, they can sense us, unfortunately," said Billy.

"Will we ever be alone?" asked Jacy. "Just me and you with no one probing our minds or knowing every move we make?"

"It's possible," said Billy. "There are small planets out there that we call vacation planets. Their environments are breathtakingly beautiful. Maybe one day we will be lucky enough to visit one.

"Samuel is sending me a message right now. He says, 'Bring Jacy and her luggage to her room, the same one you stayed in when you first arrived at the colony.' Your uncle is very fond of you, Jacy, and I believe a little protective."

"You think?" said Jacy. "You know he is my favorite uncle."

"He is your only uncle," said Billy.

"I know, but if I had ten, he would still be my favorite."

Billy opened the trunk on Jacy's car and took out her two suitcases.

"Do you want to walk to town or ride?"

"I think we should walk," said Jacy. "I need the exercise."

"Let's go," Billy said, and they headed toward town.

They smiled at each other as they walked. Walking, running, or riding, as long as they were together happiness flowed.

"I've got news," said Billy as they walked.

"What is the news?" asked Jacy.

"I met my brother Jeff. He had an accident, and I rescued him. I touched him, Jacy. I touched my brother for the first time in my life. It was awesome. He opened his eyes and looked me in the face. He knows now that I exist. That is a great feeling. I kind of feel like part of the family now—of course, from afar, though."

"Is he all right?" asked Jacy.

"Yes. He was in a plane crash, a crop dusting accident. I sensed it after I took you home and went to his rescue."

"Jeff is very lucky," Jacy said, "that he has a brother living in the colony; otherwise, he might not be alive today. Sometimes things work out for the best. In this case they did. I bet he is still wondering who you are. He will never figure it out, so he will settle on a guardian angel. You will be his guardian angel. No one will ever convince him differently."

"Hopefully I'll always be able to help my family if they are in need," said Billy. "But I'll settle for guardian angel for now."

As they got closer to Jacy's room, they saw Cindy skipping toward them. Jacy stooped down and held her arms out as Cindy ran into them and hugged her neck.

"I'm home, my princess little friend," said Jacy. She picked Cindy up and took her with them into her room. "You're staying with me for a while. I'm going to enjoy every minute of my stay by being with my loved ones."

She looked at Billy and realized that could not be with his loved ones, even though he yearned to be.

"I'll come back later," said Billy. "Lavern will be here soon."

Jacy said, "Thanks, Billy. Don't be gone long."

Cindy waved at Billy as he walked away.

Jacy began to unpack her luggage, and Cindy helped. Then Lavern knocked at the door, anxious to see her granddaughter. Cindy opened the door, and Jacy and Lavern held each other, happy to be together again.

Lavern said, "Knowing you will be visiting the colony often makes me very happy, Jacy. In a way, it's like being close to my son Murphy. I love and miss him very much."

Cindy watched the two women for a while and then said, "Let's play."

"Play what?" asked Jacy.

"Ring around the roses," said Cindy.

Jacy, Cindy, and Lavern walked outside holding hands and played the game. Cindy was so happy to be with the two women in her life she truly loved, and they both only had human traits, just like her; it was good to be around friends sharing her characteristics.

Jacy and Lavern were ready for a rest and dropped to the ground.

"We need a break," Jacy said to Cindy.

"Okay," said Cindy, and she ran off to play with her friends in town.

Lavern looked at Jacy and said, "That little girl is full of energy, which is a good thing, but I can hardly keep up with her."

"Grandmother," said Jacy, "don't try to keep up with a six-year-old child. It will wear you down. Take care of yourself, please—for me."

"I'll try," said Lavern, "but I really love that little girl, as you do, Jacy."

The women got up from the ground, and Lavern went back into town while Jacy went back into her room to wait for Billy. She lay on the sofa, put her arms on her forehead, and wished somehow she could let her family in Yelgar know how happy she was. She knew she would have to keep in touch with her mother and grandmother or they would drown themselves in worry.

When Jacy heard Billy coming up the steps, she jumped up from the sofa and opened the door.

"You ready?" asked Billy.

"Ready for what?" replied Jacy.

"Ready for some real excitement—excitement humans never experience."

"Should I be scared?" asked Jacy.

"Not as long as you're with me," said Billy.

"Could I have that in writing?" Jacy asked jokingly.

"It would mean nothing here, but if you insist."

"Never mind. Let's go for it," said Jacy, and they walked outside.

"Look up," said Billy.

When Jacy looked up, she could see a small spaceship hovering above.

"Is that Zen and Qua," asked Jacy.

"Yes. And here we go," he said as a beam of light zapped them into the ship.

The small ship went straight up, and Jacy found herself in the mother ship, once more reporting to Philip. As they approached the main deck, she sensed Philip as he spoke to her mentally.

She looked at Billy and said, "Philip is speaking to me."

Billy smiled. "It's about time you gained that power."

"How spectacular," said Jacy. "No human could imagine such a power."

"Some do," said Billy. "You're just not aware of them."

"Wow, good for them," she replied.

Jacy was happy to see Philip again. He said nothing to her orally; he only spoke to her mentally. Jacy just stood still and listened in amazement.

Not knowing how to answer him mentally, she spoke to him verbally. "How did you do that, Philip?" she asked.

He answered, "You have the gift now, Jacy. As long as you are in the colony, you can communicate mentally. You were brought here to prepare for your travels.

"I have a bracelet that will allow you to maintain your memory as you enter and leave the colony's light."

He then showed her a beautiful bracelet. It was made of a midnight blue metal. It was flat and round and looked like it had been rolled in diamond chips. It shined and sparkled. Jacy put out her right wrist, and he clamped it securely.

"Remember, don't remove it for any reason."

Jacy looked down at the beautiful bracelet then at Philip. "I promise I won't remove it until you say so."

"You may go now," said Philip. "Enjoy your stay." He then looked at Billy and said, "Be safe."

The two reported back to the small spacecraft where Zen and Qua were waiting for them. Zen spoke mentally to Jacy. *It is good that Billy has reunited with you.*

Qua then said mentally, *I agree.*

Jacy answered them mentally, *Thanks for your support.* Then she asked aloud, "Did you receive my answer mentally?"

Zen responded, "Yes, we did Jacy. You thanked us for our support."

She had done it. She had answered them mentally. She could tell Zen, Qua, and Billy were pleased with her new power.

When Zen beamed Jacy and Billy down to the colony, Samuel was waiting. He welcomed Jacy back and walked her and Billy into town. They sat down, and Samuel took Jacy's hand and said, "You have now been officially accepted by our people and are considered part of the Tavie colony in Louisiana. You will be able to come and go as you please. When in need, Billy will be at your beck and call. Lavern and I are family, and we hope you feel for us as you do for your family from Yelgar."

Jacy said, "Stop," and looked at her uncle Samuel. "I love you, Uncle Samuel, and Grandmother as much as my family in Yelgar. I missed being with ya'll tremendously. This colony is exceptional, and I'm so privileged to be welcome here."

Lavern walked up. She had heard Jacy speaking about her family in the colony and smiled. Samuel listened to everything Jacy had to say and then patted her head. He then took a small bag out of his pocket and handed it to Billy.

"This is your emergency kit. It has all the essentials you will need in case of an accident."

The bag was made of a material that resembled brown leather and was about five inches long and two inches wide. There was a drawstring at the top, and it was stuffed full. Billy took the small bag and put it in his pocket.

Samuel said, "Keep it on your person at all times."

"I will," he answered.

Samuel got up from his seat, told Jacy to enjoy her stay, and walked away. The other colonists then began to walk by, and they lifted their hands to Jacy. She really did feel welcome.

Carol walked up and sat next to her. "Jacy," she said, "you must find time to spend with me. I've got things to tell you."

"Definitely," said Jacy. "I'll be here for a while for this visit, so we can catch up on what's been happening in our lives—or should I say, our love lives."

Jacy looked up at the sky and wondered what was going on. There were at least ten small ships slowly moving around the colony. Suddenly she found herself and Billy inside one of them. This time the ship was navigated by Ebe, Carol's father, a full-blooded Tavie, and three of the colonists of mixed blood. Billy introduced everyone.

"Where are we going?" asked Jacy.

Billy answered, "England. England is the Earth's Tavie colony meeting place. The colonies from all over the world communicate over England. If there are alien visitors from other planets hanging around, we are notified by different signs located in some part of England. Philip is sending us to England to alert the colonies of some alien sightings in three different countries. There are so many planets in the universe, we don't have a name for all them or their inhabitants, so we leave an image of the ship or the formation of ships so they know what to watch for."

Jacy took a seat next to Ebe and watched the universe go by as they made their way to England.

She looked up at Billy as he stood next to her and said "This is like a dream. Nothing could be this amazing."

"It's no dream," said Billy. "You are now a space traveler."

Suddenly the ship came to a standstill and then began to move very slowly.

"I guess we're here," said Jacy as she glanced out through the windshield, though she saw nothing but space.

"We are here," said Billy.

The ship was now going straight down. Finally Jacy saw land as the ship got closer to earth.

"What a sight!" she said as the ship hovered over a sea of wheat fields.

As the wind touched the tips of the wheat, it looked like ocean waves moving back and forth.

Jacy thought, "From the air God's creations take on a different beauty—an unforgettable beauty."

Jacy watched Ebe as he drew three circles on a small computer tablet. He drew one large circle and then two small ones. Inside the circles he drew stars, and on the sides of the circles he drew lines. Billy told Jacy to look down into the wheat fields. As she looked down, the impressions of the circles Ebe had drawn were left in the field.

"A crop circle!" said Jacy. "That's why there are crop circles?"

"Yes," said Billy. "That's what the bottom of the alien ships look like. There are three of them in formation. Now the colonies can be aware of these ships."

"A real crop circle," said Jacy and shook her head in wonder.

"Another lesson in life, Jacy," said Billy. "These circles can be viewed easily from space. They pay colonies to be on the lookout for these alien ships. And if you happen to be one of these alien ships, I would advise you to go home and leave the Earth's atmosphere. We know you are here."

"Why do you think they are here, Billy? What do they want?" asked Jacy.

"Many alien visitors are curious and just want to look the planet over. Some are searching for different minerals they need for survival. Others are looking for a new home because their planets are failing. There are many reasons, Jacy. Some I won't discuss with you because they would scare you. Just know, as I've told you before, that only the strong survive in this universe, and we are survivors. We mind our own business and have many allies we can call on in an instant. Most of our allies are neighboring planets. We protect each other from hostile invaders."

"Has Earth ever been threatened by another hostile planet?" asked Jacy.

"Every day, Jacy," said Billy. "There are always aliens in the universe searching for planets they could survive on. The trick for us is to locate and stop the investigation before it gets in progress. When a ship is spotted looking down on what they would consider a primitive world and an easy takeover, our ships attack and show them that Earth is a protected planet. If the attack is not swift, they could return to their home planet and come back with a fleet of ships. This would cause a great war in the universe."

"Has there ever been a great war in the universe, Billy?" asked Jacy.

"Yes," said Billy, "before we were born. A planet on the other side of our universe was totally annihilated. Its inhabitants were forced to come here looking for a home. Earth was one of several planets they were looking to take over. Hundreds of ships entered Earth's atmosphere. The Tavies were alerted, and they forced the invaders up and out of the atmosphere. Most of them, anyway. Some were shot down as they attempted to flee. Three were shot down over the oceans, and one unfortunately fell to earth. A major war was fought in the universe. Many ships on both sides were destroyed along with the lives inside. The whole war was unnecessary. If only the aliens had contacted our ships before entering our atmosphere, the war would have never happened."

"Why didn't the aliens contact our ships?" asked Jacy.

"Because," said Billy, "they underestimated our strength. They thought we would be an easy conquest. The aliens weren't evil; they were just looking for a home so their kind could survive. The will to survive will drive a living being to do anything. Keeping your species alive means you are protecting your family and their families to come."

"Too bad they picked the wrong planet to invade. What happened to them?" asked Jacy.

Billy answered, "They were captured and brought to what we call a *multi planet*. It is used by Earth and all its neighbors. It has four different environments. One section is like Earth. One section is dry and has no water at all. One section has very little water and almost no humidity, like Tavus. The last section is very high in altitude and unlivable to many species. You would call it mountainous. Nothing lives on this planet but vegetation.

"Our ships forced them to land on the section of the planet that has a Tavie environment. The doors of their mother spaceship opened, and these small beings about four feet tall came out. They had pale skin, large eyes, and no hair—just like the Tavies. They looked like miniature Tavies, with some differences.

"They walked up to our commanders and just stood there.

'Where are you from?' they were asked by our people.

'We are from a planet that no longer exists, a planet far from this part of the universe, it was called Novae. We are dying and have not stood on the surface of a planet for two of your years. We were forced to fight. We can't survive much longer. We are in desperate need of a home. Our fight with you was a fight to save our families.'

"The Tavies then walked away and discussed what was to be done with this dying breed. They turned back and looked at the sad big eyes of the Novas. They weren't really bad, and they weren't any threat to Earth anymore. As the Tavies looked on, hundreds of Novae spaceships surrounded them, and our ships were hovering over them just waiting for the word to destroy. The Novas were in the hands of the Tavies, and lucky for them we are a humane and good breed.

"Our Tavie leader summoned the leader of the Novas, and they approached. Our leader asked the Novae leader if the environment he was in would be livable for them.

"The Novae leader answered, 'Yes, this would be a good home. We are vegetarians and have the plants we eat with us. They would grow easily here.'

'Land your ships,' said the Tavie leader, 'this is your new home.'

"The Novae leader looked at the Tavie leaders and said, 'Thank you. We will be eternally devoted to you. Our lives belong to you.'

"The Novas landed their ships and walked out onto the soil of their new home. Small men, women, and children ran and jumped as they looked at their new surroundings. In their language, they said, 'We were given our lives back today.'

"The Novas are our friends now, and our strongest allies. We visit them, and they visit us. Rice is a delicacy to them. We have taught them to grow it on the section of the planet that has Earth's environment. It is now their favorite food.

"The very strange thing about these people is that they came from so far away from our planet but have our look, eat the same food, and breathe the same air as we do. The inhabitants of the planets around us have different, distinctive looks. No one really knows what lives in the great beyond. We learn something new every day."

"How did the Tavies communicate with the Novas?" asked Jacy.

"They are very intelligent and can also communicate mentally, as we do. They used a basic language every planet can understand. This is the way all aliens communicate, unless a shield is thrown up by our side, which means that the aliens don't want to communicate. No communication means trouble. Those aliens are always evil and don't want to be found out."

Jacy had listened to everything Billy said while still looking down at the crop circles. The ship began to move slowly away from the crop circle site. They entered the clouds and came out again.

"I've never been to England," said Jacy. "It is very beautiful from the air. Look, Billy!" Jacy pointed to a circular formation of huge stones. "Is that Stonehenge? It's in our history books, but no one really knows how it got there. I can see it so good, although we are so far away."

Billy said, "Some of it has fallen over the centuries. It was one of the landing sights the Tavies used when visiting Earth. The spaceships actually landed on top of Stonehenge for many centuries. Time has slowly crumbled the earthy stones the circle is made of. Many people call it mystical, and little do they know just how mystical it is. Many people come to Stonehenge with problems or to find contentment, and when they walk away, they are different than when they had arrived. They are stronger mentally and can handle their problems. They appreciate life more and feel our presence. Anyone that stands in the circle is better for it.

"From this great country England comes most of the world's greatest knowledge. It is an old country, and most of the English have Tavie blood. Just about any question can be answered here, and most of the world's problems could be solved. The English communicate with Tavie scientists and doctors often. The Tavie consider all of the English family.

"Evil aliens from distant planets were brought here years ago to prey on these people. The English have witnessed evil you can't imagine. All the myths you have read about in books involving vampires and werewolves actually happened. These beings were trying to change the English into their own kind and eventually take over Earth. It was a vicious attack on Earth. Eventually they were all found and destroyed, but not before many lives were lost. It was a very scary and sad time for England, but the country recovered quickly."

Jacy sat back in the chair, not believing what she had just heard. Werewolves and vampires?

"This is unbelievable," she said.

He looked at Jacy and said, "There have been many creatures roaming the earth from time to time from other planets. We always find them eventually. The Tavies are alerted by their spaceships always hovering close to their creatures. Once they are in Earth's atmosphere, the ships are easily detectable. These ships have no idea that Earth is protected. All they see when they look down at Earth's surface is an easy takeover."

Jacy shook her head. "I think people on Earth are better off not knowing what is taking place above the clouds with the visiting aliens. They wouldn't sleep at night if they did."

"Right you are," said Billy. "What you don't know can't hurt you."

Jacy and Billy noticed that the ship had landed in a wooded area.

"Where are we?" asked Jacy.

Billy answered, "An Irish colony."

When the ship landed and the doors opened, they were greeted by four Tavie colonists that looked very much like the colonists in Louisiana. They seemed excited to see the crew as they walked off the ship. They had very distinct Irish accents. Jacy had read books and watched movies about Ireland, but to actually be there was more than cool.

"Welcome to Ireland," said the colonists. "We are glad you are here."

One of the colonists looked at Jacy with his big green eyes and seemed to be probing her mind until another colonist interrupted him by moving between them.

Billy said, "Don't be frightened. These are very friendly people. They are just not used to seeing humans traveling with Tavies, except on special occasions."

Jacy stood close to Billy as they followed the Irish Tavies into their town. The town resembled the Louisiana colony. It had the same familiar streets made of brick and many small businesses. On both sides of the streets were colonists going about their business—whatever it might have been at the moment. No one even looked up at the visitors.

Even though Jacy had been already exposed to the mixed breeds of Tavie and human, it still made her a little nervous being so far away from home. All of the colonists definitely had Irish looks, some with red hair and freckles. There were no different nationalities here. They all seem to be an Irish-Tavie mix.

The crew followed the Tavie colonists into a building while Billy walked with Jacy toward the end of the town area. All she could see was forest—beautiful forest.

Billy said, "Isn't it great here? Smell the fresh air." He inhaled deeply.

"Very nice," said Jacy. "I can't believe it's so cool and humid."

Billy laughed. "Better than hot and humid, like our state is right now. It never reaches those high temperatures here that we have back home. The weather is perfect. I like it. This is one of my favorite colonies to visit, and I had to bring you with me. I have a surprise for you."

"What is it?" asked Jacy. "I hope it's a pleasant surprise."

"Oh," said Billy, "I think you'll be amazed. I want you to meet some friends I've had for a very long time. I've been coming here since I was a small child, and even as a man I get excited when I know I'm coming for a visit."

"How much farther?" asked Jacy. "We have been walking for twenty minutes."

"Not much," said Billy as he pointed to a part of the forest that had a slight mist rising above it.

As they approached the special patch of the forest, there were flowers and all sorts of berries growing wild, and butterflies were gliding slowly through the air.

"What a sight," said Jacy.

Billy continued to walk along a small path as Jacy followed him. Suddenly the two heard a voice coming from a tree. Billy looked up and saw a very small man hop down from a low limb in a tree.

The small man said, "Billy, my boy, it is so good to see you. And I see you have brought with you a fair maiden, and very pretty she is."

Jacy put her hand over her mouth, not knowing how to respond to such a sight.

Billy took a seat on the ground in a patch of green clover, and Jacy sat next to him.

"Clancy," Billy said, "this is the girl I love. Her name is Jacy."

Clancy came close to Jacy and looked her directly in her eyes. "She's a good one, Billy. I think she's a keeper."

Jacy said, "Thanks, Clancy. I'm glad you approve of me."

Clancy said, "We are the little people you have heard of and read about in books about the isle of Ireland. There aren't as many of us as there once was, but we still exist, protected in the colony."

Jacy guessed Clancy was about forty years old and maybe two feet tall. He looked pure human, except for his size. He wore a red hat that came to a point that flopped slightly to the side. He had a beard and was dressed in blue pants, a white long-sleeve shirt with a purple vest, and a belt at his waist. His shoes looked like they were made of wood. His eyes were blue and bright, and his ears protruded a little. Jacy couldn't take her eyes off him.

Then two more little people came up. "Billy, my boy," they said as they ran up to him.

It was obvious Billy was well-liked by these little people.

"Jacy," said Billy. "This is Donovan and Branigan."

"So pleased to meet you," Jacy said as the small men also came close to Jacy's face and stared in the eyes. She just sat still and let them look. They touched her face and then sat next to her.

Donovan looked to be a little older than Billy, maybe thirty years old. He had green eyes and was wearing brown pants and a long-sleeve red shirt with a tan vest. His hat also came to a point, and he also had a beard and wood shoes. He was maybe two feet five inches, a little taller than Clancy.

Branigan looked a little different. His ears were normal-sized but came to a point on the side of his head. He was about the same size as Clancy and wore red pants and a brown long-sleeve shirt that had wooden buttons up the front and a brown belt around his waist. He also had a beard but brown eyes. His shoes were also made of wood. His hat was a subdued shade of red. He was about fifty years old.

These little people had their own look and definitely no Tavie blood in them, Jacy observed.

Billy leaned back and put his hand behind her back while he talked with his friends, and Jacy took in the beautiful sights surrounding her. She could see more little people—men, women, and children—walking around. Some sat in the trees. Each tree had a large rope made from twisted ivy hanging from it. The little people looked down at her and waved. The women wore brightly colored bonnets, skirts, and blouses in solid colors with colorful aprons tied around their waists. Their skirts were long and reached down to their ankles. Their shoes resembled the men's clogs and were also made of wood. Their faces were round, pretty, and very human looking. They looked like living dolls. The women were about one foot five inches to two feet tall.

The children were dressed like their parents and so small it would be dangerous for a full-sized person to walk around them. They could easily get stepped on. Now it made sense to Jacy why Billy had set the plane down at the entrances of the forest and why the little people lived on their own away from the normal-sized people.

In the distance, Jacy could see small puffs of smoke coming from all over the forest. She touched Billy to get his attention and pointed at the puffs of smoke. He knew what she was wondering about, but Clancy answered her question.

"That, my dear girl, is smoke coming from the ovens and stoves of our little people's cottages. The women are preparing meals for their families. The smoke is from small wood-burning stoves. We still live as our ancestors did. We have no need for electricity or other conveniences of your time. Our homes are now built on the ground and not in the trees as we did when we lived among the humans of normal size. We have no enemies here, so it is allowed.

"We are human, just very small. Our food comes from the forest. Everything we need we can find right here. The colonists bring us fish once a week, and to them we are very grateful. "

"How did you come about living here?" asked Jacy.

Branigan, the oldest of the men, answered her, "We were a dying breed, Jacy, when the Tavies collected what was left of us and brought us together in this wonderful colony. The Tavies protect us, but never do they enter this section of the colony. We still live in Ireland, the land we love, and thanks to the Tavies are able to survive without constantly running and hiding. We are all very happy here. The younger colonists sometimes come to the entrance of our forest to visit with us, which is very delightful and welcomed. Billy, for example, has come here since he was a child, and we so look forward to his visits.

"Donovan and Billy grew up into manhood together. They are great friends. Billy attended Donovan's wedding three years ago. We had many of the colonists attend. The wedding was held right here, on this spot. Of course, the little people can't mix with normal-sized people, so they were not allowed to go past this spot. It worked out great. We have many celebrations together. We celebrate almost the same holidays as you do in your country. And we have visitors every day.

"Clancy is the lookout. He lives at the entrance of the forest."

"And I love the job," said Clancy. "I love it. I love it."

Billy smiled at Clancy and tugged on the tip of his hat.

"Watch it, my boy," Clancy said, putting his fists in the air and throwing punches, "you know we are the original fighting Irish." Clancy continued to hop around like a boxer in a boxing ring and made Jacy and Billy laugh.

"Oh, Jacy," said Billy, "I forgot to tell you Clancy is a comedian."

"A comedian I am," said Clancy, "but a very dangerous man."

"A dangerous man," said Branigan, "only to yourself." Branigan put his fists up and moved with Clancy as if they were two boxers competing in a boxing ring.

"Enough," said Donovan. "You two are going to hurt yourselves jumping around like that."

Jacy watched Billy's reactions as he focused on the little people. He was genuinely enjoying this time with his friends, and they were entertaining him as they had many times before. The moment was priceless.

Jacy listened closely and heard the faint sounds of the pipe instruments the Irish were famous for.

Billy listened and then said to the three men, "You didn't."

"Yes, my boy, we did. This is going to be a celebration. We are meeting Jacy for the first time, your true love, and it is an honor to us."

The sounds grew louder, and Jacy and Billy could now see coming down the narrow path from the forest about twenty men carrying small pipe instruments of every kind. The music was very loud now, and the men clicked their heels and danced for Jacy and Billy, never missing a note. As they played,

Clancy and Branigan sang along with the music. The Irish men played on for about thirty minutes.

As the men played, they separated into lines on the left and right of the path. Five boys and five girls, who looked to be fifteen to eighteen years old, emerged from the forest carrying two halos. One was made of two kinds of green ivy collected from the forest. Billy lowered his head, and the boys placed it on top. The other halo was made of a variety of wild flowers intertwined with some ivy. Jacy lowered her head while the girls placed it on top.

"Thank you," said Jacy. "It's beautiful and smells so good." She put her hand out, and the young people all touched it. Then they bowed to Jacy and Billy. "Welcome to Ireland," they said and then turned and walked away.

Billy said, "These halos make us the guests of honor."

The music continued as four women gathered in the center of the music makers. Each one was carrying a small tray with food on it. The first young woman stepped up to Jacy and Billy as Clancy announced her.

"This is Biddy, wife of Malloy." Biddy set a tray of smoked salmon in front of them. Then she smiled at the honored ones and walked away.

Next in line was another small lady holding a tray with sliced soda bread. Clancy once more announced her.

"This is Renny, wife of Brady." She sat her tray down and walked away.

Behind her came a younger lady, maybe twenty-five years old. Clancy introduced her.

"This is Christy, wife of Donovan." She sat down a tray with two cups of potato soup with shrimp and walked away.

Behind her was the last lady. Clancy announced her.

"This is Cara, wife of Reilly." She sat down a tray with two small slices of something that looked like pie.

Billy said, "That is Irish apple cake. I guarantee you will love it. It is my favorite."

Cara smiled, turned, and walked away.

Billy and Jacy were hungry, and the food sitting in front of them looked and smelled great. The musicians stopped the music and dancing, and everyone gathered around Jacy and Billy. The women serving the food stood, and others joined them. They all watched to see that their honored guests enjoyed the meal.

Jacy put her head up to get the attention from her hosts.

"I want to thank everyone," she said, "for treating me so wonderfully. I love it here, and your people are a wonder of joy. I want to give special thanks to Biddy, Renny, Christy, and Cara for preparing this outstanding meal for us."

Everyone clapped in acceptance as they continued to look on.

Billy picked up his wooden cup with the soup and sipped it. Jacy did the same while taking a bite of her soda bread.

"Mmm," she said, "this is delicious."

The small people started playing their instruments once more. Everyone danced their Irish jigs as Billy and Jacy ate.

Jacy said to Billy, "This is the best picnic I've ever had."

Billy answered, "These are our friends, Jacy. We will visit here often."

"Good. I love it here," she replied.

Jacy and Billy finished their meal and had enjoyed every bite of it. Then they saw another lady coming with a tray holding two large cups of coffee and Irish whiskey to flavor it. Once more, Clancy did the introduction.

"This is Kiera, wife of Finnegan." She sat the tray down in front of the guests.

The coffee and whiskey smelled very good. Jacy picked up her cup and took a sip.

"This is good," she said as she looked at the crowd.

"Billy," Jacy said, "you are not to consume hard liquor. Tavies of the colony cannot drink whiskey."

Billy said, "Remember, I'm more human than most of the Tavies of the colony. I drink this every time I come here, and it does not bother me. Besides, who could turn down a drink made by their hosts especially for their guests?"

"If you say so, Billy."

As Billy and Jacy finished their drinks, the crowd of small Irishmen and women disbursed. Clancy, Donovan, and Branigan stayed and sat down on movable tree stumps.

Clancy said to their guests, "I think you may want to take a nap now."

Jacy and Billy lay back. "Not a nap," said Billy, "just a rest."

The three small Irishmen told Billy and Jacy stories of happenings from their history. The stories were very interesting to the guests. They were like children who always wanted to hear more.

Then Billy sat up quickly. "Getting a message from Ebe," he said. "Do you hear it, Jacy?"

"Sort of," she said.

"It's kind of vague. He's summoning us to return to the colony. The ship is almost ready to take off. We should leave here in about ten minutes."

"I don't want to leave," said Jacy. "This has been so enjoyable."

Billy took two bags of small jelly beans out of his pocket and handed them to Clancy. "Please give these to the children," he said. "I will be back soon. Thank you for your warm and much appreciated hospitality. And once more, thank you all for your acceptance of my girlfriend Jacy. It means the world to me. I love you. Your people are small in body but big in heart."

Billy and Jacy boarded the spaceship, and Ebe told them that Philip had ordered the ship back immediately because there was danger lurking. The ship quickly rose and headed home to their Louisiana colony.

Billy and Jacy watched the monitor as they moved. Eight small spots of gleaming lights appeared on the screen. The spots got larger on the monitor and looked to be surrounding their small spaceship. Ebe called to Billy to turn on the protective shield. Billy rushed to the control panel and turned it on.

Ebe said, "We definitely are surrounded, but by friend or foe, I do not know. They are not getting close enough to see if their crafts are ones we recognize. We will just keep moving, and they may come closer."

Billy said, "I'm sure we have help on the way from the colonies in this area."

Within seconds, the strange ships surrounding them moved in so close that their ship had to slow down. Ebe tried to communicate with the ships, but they would not respond.

"Not good," said Billy. "We have never seen these ships before, and I do not think they want us as friends. It seems to be their first trip to Earth, and they're trying to size us up."

"We seem vulnerable to them right now," said Ebe.

"Eight against one is not good odds," said Jacy as the strange ships approached, forcing their ship to stop in midair.

Ebe yelled, "They're trying to attach themselves to our ship and take us somewhere! We cannot leave Earth's atmosphere. No one will ever find us."

Jacy screamed, "Look!" The monitor had lit up with a hundred lights surrounding the strangers.

"That's our help," said Billy.

Philip had contacted the local colonies, and they were ready to defend their Cajun friends. The strange spaceships seemed to be under arrest. They rose straight up into the universe and disappeared.

"I'm sure they will be back," said Billy, "but maybe they will be more discreet next time."

As Jacy watched the screen, the one hundred lights left and returned home.

"Wow," she said, "this trip could have ended badly. They were trying to kidnap us."

"Yes, they were," said Billy. "Their intentions were to take us home to their planet where they would question us and study our bodies and brains. They would have checked out our intelligence and used us for their advantage—maybe through breeding, maybe as slaves, or maybe one of the fifty other uses that aliens have for humans. I'm sure right now they know Earth is a protected planet, and they are not too anxious to return.

"The ships that had surrounded us were only information gatherers. Their job is to go from planet to planet. Earth is a peaceful planet, so they got away without being destroyed. Believe me, Jacy, many planets would have attacked them on sight. They have a very dangerous job. Tavies don't visit a planet unless we are invited or we are contacted first, so we can be sure we are welcome. The universe is never ending. There are so many different worlds out there. But you just mainly stay in your own neighborhood as planets go."

As Ebe navigated the ship toward the swamp island, Jacy breathed a sigh of relief.

"Home," she said. "I love heat and humidity, even Raspas and gators. Don't scare me anymore after that trip. Thank you, Ebe, thank you."

Ebe smiled at Jacy and nodded his head as she walked off the ship.

"No more trips for me this week."

Billy heard her and replied, "Jacy, we know they're here now and what their ships look like. They are no longer a threat to us…relax.

"Let's get a good night's sleep, and tomorrow we will take the airplane up and do some sightseeing."

Jacy asked, "Billy, can we stay within three states—Texas, Mississippi, and Arkansas?"

"Yes," said Billy. "We have colonies in those states. You know, the Tavies are bigger in Texas."

"Ha ha," said Jacy. "Everything is bigger in Texas."

Jacy's favorite little friend greeted her as she walked into town—Cindy. Cindy grabbed Jacy's hand as they continued to walk and asked, "Can I go on the plane ride with y'all tomorrow, Jacy?"

Billy heard her ask and shrugged his shoulders. "That's up to Samuel. Ask his permission, Cindy."

"Okay, Billy, I will be good," said Cindy. She skipped off to get her permission from Samuel.

Billy looked at Jacy as they took a seat on a bench. "There's no way Samuel is going to let Cindy go with us tomorrow in an airplane."

"Why?" asked Jacy. "She'll be no trouble. I will take care of her."

"I'm only half Tavie. I could not control her. She has much stronger powers than mine," Billy said. "Samuel will only let her go with equals like Zen and Qua. They are pure Tavie—her match."

"I really do not think she would be a problem," said Jacy, "but I understand."

"You understand, but will she? Hopefully this won't be a problem. Cindy could stir up a storm. Watch for it," said Billy.

An hour went by and then Jacy spotted Cindy sitting alone with her head down. She looked very sad.

"Oh no, Uncle Samuel has said no to Cindy, and she is upset. I'm going to go talk to her."

Billy quickly stood and said, "Please leave the situation alone. She will be okay. Pity is not what she needs."

Jacy sat back down and said, "All right, Billy."

Lavern then walked up and gave Jacy a big hug. She sat down to visit for a while. They discussed Cindy's sadness.

Lavern said, "Cindy has a big problem with 'no.' I will get her favorite dessert, and it will make her happy for a while. She is still young. It's when she gets older that concerns me. My love for her helps with my control of her. She feels protective of me. I'm weak in this colony, being pure human. It just goes to show you, Jacy, how looks can fool you. Her strength and powers are far beyond anyone on this island. The only human trait she shows is devout love, but devout love is considered a weakness among the pure Tavies. Well, Cindy needs me. I'll see you later, Jacy." Lavern then went to Cindy with her arms open.

Jacy told Billy she was tired and would like to get some rest before the next day's plane trip. Billy walked with her slowly and kissed her passionately before she disappeared into the room. He then went back to his sleeping quarters.

Night fell, and Jacy felt like she was at her home away from home. Her strange day of space travel had been very tiring. As she lay in bed, she thought, "If I told someone in Yelgar about what I have experienced here, I would surely be put in a padded room and called crazy."

Morning came, and Jacy got ready for another day of visiting Tavie colonies. But this time, the colonies would be in neighboring states. "Sightseeing will be just as much fun," she thought.

As Billy and Jacy headed into town for breakfast, they saw Lavern. She stopped the couple and asked if they had seen Cindy.

"No," said Billy. "I'm sure she's playing with her friends somewhere."

"You're right," said Lavern. "I should let her play for a while."

"I will tell her you're looking for her, Grandmother, if I see her," said Jacy.

"Thank you," said Lavern as she walked away.

Billy and Jacy finished their breakfast and boarded the small plane. They put their seatbelts on and headed up into the sky.

"It looks like rain," said Jacy.

"Don't worry. We'll fly over it. There are plenty of colonies to find refuge at if the weather gets too bad. And remember, Zen and Qua are patrolling this area in case we need help." Billy took the plane higher into the sky, trying not to get bombarded by the rain and wind.

"I told you it looked like rain," said Jacy.

"Yes, and I told you we would fly over it, and that's just what I'm doing."

The small plane rocked from the wind and pounding rain.

"This is scary," said Jacy.

"We're all right, Jacy. Just hang on.

As they descended into the clouds, the rocking stopped, and they only saw sprinkles of rain on the windshield. Billy turned on the radio, and they enjoyed the music.

Suddenly a message flashed on the communicator: - NO COMMUNICATION - NO COMMUNICATION - SIGNAL LOSS - RETURN HOME IMMEDIATELY.

"That's impossible," said Billy. "What could be blocking our communication? This has never happened to me, ever."

Just then a sound of metal on metal blasted their ears.

"Oh my God, no!" yelled Billy. "We've just been taken by an unknown spaceship."

"What does that mean?" screamed Jacy.

"It means were in trouble, deep trouble, with who knows who. Jacy, no one knows where we are because of the loss of our communications. This is a nightmare. I have no idea what's happening."

The plane was now in an enclosed area surrounded by darkness. It was disabled. Billy tried to start it over and over, but it was no use. He looks at Jacy with fear in his eyes. All they could do was wait. Twenty minutes went by and then a dim light took the place of the darkness. They could see a door open, and three strange creatures approached the plane. One of the creatures waved to Billy to open the door, but Billy just sat still and hoped the creature would think he did not understand him. The creature hit the door so hard it dented. Jacy opened it and got out. Billy followed.

Jacy asked, "Billy, what are these things?"

"I do not know," said Billy. "I've never crossed paths with these creatures before."

Billy and Jacy stared at the unusual beings. They were about six feet and had rough green skin all over their bodies. Their faces had two holes for their noses, one on each side of their heads for ears, and small round yellowish eyes. They had protruding round mouths like monkeys and scales on top of their heads instead of hair. Their bodies were humanlike, except they had stubby arms and legs with clawlike nails on their fingers and toes. They each wore a skirt that tied around the waist that covered their knees. The skirts looked as if they were made from some kind of weeds that would be found in water.

Billy tried communicating mentally with the beings, but there was no response. They just stood and stared at Billy and Jacy. Then one of the creatures rubbed his finger over Jacy's jeans and then Billy's. The creature mumbled something to his friends, and they walked to the corner of the huge holding facility.

Billy said, "They think our jeans are our skin, I bet."

The creatures came back and looked at the tops of their bodies from the waist up. Both Jacy and Billy had on T-shirts that were a bit loose. One of the beings pulled on Billy's T-shirt, and as it stretched away from his body, the creature stepped back quickly, as if he had been startled. They looked at each other in wonder. Apparently the creatures had never come across humanlike beings before. They were flabbergasted. Billy knew they were definitely going to dissect them to understand more of their makeup, but there was nothing he could do.

The creatures were getting more aggressive. Now they were touching their hair, pulling on their noses, and putting their fingers in Billy's and Jacy's mouths. Billy pushed them away from Jacy, and one of them pushed him onto his back, scratching him with his clawlike hands and ripping his shirt. Their strength compared to the Raspas of the colony. Billy was no match for them.

Blood was coming out of the scratches the creature had made and staining the white T-shirt Billy had on. One of the creatures touched the blood and tasted it. Then the other two did the same. They shook their heads in joy, like they had found another food source. Jacy just stood frozen in fear that they might try and eat them. Their teeth were sharp and jagged, which meant they were not vegetarians.

The creatures pulled on their T-shirts so hard that their bodies were moving around, back and forth. One of them took his claws and ripped Billy's T-shirt off. As they looked more closely to find more blood, they saw the scratches—the real source of the blood.

Then they turned to Jacy who was still frozen in fear. Her long hair had been up in a clip on her head, but all the shaking with the T-shirt had caused her hair to come loose. It was now hanging around her face. All three creatures began to touch, pull, and stick their tongues in her hair. Then one of the creatures began to sniff her whole body.

Billy once more tried to save Jacy from them. He jumped in front of her and offered himself instead. The beings were not stupid. They had quickly realized that Billy was the male and Jacy was the female, his mate. One of the creatures grabbed Billy as the other two ripped off Jacy's T-shirt. She had on a lace bra and the necklace Billy had given her. They rubbed the bra and licked it, but it had no taste. They left Jacy alone and focused on Billy again.

Billy talked to the beings and yelled at them. He hoped to get a response of some kind.

"Stop! Stop!" he said as one of them pulled on his jeans. "Leave me alone, you lizard man."

The creature grabbed Billy's face, showed him his jagged teeth, and growled. He took one claw and rubbed it down the leg of Billy's jeans, opening them but not cutting him.

It seemed the creature thought he was skinning him. The creature pushed on the flesh of his leg, and tore Billy's jeans off completely. Billy stood with only his boxer shorts and boots on. One of the creatures took its foot and kicked Billy's boot. It jumped back and made sounds as though it was in pain. The creature sat down and stroked its foot. The other two got closer to the boots and ran their clawed fingers down the side. When nothing happened, they looked stumped. The only damage was a slight scratch along the side of the boot. The creatures then sat beside each other and talked among themselves, still looking at the boots.

Billy thought, "These lizard men are going to try and take over our planet. They are testing us to see what kind of beings they will be up against." He felt guilty about the situation. He was very worried about Jacy. This was all his fault. He should have stayed close to Zen and Qua. He hoped everyone would be looking for them by now. "These are probably the ships we escaped earlier. Apparently they are not going to be scared off, so they must be destroyed," thought Billy.

Jacy asked, "Billy, how has this ship not been found by the Tavies?"

"Good question, Jacy. No ship can hide from the Tavies. They must know they cannot hang around long without being spotted. Just pray they do not take us to their planet, if they have one. These things look like they would need a lot of water around them to survive. Our planet has oceans. They could be looking for a new home."

The trio of creatures got up, and their demeanor had changed. The boots had made them look at humans as threat. They charged Jacy and ripping at her jeans, cutting up the skin on her legs with their claws. Jacy screamed loudly as one of the creatures started to run his claw down her spine. The creature stopped to look at Jacy.

Then the door of the plane opened, and a girl child stepped out. It was Cindy. She had hidden in the back of the plane and fallen asleep. Jacy's screams had awakened her. She rubbed her eyes as one of the lizard men went to grab her.

Jacy screamed at her to get back in the plane. Then Cindy saw all the blood running down Jacy's body and her face turned red. She focused on the creature who was trying to grab her. She clenched her fists and hummed a loud noise in fear. The creature exploded, and blue blood covered everyone in the facility.

She was now focused on the creature next to Billy. She once more clenched her fists and hummed with rage. The creature exploded and more blue blood went everywhere.

The last creature fell to his knees and grabbed an instrument to open the hole in the spacecraft to let them out. Billy and Jacy, half-dressed and covered in blue blood, rushed to the plane. They put Cindy in first and then Billy started the motor and their plane was released. As they raced away from the ship, it was attacked by what looked to be close to fifty Tavie ships and completely destroyed.

"Well, that's the end of the lizard men," said Jacy.

"Maybe," said Billy. "They were pretty determined. The whole time we were captured, that ship was surrounded. The alien ship would not respond to any communication, and the Tavie could not destroy the ship knowing they were holding us."

"My scare is elevating to horror," said Jacy. "No more trips for me."

She held Cindy in her lap and hugged and kissed her.

"How did you do that, Cindy?" asked Jacy. "Those creatures were going to kill us and maybe even eat us. You saved our lives. Thank you!"

Cindy just sat quietly on Jacy's lap and enjoyed the affection. Cindy hugged Jacy and said, "They were mean. They made you bleed and took your clothes, so I got mad at them." She looked at Billy. "Will Samuel be mad at me?"

Billy said, "Cindy … Cindy … Cindy. Why didn't you tell Lavern where you were? I bet she was worried sick looking for you."

"I'm sorry," said Cindy. "I just wanted to go on this plane trip with Jacy. Can we get something to eat? I'm hungry."

Billy landed his plane on the island. Samuel had sheets for Billy and Jacy to cover their partially naked bodies. On their way to their dwellings to get the blue blood off, Cindy kept asking Lavern, "Am I in trouble? Am I in trouble?" Lavern said nothing.

Samuel summoned Billy for a meeting with Philip. Billy was fresh out of the shower but still had untreated claw wounds on his back. He headed to the main ship where Philip had doctors waiting for him. Infections from other planets could be in his body. Jacy had also been summoned as she had claw wounds on her legs. She arrived just as the doctors were finishing with Billy. The doctors quarantined them in different quarters of the main ship. Neither Billy nor Jacy could leave until released by the doctors and scientists. Philip contacted them through the two communicators Samuel had given them. He needed information about the aliens that had captured them, in detail.

Billy first gave a description of them and explained how they were confused when they looked at their bodies. He also told Philip about how they had reacted when they tasted the blood and how they had become hostile when they could not hurt his boots.

Then it was Jacy's turn to be questioned. She replied, "I was so scared I only remember those horrible, sharp, jagged teeth and their small yellow eyes that glared at us. It was so painful when they ripped at my jeans. All I could do was pray. Then my prayers were answered when Cindy came out of the plane. She walked out as they were about to remove my spine. They were going to dissect me. My loud screaming made them pause for some reason."

Philip said to the two survivors, "I'm glad you have made it home with only minor scratches. It could have been a lot worse. You know they will be back because there were no survivors to tell of their horrible deaths caused by a child. It sounds as though the creatures were looking for a place to call home. We will get rid of them all now. We know they are hostile. Where there is one ship, there are hundreds. We will find them all and exterminate them."

Billy asked, "What will happen to Cindy?"

Philip replied, "Think about what she did to those creatures. What do you think?"

"Please, Philip, she saved our lives. Do not send her to Tavus. I've been there. It is intimidating, and I'm only half human. She looks 100 percent human. They will make her sad."

"They may make her sad," said Philip, "but that's all. Her powers may exceed even theirs."

"Lavern would be devastated," argued Billy. "I do not know if she could handle losing Cindy."

Philip replied, "Who said she would be taken away from Lavern? She would go with her."

"Lavern is human. She could not stay on Tavus," said Billy.

"Cindy is to be quarantined also, until we decide what we are going to do with her. She knows how to use her powers, and they are so strong. We may have a big problem," said Philip. "She is a good child, but what if she gets mad at someone that's not as strong as her, like you, Billy? The Tavies can fend off her mental anger, but the colonists would be at her mercy. The older she gets, the stronger she will get. She saved your lives, and that was a good thing. I'll make my decision when I have examined the situation completely."

Billy and Jacy felt guilty that Cindy might be removed from the colony. Her powers were amazing, but she still had a little girl's love and feelings for her friends and family. They believed there had to be a place in the colony where she could be controlled. There would be no problem with her as long as she was not provoked.

Billy knew she would not be able to cope in Tavus, and Lavern would never be accepted there. Hopefully Philip would not send them there. Cindy had to be confused. She did not understand her powers and only used them when forced to. Yet she knew in her innocent mind that she had done something wrong. Philip knew it had to be handled carefully.

The results of the blood tests for Jacy and Billy were negative. There was no blood infection from their wounds. They were removed from quarantine and immediately went to be with Lavern and Cindy. Cindy ran to them and asked why she could not go play with her friends. Lavern just shook her head with a look of fear on her face.

"I want to go home," said Cindy. "Please, Billy."

Billy sat down, and Cindy climb onto his lap.

"You must stay here with Lavern and Jacy for right now. I will be back with y'all soon. I have an idea I need to present to Philip." Then he stood up and set Cindy by Lavern.

"Good luck," Jacy said to him as he left the room. He turned and winked at her.

Making Cindy happy was important to Philip as well as all of the other colonists. When Billy came to him with an idea to keep Cindy happy and everyone else safe, he immediately sent a Tavie to get Cindy, Lavern, and Jacy and had them come to the ship. The idea was to surround them with only pure bloods from Tavus—men, women, and children. Cindy seemed all right with the situation as she played with the Tavie children. But she tested the Tavie children by moving chairs with her mind and flickering the lights by blinking her eyes. The children responded to her powers by doing the same thing. They were nearly as powerful as her. There would be no problem with these Tavies. They could protect themselves from any misunderstandings with Cindy. The children on the ship would be taught to control their powers by their parents and teachers. They would not have a lot of interaction with the people of the colony.

"For now, all is well," Jacy thought as she sat and watched Cindy play games with the Tavie children. The experiences of her summer in the colony had been overwhelming, and she would never be able to share them with her family or any of her friends. Would Philip take this memory from her when she left the colony? There was nothing Jacy could do but wait for his decision.

One thing Jacy had learned from her adventures to the colony and the great beyond was that there was no place anywhere in the universe that was completely safe. Everyone everywhere should enjoy the people and places they loved because life was fragile and could be taken away at any moment.

Jacy thought, "If only the people of Earth knew of the Tavies and how hard they work to keep us all safe from invaders. And I thank God for my life and for putting on Cindy that plane with us. It was good against evil—and good won."

Jacy gave Cindy a big hug and left the ship. She walked alone to the place where she had docked her grandfather's boat on her first visit. She sat and stared at the bright light that bordered the swamp.

"This is where it all began. I met the love of my life, the family members that I didn't know existed, and a little girl that has been my guardian angel. Life takes many turns, and I'm glad mine took this wonderful one. I would not change a minute of it. I'm such a lucky girl to have two loving families," thought Jacy.

Then she leaned back and saw Zen and Qua in their small spaceship hovering over her. She waved, and they sped off.

Summer was ending. The months had flown by. Jacy had witnessed many things—some good, some bad, but all with family and friends around her. Each time she left the colony, a sadness overtook her … not knowing whether she would ever be allowed to return.

www.ingramcontent.com/pod-product-compliance
Lightning Source LLC
Chambersburg PA
CBHW051243260626
47162CB00002B/574